THE PAPER PIRATE

DAWN MCINTYRE

CONTENTS

Chapter 1	1
Chapter 2	7
Chapter 3	20
Chapter 4	30
Chapter 5	37
Chapter 6	44
Chapter 7	52
Chapter 8	61
Chapter 9	69
Chapter 10	80
Chapter 11	86
Chapter 12	94
Chapter 13	100
Chapter 14	108
Chapter 15	115
Chapter 16	121
Chapter 17	128
Chapter 18	137
Chapter 19	145
Chapter 20	155
Chapter 21	164
Chapter 22	172
Chapter 23	179
Chapter 24	185
Chapter 25	192
Chapter 26	198
Chapter 27	205
Chapter 28	212
Chapter 29	218
Chapter 30	225
Chapter 31	233

Chapter 32 242
Chapter 33 249
Chapter 34 260
Chapter 35 266

Acknowledgments 273
Author Bio 275
About Running Wild Press 277

Edited by Benjamin White

Published in North America and Europe by Running Wild Press. Visit Running Wild Press at www.runningwildpress.com Educators, librarians, book clubs (as well as the eternally curious), go to www.runningwildpress.com.

ISBN (pbk) 978-1-955062-18-3

ISBN (ebook) 978-1-955062-19-0

CHAPTER ONE

June 29

Charlie's head drooping to the left startled him awake. He had hoped that daytime napping would help him stay alert through the nights, but that was far from a sure thing. Sleep had never been the enemy before, but these last few nights were different. He sat forward and listened intently, but thankfully the house was silent. Leaning with his elbows on his knees would probably help.

Can't sleep that way.

How long could he keep this up? It would be hard enough if he were a younger person, instead of seventy-one. But it was too late to turn back now.

He'd made himself and his injured, vulnerable condition obvious, working his scheduled shifts, running his usual errands, even making a point of taking some short walks on Main Street or in the park while leaning on his cane. He had bent the truth a little by reporting someone sneaking around his house a few nights ago to encourage the police to take a spin down his block a little more often. It hadn't been a blatant lie—he *had* spotted his neighbor roaming around on his property, calling for her misbehaving dog. It was a harmless editing of information that just might save his neck.

Charlie concentrated on the pattern of shadows in his darkened living room, the soft whoosh of the air conditioning, the tick of the clock behind him in the dining room. Training himself to recognize every normal nighttime sound would allow him to hear the one click or bump or scratch that would put his mission into motion. So far, everything was as usual, just like last night. A car slipped by slowly, then the sound faded. Too bad his long-ago Army training hadn't prepared him for a post with the military police. Maybe he'd be better equipped for this sort of—

A rustle outside the picture window caught his attention. Sitting in the recliner meant that his back was toward it, but he hunkered down just to be sure he wouldn't be noticed by anyone peering inside. There was a muffled sound—someone was trying both window sash and finding them locked. Then he heard the light padding of footsteps on the stone path heading around the corner of the house, no doubt toward the dining room window. Charlie rose too quickly, nearly knocking his cane onto the floor. Twisting to catch it produced a sharp pain in his back.

Shit.

Grabbing his cell phone and handgun, he hurried to the shadows at the side of the room that would conceal him from prying eyes.

The locked dining room window was pushed a little harder. So was the patio door, which jiggled a little as it was being tried, making the suncatcher tap gently against the glass. A sound like the heel of a hand striking the siding made Charlie smile.

Growing impatience. Good. Hope it makes him careless.

Knowing the intruder wouldn't bother with the casement over the kitchen sink or the small bathroom window, Charlie risked moving over to the picture window, where he pushed aside the blinds and peered outside. There had been a cruiser parked across the street for the last couple of nights, but none was in sight now.

Crap.

Oh, well, there'd been about a fifty-fifty chance that help would be just a few steps away at the moment Charlie's plan came to fruition, and although he'd hoped for that scenario, he hadn't really counted on it.

A rustling in the bushes at the back of the house made Charlie take up another position in the living room's shadows. The guy must be nearing the spare room window now, but it seemed to be taking him a long time to get there.

Come on, asshole. Keep trying. There's one waiting for you.

One window in that room was only half-latched—as if he'd forgotten to slide the lock home—and could easily be jiggered around enough to open from the outside. The sound of a forceful push made Charlie snap to attention and remember his plan. But, to his disappointment, he was hit with a bout of conflicting emotions.

He knew he should call the police—should have, in fact, called them five minutes ago. He squeezed the case and powered it up, but the glare of the light startled him and he hugged it against his chest to hide the glow. He raised the gun and pointed it in the direction of the narrow ranch-house hallway that served the private rooms, knowing that was where the jackass might appear. He felt both hands trembling, and, shifting his weight, he almost dropped the cane again.

The gun in his right hand and the cell phone in his left

acted the parts of the cartoon angel and devil perched on a character's shoulders.

Call the police.

You can handle this.

Make the call. You've done what you set out to do. Let the pros finish up.

You wouldn't have started this if you knew you couldn't follow through. The Glock will help you hold the guy until help comes. You deserve to be the hero.

Don't be a moron. A real man would know enough to play his part and share the glory. Call the police.

Don't call.

Charlie felt his heart quicken and he drew in a deep breath. He found that he'd inadvertently edged past the kitchen and a few feet down the hallway rather than retreat to the basement as planned. Nervous as he was, his curiosity was working overtime.

Who was the bastard, anyway? Who had caused him and his business partners weeks of aggravation and fear?

Finally discovering what the guy was after, and why, had pleased Charlie, but that, he realized now, had been the easy part. No danger involved there. Of course, he could have avoided tonight altogether—he didn't have the item the man was after. He could've spent a few nights with various friends, let the idiot come in, poke around, find nothing, and then go on his way. The police may even have been parked behind the neighbor's bushes on that particular evening and might've caught the guy. But the man had wronged and terrified Charlie's friends. And once done with them, wouldn't he seek out and trouble someone else in the quest for his treasured object?

A click, a sliding sound, and a light thud made Charlie realize his options had narrowed. He heard the heavy steps of the burly man who'd been big enough to knock his friend into next Tuesday, and he knew he was no longer safely alone in his home. The door to the spare room that Charlie used as his office was ajar, and he could see a dark figure moving around, pointing the beam of a tiny flashlight, no doubt scanning the shelves that lined two of the walls. There was plenty of stuff stored there; he'd be at it a while. Charlie slipped the phone into his pocket and raised the gun with two hands and took a step forward—then turned, lowered it, and pressed his back against the wall.

You didn't choose an honest life for all this time just to lie in wait and possibly have to shoot an unarmed man.

Drawing a careful breath, Charlie fished the phone out of his pocket.

A bump, a crash, and an oath issued from the office in quick succession. The man must've backed into the desk, knocking the green glass-shaded lamp onto the wood floor. So far, at the other locations, the jerk had been fastidious, and Charlie hadn't expected any damage. The lamp was a favorite of his, and some of the shelves held his mother's collection of Staffordshire—a growling sound and another shattering of something breakable pushed Charlie forward and down the hall.

Now that didn't sound like an accident. Keep your goddamned filthy hands off my things.

He covered the length of the hall in a few seconds, pushed the office door open, and slapped a hand on the wall switch, flooding the room with light. A beefy, dark-clad man with a stocking obscuring his features jumped and whirled to face him. The room wasn't large. They stood about ten feet apart. Charlie didn't give him much time to think.

"That's enough. Sit down and keep your hands where I can see them." He pointed the weapon at the desk chair then at the intruder's heart.

The man stood frozen for a moment.

"I said sit." This time, his command was obeyed.

Charlie hooked the cane over the door handle and lifted his phone. "Let's see if I can call an Uber for you. One with flashing lights on top." He hadn't meant to taunt—the situation was delicate enough, but the sight of his broken objects had thoroughly pissed him off. Before he could get the phone up to eye level to punch in the three magic numbers, he saw a sneer creep across the guy's face—visible even through the dark stocking. Charlie barely had time to wonder if perhaps the bastard wouldn't flinch at harming a lame old man when his opponent stood and threw the heavy rolling chair at him as easily as if it had been one of those cheap, stacking vinyl chairs that could be tossed around in a light gust of wind. Instinctively, Charlie flung his hands up to protect himself. The phone clattered to the floor, and the bulky, barrel chested figure hurtled toward him.

CHAPTER TWO

April 22

Rainwater slithered down the many-paned window and thunder growled in the distance. Al Rockleigh contemplated Brookdale's drenched main street with folded arms and a worried expression. Not quite tall and of medium build, with greying, thinning light brown hair and green eyes, Al was often told he looked young for sixty-three, but his grim reflection in the window seemed ancient to him today. The late April afternoon had been warm and the door to the bookstore he had purchased five years ago with his writers' group colleagues was propped open, but now Al walked over to close it. His store uniform of rumpled khakis and untucked, oversize shirt quickly became speckled with raindrops. Cars sloshed past, sending little waves toward the curb. The dark clouds had created an early twilight, and the film of water on the road was streaked with brake lights and low beams. Al watched a dark green pickup roll by The Paper Pirate and negotiate the curve that would take it past Wilson Lake.

He turned to walk back to his post at the antique apothecary counter that served as the sales desk. The old floorboards creaked just enough to be charming but not enough to incite worry about the condition of the building's structure. Good thing, since the extensive repairs they'd been forced to make after the water damage to the basement last fall had nearly wiped out their savings. Al glanced at the bulletin board, hoping the lively crayon drawings left over from Wednesday's Children's Hour would cheer him. The posies and sailboats and kittens were sweet, but the orange and red hot air balloon contributed by a boy named Blake made Al pause his step. Breathing a deep sigh, he slipped behind the counter and dropped into the vintage leather office chair.

Balloons probably symbolized fun to young Blake. Parties, birthday gifts, maybe his parents had even taken him for a ride in one. As Al awaited the arrival of his partners for their bimonthly Friday business meeting, he imagined Blake's colorful silk orb collapsing above him, and floating down around him on all sides. Maybe he'd get up and run. Maybe it would simply suffocate him. He wasn't sure he cared, either way.

The balloon mortgage obtained by the group of friends had been the only one they'd been able to qualify for, and since the book shop had been a steady, modest success for the elderly former owners for decades, they were confident about their own chances for success. But time had flapped its wings pretty quickly, meaning that a huge payment was due in three months, and negotiating a second loan had proven to be problematic. They had to come up with a 20 percent down payment, and after the unexpected bill for the flood damage repairs, there weren't enough funds in the till to cover that surprisingly huge amount. Nearly all the partners were retired, some comfortably, but none of them would be able to spare a sizable portion of their personal savings to contribute. Selling the business they loved was an option they had to consider. All of this had been discussed at the last meeting, but denial had run rampant, and they'd all looked forward to finding a solution next time.

Tonight.

There was a scraping and scuffling at the rear of the store, then the door banged shut and Felicia's voice rang out. "Brownies. Caramel brownies, everyone."

Al turned his head slightly, but didn't rise from his chair. "It's just me, Felicia," he called. He pulled himself up taller and ran a hand through what was left of his longish hair when he heard her footsteps approaching. No use looking as depressed as he felt. Felicia had annoyed him when she first joined the writers' group, but she'd been so sweet and nervous and had a neat habit of providing baked goods, so he'd wisely put his sarcastic, take-no-prisoners attitude on hold and given her a chance. Turned out she'd had a bullying son-of-a-bitch for a husband and her patronizing grown son wasn't much better, which explained her meekness and occasional passive-aggressive comment. He wasn't sure her home life had improved after her husband's passing, but, as she'd gotten comfortable with the group she had blossomed into the warm, funny, slightly irreverent lady she probably always had been underneath, and Al had decided that he liked her.

Felicia Cocolo brought the scent of fresh, damp air and a warm smile onto the sales floor. She rolled a second antique office chair out of the corner and parked it next to Al's. Shaking out the folds of her flowered skirt before sitting down, she said breathlessly, "Look at me. I'm drenched. I used my umbrella and I jogged from the car to the building, and I'm drenched anyway." She was a short and pretty sixty-year-old, and the wavy brown hair that settled around her shoulders seemed to be the only part of her that was completely dry.

"It's warm in here. You'll dry out."

"Yeah. That should be the worst of our troubles." Felicia's dark eyes were suddenly filled with sadness. "What's going to happen to us, Al? Have you had any brilliant ideas since last time?"

Al shook his head. "You?"

"No. I asked my daughter for advice, but she couldn't think of anything either. I almost broke down and asked my son, but I'm glad I didn't do it. He treats me like I'm a loser even when he thinks the business is doing well."

"Best to leave him out of it," Al said. He'd never met the younger Mr. Cocolo, but he was certain they wouldn't like each other. "Whatever happens, we'll make the decisions for ourselves."

A pair of those awful, bright bluish headlamps illuminated the streetscape as a car pulled off to the curb and parked directly across from the book store. Al recognized the cute little BMW, and apparently, so did Felicia.

"Oh, Lenora's going to ruin her nice shoes," she predicted, rising to her feet and then to her toes to watch the petite, slim young woman negotiate the scattering of cars with the natural skill of someone born and raised in New York City. The "little sister" of the group at forty-six, Lenora Stern had black hair cut in a short, angular style and fair skin. She hopped up onto the curb on their side of the street and hurried to the door of the shop. Every step raised a splash that wet her to the ankles. Even though she was wearing those pants that women insisted were stylish, but to Al looked like they were just too short, the hems were soggy by the time she crossed their threshold and she had to push against the wind to get the door closed behind her.

"It's a monsoon. The street's one huge puddle. We're going to be inundated."

Felicia had jumped up and fetched a roll of paper towels,

and now she squeezed past Al and hurried toward her dripping partner.

"More likely just an inch or two, but it's coming down all at once," Al said, but the women were focused on trying to salvage Lenora's no doubt expensive shoes. He watched with some amusement. There was a good deal of hopping around, stooping and standing, and flailing of arms as Lenora shed her smart, Burberry trench, and finally a theatrical gasp when Felicia realized they were sprinkling the merchandise with raindrops. She set to work blotting books while Lenora padded toward the sales desk in her bare feet, carrying her soaked shoes by their straps. They were that odd combination of short boots and sandals whose purpose Al couldn't guess. "Maybe if your galoshes didn't have so many holes in them your feet would be drier," he teased. Lenora shook her dripping umbrella at him as she brushed past.

Felicia returned to her seat beside Al, laughing and panting from her exertions

"Oh, who made brownies?" Lenora's voice came from the back room.

"I did," Al said.

"You're full of shit," came the conversational reply.

"Well, then why did you ask?" He turned to Felicia for support, but she waved him off, with a smile and a shake of her head. The bathroom door banged shut.

"It's slow for a Friday evening," she said instead, glancing toward the street again.

"Yep." Al's somber mood, interrupted by the comical gaiety of the rain dance, began to settle on him once again. "Business has always been good," he said, earnestly. "Okay, not tonight, but no one's strolling around in this mess. If we'd been able to get a garden variety mortgage, or if we didn't have to clean out the business bank account to fix that damage to the foundation, we'd be okay. We'd be doing just what we had set out to do: pay all the bills and provide a modest second income for each of us with the leftovers. We *were* doing that for over four years."

Felicia smiled sadly, and reached out to squeeze his arm.

The bathroom door and the rear entry door opened almost at the same time, and the pair heard Lenora and Vinnie greeting each other in the back room.

"Uh-oh, it's the Frost Queen," Al whispered.

"Shh." Felicia turned to the rear of the store and called out, "There's brownies."

Al didn't know exactly what he disliked about Lavinia Holcomb. She certainly was attractive—nearly as tall as he was, blonde, with fine, patrician features and an athlete's build. She looked about ten years younger than sixty-four, and still was able to turn the heads of male customers much younger than she was. Her writing was poetic, literary and polished, especially for someone who was not yet published. Her political views were left of his own, but not by much. Maybe it was the air of secrecy that hung about her that was unappealing. Why on earth did she act like she had to hide something from the world?

Both women appeared in the doorway to the back room munching brownies.

"Oh, I'm going to join you," Felicia said, rising. "Let's put on a pot of coffee."

Al checked his watch and rose too. He saw Charlie's dark 1997 Cadillac sedan pass by and signal a turn onto the side street, and his arrival would mean the group was complete. It was not yet six, but Al locked up and switched to the night lights, climbing the open staircase to do the same thing in the used book section on the second floor. He stepped into the back room just as Charlie Santorelli came through the rear door and stood, calmly dripping on the floor mat. Vinnie took the two pizza boxes he handed her and set them on the counter in the little kitchenette area on Al's right. The center of the beadboard-paneled room was filled with an oval, turn-of-the-20th-century oak table ringed by many mismatched chairs, and to his left sat a couple of overflowing desks squeezed in between the doorways to the bathroom and a small private office that overlooked the parking area out back.

Charlie unbuttoned his coat deliberately, nodding and smiling at the women. Al liked this urbane, bookish man, even though they didn't have enough in common to become true buddies. Nothing ruffled this guy. He was confident at all times and at home everywhere. He was a bit shorter than Al, maybe five-eight or nine, but he was slimmer, silver-haired and just past seventy, and still stood as ramrod straight as the military man he once was.

Charlie caught Al's eye with a melancholy gaze, and Al slipped past the women brewing coffee and setting the table and reached out his hand. Charlie grasped it firmly.

"The rain," he said, wearily. "I just can't feel the same way about the rain ever again."

Al nodded. Main Street Brookdale wasn't in a flood zone, so the former owners of the book store didn't have flood insurance and everyone assured the new group that they didn't need it either. The town was established in the 1830s and never had experienced more than modest flooding of the creek beside the railroad tracks, in an area obviously downhill from the shopping district. But last October, the Atlantic kicked up a demonic tropical depression that pummeled the southeast and then curled up the coast, producing downpours that created a hundred-plus year flash flooding situation in northeast Pennsylvania that set all the pimply-faced young weather geeks chattering, giddy with excitement. The little creek did spill over its banks, but did no harm on Main Street. What roared down the wooded hill behind the town and tore a gash through yards, lifted sidewalks and scoured out pavement was instead a white-water torrent of run-off and a temporary Niagara, and the back-yards of the row of brick storefronts on their side of Main became its plunge pool. Four or five doors down in either direction, the shopkeepers had only to contend with washed out parking areas and flooded basements. The Paper Pirate and her immediate neighbors got the worst of it, each experiencing gaping holes torn into hundred and thirty year old stone foundations.

Al and Charlie, and Vinnie too, as a matter of fact, had climbed down into a ten foot deep depression to inspect the damage, wearing expressions of solemn disbelief. The others had stood on the brink, Felicia crying and Lenora trying her best to comfort her. The entire back wall of the two-story brick building had been threatened. There had been no choice but to act immediately and make repairs.

Coffee was ready, the pizza had been distributed, and the meeting was about to start. Al shook off the bad memories and found a seat at the table. Naturally, Vinnie seated herself at the head, and took charge.

"I hope we don't have to rehash everything that was discussed at the last meeting. Given the situation, I doubt anyone has forgotten a word of it."

Heads shook and other members murmured their agreement.

"First of all, has anyone come up with a mortgage product that suits our needs?" No one had. "Okay, so that leaves us with the same three prospects, none of which we can afford. I hate to entertain the thought of having to sell the business, but I don't think that we can avoid the subject completely."

Felicia groaned. "Vinnie, don't say that. This store means so much to me. It represents freedom, and truthfully, my independence wouldn't be possible without it. My late husband's pension isn't much, and I won't be able to collect Social Security for another seven years. Unless I take it early, and—"

"Don't do that," Al said, still chewing.

"And Al's always telling me not to make the mistake he made. I love this area and although my daughter would take me in in a heartbeat, I really don't think I'd like Florida. I do want to be on good terms with my son, but I simply cannot move in with him. It'd be like living with his father all over again." She covered her face with her hands for a moment. "I just can't let that happen."

"No one wants to see any of the members hurt," Vinnie said, gently. "The income is helpful to me, too. Not to mention the fact that I truly love the store." She glanced around the table, and members took it as a cue to speak up in turn.

"I screwed myself out of three hundred and fifty dollars a month by taking an early retirement last year," Al said. "Okay, water under the bridge, and you've all heard it before. Honestly, I couldn't live comfortably without the income from this place. I don't mind getting a different part time job, but I hate the idea of working for some kid. I was the boss for thirty years."

"This place suits me fine," Charlie said. "Everyone knows how much I love books and always wanted to make a living among them. Okay, so I'm doing all right financially, but this place fulfills a different need for me."

Al smiled, slightly. Occasionally, Charlie would use the little private office next to the bathroom for quiet conferences with seemingly well-to-do clients. He dealt in rare and expensive books, buying and selling through The Paper Pirate, serving a clientele that valued privacy highly. The others left him to this little side-business, since he stepped on no one's toes and shared his profits with the group.

Lenora set down her slice of pizza and dabbed at her lips with a napkin. "You all know that in spite of the fact that I moved here to marry my ex twenty years ago, I'm a dyed-in-the-wool New Yorker with a foot in both worlds. I won't lie—I've been thinking that selling would, at least, give me an opportunity to move back home. I miss the excitement and the culture, but on the other hand, it's not even three hours away, so it's still available to me. I love to drive, and it's nothing but a pain to keep a car in the city. I have a beautiful home here, right on the lake. I've asked if the old employer that I freelance for would take me back full time, and the answer was no. Even if I were to find another job in advertising comparable to the one I left twenty years ago—which is a big 'if'—I'd only be able to afford a cramped hallway with one window and granite countertops that they call a studio apartment. Unless I wanted to have a long commute from some God-forsaken place like Queens or New Jersey." She shuddered. "I don't know which would be worse. And despite the fact that everyone here thinks of me as a young girl, I'd be a middle-aged woman to the companies I'd be applying to. One who's been out of the big-time ad business for two decades. I didn't think I'd fit in up here, but now that I have, I wonder if I'm the same person who used to fit in in New York.

"Anyway, my decision was that I want to stay."

"Okay, so we can all agree that we would *like* to keep the store open, but that's really not news. If we can't arrange suitable financing in less than four months we are going to lose The Paper Pirate." Vinnie let that obvious fact sink in for a moment. "Assuming that we can't do that, which would you prefer—selling the business and making the best of it, or having it taken away from us? I don't mean to play the devil's advocate, but these are the two choices we're most likely going to be faced with. And remember that being an LLC only protects our personal assets. It doesn't mean we can't default on the loan and lose the building and the store along with it."

The evening had come on, and the dim lighting added to the general gloom. It was Al who had originally suggested that they form an LLC, a move which he knew would protect everyone's savings. He had felt like a hero at the time, but now the victory seemed hollow. Acting on Vinnie's suggestion, they'd applied for small business grants late last year, hoping to replace the lost savings. They'd already been awarded a very small one, but by the time they received what they hoped would be approval of the others, it might be too late.

"If we only keep thinking positively," Felicia said, "we can get through this."

"I like positive thinking as much as the next person," Vinnie said. "But we've tried every local bank, every Scranton and Wilkes-Barre bank, on-line banks, the credit union. I don't have to repeat what we've been told. If we still had the money we spent on the storm damage we'd be all right, but we don't. It kills me to say this but we have to face facts."

"Okay, I understand, but look," Lenora held up both hands and Al inspected them as if she might have the answer clasped in one of them. "A bookstore has survived in this spot for forty years. We've made so many connections with the community since taking over. Children's parties, author readings, book clubs, even our own readings of our works-in-progress. We've volunteered at community clean up things and recycling things and food bank things, always wearing our Paper Pirate T-shirts."

Al smiled. "All thanks to you. You're not so out of touch with marketing as you think you are."

Lenora glanced down at her hands on the table. "Well, thanks, but we've all made the connection, we're all known in the community."

Some of us more than others, Al thought, with a sly glance toward Vinnie, but he kept his smart mouth shut for once.

"I believe we're valued," Lenora said. "Why not tell the town we're in trouble and ask them if they want to help us raise money so we can stay here? A couple of days ago I mentioned the fact that we might have to close to a lady who often stops in on her lunch hour, and she suggested a Go Fund Me page."

"We can do a bake sale," Felicia suggested. "Or some type of auction."

Vinnie looked doubtful. "We could, but how much money would those things bring in? And how much could we get from Go Fund Me in the short amount of time left to us?"

Charlie shrugged. "We don't know that right now. But why not try it? Maybe a fancy dinner dance, like the library held at The Maples on the Lake. Let's try everything we can think of. And since we don't have much time, we should start soon. We should start tomorrow."

"I'm with Vinnie, I have my doubts," Al said, reaching out for another slice of pizza. "But it doesn't hurt anything to try."

Vinnie sat back in her chair, looking exhausted. "Well, I was only trying to be realistic. But, okay, I'm in. We'll give it all we've got."

Charlie nodded. "Done."

* * *

Al piloted his battered Jeep Cherokee toward home. The storm had wound itself down to a pattering of small drops. The wind had died out and the power was still on, so that was encouraging, at least. He'd go along with anything the others suggested, and try to have hope, but that didn't come easily to someone of his nature. He hadn't brought it up at the meeting, but things might be worse than they seemed. With the popularity of brick-

and-mortar bookstores on the wane, they might not even find a buyer for The Paper Pirate.

At the end of the business district, just before Al turned onto Forest Road, he passed a dark sedan that reminded him of Charlie's, causing him to slow down and notice the driver, who met his gaze boldly. The man definitely wasn't Charlie, and in fact, he wasn't someone even remotely familiar. Nor was the woman who sat beside him.

Strange, Al thought, looking back at the road ahead. Brookdale was mostly peopled by locals at this time of year. Sure, some of the summer residents started coming up on weekends as soon as the weather turned nice, but today's downpours were supposed to usher in an unseasonably chilly Saturday and Sunday. Al was too weary to question the stranger sighting further. Probably someone just passing through town. His warm and dry home beckoned, and Al signaled a turn.

CHAPTER THREE

Nina Bartov clicked the coffeemaker's switch and reached out to push aside the white eyelet half-curtain that covered the kitchen window. Ruffles and lace were not her style at all, but they had come with the furnished log cabin when she and Rick—well, when Rick had rented it two months ago. Since then, he had spent his weekend days searching the shelves of every book store and antique shop in Northeastern Pennsylvania for a mysterious volume, while refusing to explain his mission to her.

She cranked open the window and breathed in the fresh spring air. It was a bit chilly for the end of April, and Nina folded her arms tightly, but left the window as it was. She hated the smell of the closed-up house. Good thing the coffee aroma was starting to bloom. She opened the outdated fridge and pulled out the breakfast things they'd purchased at the market outside of Brookdale yesterday evening.

Slender, shapely and petite, Nina made fifty look good. Her black hair swept well past her shoulders and her fair skin made her sultry, dark brown eyes stand out beautifully.

Although she never had been lovely, she had a handsome, bohemian look about her that she had always used to good advantage.

The sound of heavy footsteps and creaking stair treads made her hurry to get mugs out of the cupboard and pull a frying pan off the pot rack in an effort to look like she'd been starting breakfast prep rather than staring out the window and daydreaming.

Rick Foster was demanding, but rich, quite good in the sack for a man in his early sixties, and had an interesting lifestyle that she wanted to share. So she toed the line, although at times, she herself quietly set the position of that line, and that made things bearable.

Rick paused in the kitchen doorway, hair wet from the shower, dressed in his customary dark slacks and collared shirt, even though they were in the country for the weekend. He flashed the facial expression that, for him, passed for a smile, and headed for the hideous faux-Colonial pine table. He was of medium height and stocky build, with average features that perpetually wore a hard-edged expression. His hair was as black as hers but his skin had a year-round tan.

Nina sauntered over to the table with placemats and cutlery as if she had been just about to do that anyway, whether or not he'd given the signal that it was time to do so, and planted a light kiss on his forehead for good measure.

"Are you going there today?" she asked, with a casual glance over her shoulder, knowing perfectly well that Rick did whatever he wanted at precisely the time at which it pleased him the most, and rarely consulted her.

Obviously playing the game—because she was, after all, an attractive younger partner for him and not completely desperate for companionship—Rick nodded.

"Yeah, this morning. I hope it's still where you said it was.

I'd rather not hang around the store for an hour searching the shelves." He sighed, and shook his head, a bit sadly. "I only wish you had done the right thing when you had the opportunity."

Facing away from him, dutifully scrambling eggs, Nina scowled, but she kept her tone of voice light when she replied, "I did what I thought was best at the time. I made a choice." She shrugged, and butter hissed when it hit the hot pan. "I'm sorry it wasn't the right one."

Rick leaned over and grabbed the black messenger bag that he'd left on the other kitchen chair last night, and extracted an old hardbound book. Its dust jacket was missing and the page edges were yellowed and crumbling.

"*The Chart Room*," he read aloud. "A much better effort of Conway's than *The Stargazer at Dawn*, but no matter. Some desperate soul found a copy of *Stargazer* close to hand when he needed a place to write down his tragic and incriminating story. The timing wouldn't have been right for this volume which was published two years later. Our man had been killed, no doubt, long before this," and he waved the book in the air a bit, "hit the shelves."

Nina was looking in his direction now, heading toward the table with two mugs and the pot of coffee, so she smiled, and hoped the expression looked somewhat genuine. "I didn't know the title of the book you were looking for—only that it was an old Benjamin Conway," she said casually, repeating the excuse that had not impressed him the first time and was unlikely to win her his forgiveness now. "The right one, if it is the right one after all, had a much better general appearance, so I assumed it was newer. Anyone but a true expert might have been fooled." Nina hoped that she wasn't laying it on too thick, but a glance at Rick sipping his coffee confirmed that she hadn't overshot the mark. It would be difficult to imagine Rick taking any compliment as anything other than sincere, but he wasn't stupid, either, and Nina was forever on her guard.

"Not surprising since it spent much of its life in seclusion, rather than circulating freely among the book-buying public."

"I was bored to death sitting around here. I only tried to help." Nina brushed a tendril of hair off her face impatiently, setting two plates down on the ridiculous homespun mats. She dragged out a chair for herself, regretting the annoyance that had crept into her voice, but she didn't risk making matters worse by covering with a phony smile. "Maybe if you had taken me into your confidence and told me what on earth you were after," she said, facing him squarely, "I would have known which book to buy. Maybe you ought to do that now so that I can help you look."

It was an acceptable touché moment and Rick leaned back in his chair and regarded her with an almost respectful expression. "You may be right. For now, let's have our meal in peace."

* * *

Felecia hummed as she gave the books on The Paper Pirate's main floor a once-over with a fluffy duster and plumped the throw pillows on the easy chairs scattered about the place. The store encouraged patrons to sit and relax with their purchases, and even offered free Wi-Fi so people could buy e-versions online.

The morning air was chilly, but the sun warmed the shop's front windows at this time of day, so she and Lenora had decided to prop open the front door for some fresh air.

"There. That's presentable. I think I'll leave upstairs for now. A little dust adds to the atmosphere in the used section."

Perched on a stool behind the old oak counter, Lenora looked up from her laptop and grinned. "I like that. There's plenty of atmosphere at my house," she said. "I've started to make a little more effort because of Jason, but he doesn't really seem to notice."

Felicia leaned on the counter opposite her young friend. "How're things going with Mr. Jason?"

"Pretty well," Lenora said, a bit guardedly.

"He still hasn't had you over to his place?"

Lenora shook her head, tapping away. "He says he likes my view of the lake." Looking up, she seemed to recognize the pained expression that Felicia had tried to wipe off her face. "I know, I know. Something might be up, but maybe not. I really like this guy, Felicia. He was burned pretty badly last time and maybe he's just gun shy. I'm going to give him a good, long chance."

"Nothing wrong with that," Felicia said. *Poor Lenora.* She had the worst taste in men. Felicia hadn't done much better with her late husband, but she had been very young, innocent in every sense of the word, and pressured by both sets of parents into making the leap into an unhappy marriage. Lenora was a grown woman of the world, attractive and educated, and really ought to be a better judge of character than she actually was. Felicia stowed the duster and moved to glance over Lenora's shoulder.

"Oh, is that our Go Fund Me page?"

"Uh-huh. What do you think of it?"

"Looks great. I can't believe this stuff really works, but my son says it's true. I checked it out for myself, and I guess I'm a believer now."

"Worth a shot, anyway," Lenora said. "There, that's finished. Now I'll just tidy up our web page, and insert that little piece Vinnie wrote for us."

"Remind me how she got elected to write it?"

"Um, I believe she elected herself when she realized she didn't like any of our suggestions." The two women grinned at each other. "It's pretty good, actually. It lays out our predicament and asks for support without seeming like we're throwing ourselves at our customers' feet begging for pity."

A patron in a red jacket entered and Felicia looked up with a smile. "Good morning, ma'am." To Lenora she murmured, "I'm kind of nervous about finding out just how much the town really wants a print book store. Everyone says they do, but, well, I guess we'll see."

A young woman with a toddler walked in next and was dragged by the little one to the children's section. *Adorable*, Felicia thought, missing her own grandchildren in Florida and on Long Island. The woman in red came up to the counter with a question about a romance novel and a man in dark slacks and a windbreaker crossed the threshold and immediately slipped upstairs.

It wasn't long before the Saturday morning regulars were ensconced in the easy chairs, coffees and pastries from the Lakeside Bakery sitting on the little tables close at hand. Felicia noticed a couple of weekenders from New York among the group. By this time next month, around Memorial Day, the scales would tip and the "summer people" would outnumber the Brookdale residents. Al and Charlie would set up the awning and she and the girls would drag the folding beach chairs out of the basement storeroom and line them up in front of the shop to handle the overflow. Al always planted two beautiful containers of annuals and Felicia herself kept a vase on the sales counter filled with fresh flowers, either from her garden or the field across from her house.

Felicia sighed deeply. Those things would only happen if

she and her partners were able to keep the store open. If not, there would just be memories of summers past.

The man in the windbreaker descended the stairs empty handed after about a half an hour and seemed to hesitate to approach the counter. Lenora beckoned to him with a warm smile. "Didn't find what you were looking for, sir? Can I help you locate something?"

He came toward them reluctantly. He was dark—swarthy like her late husband. "Do you have. . . Anna Karenina?" A New York accent, Felicia noticed.

"Well, I have her in the Classics section, over here on your right. I don't think I have a used copy upstairs. Felicia?"

Lenora turned to her and Felicia shook her head. "I haven't seen one, either." Although a complete stranger, the man struck her as the last person on the planet who would be interested in a copy of Anna Karenina of any vintage.

Just as the man began to reply, one of the local librarians hurried into the store and flung herself at the counter, clutching a flyer. "Is this true? I was in the Lakeside for coffee and muffins and I saw a stack of *these*." She flattened out the sheet of paper on the counter and gestured dramatically. "I can't believe you guys are in trouble. I can't imagine this town if you close."

Lenora nodded, and Felicia glanced between the librarian and the odd gentleman, who waved her off and wandered in the direction of the Classics Section.

"So many of our customers come in with Lakeside Bakery bags, I thought it would be a good place to start," Lenora said. "We're trying everything we can think of. We're going to start with this bake sale next weekend, and go from there. Vinnie thought of maybe doing a Pirate Prime thing, you know, like a membership. Pay X-dollars now and get an equal amount off your purchases, spread out over time. Like, two dollars off every book, or some such thing."

"We'll drum up as much support as we can, back at the library," the woman promised, wringing her long, skinny hands. "I hope you don't need much money, though. Bake sales and such are only going to bring in small change."

Felicia and Lenora glanced squeamishly at one another, then faced her with brave smiles.

The woman's features sagged. "Oh, dear. Oh, dear. Well, we'll be behind you all the way, and I'll see if I can't get any ideas out of the crew at work."

The three of them chatted a bit longer, then the librarian pressed a twenty-dollar donation on them and rushed out. A middle-aged couple had overheard the conversation and offered their thoughts and good wishes to Lenora while Felicia scanned the tables—the Classics Section was empty, and the Tolstoy fan was gone.

* * *

"What's this flyer I picked up at the Lakeside?" Dominick Jr. asked, waving it in Felicia's face as she stirred pasta in a pot of boiling water.

Felicia mock-flinched, to show her annoyance. "Boy, bad news does travel fast in a small town, doesn't it?"

"Fine, Ma, be sarcastic. Your only source of support is going belly-up and you're making faces at me." He tossed the flyer onto the kitchen table and pulled open the fridge.

"Help yourself to a beer," Felicia cracked, because he already had done so, despite the fact that he no longer lived in her house and really ought to have asked first. "And the business is not necessarily going belly-up, Mr. Optimistic. It's just a rough spot and we'll get through it."

"Fine. Whatever. Give me your car keys."

Felicia's blood ran cold when he sounded precisely like his dead father. She turned slowly, drawing in a deep breath to calm herself. "What on earth for?"

Although pushing thirty-nine, Dominick regarded her like a petulant child would have done. "I came here to get your wiper blades changed. I don't have all evening."

Felicia tilted her chin slightly and turned back toward the steaming pot. "No need, Mr. Important. They're done."

"They're done? How?"

"Al took me to the A & A," she said, airily. "He got me the best ones, he had cut out a coupon for me to get one at half price, and he even showed me how to take the old ones off and put the new ones on so I can do it myself next time."

Dominick scoffed and paced the kitchen floor. "That jerk is after your ass."

"Al isn't after anything. He's my friend and we all help each other out. You should have some respect."

"I don't even know him," Dominick grumbled.

"I meant for *me*, for crying out loud." Felicia flung both hands in the air, and the wooden spoon she held in one of them sent droplets of pasta water flying. "Now stop being yourself and set the table. The raviolis are done and I have some leftover homemade sauce." She glanced heavenward. "God give me strength."

* * *

Nina drew in a ragged breath. Her heart thumped in her chest and she kept an eye toward a handy exit. Rick had never hit her, but he certainly was known to throw heavy things about. "Gone?" she whispered, failing in her pitiful attempt to sound casual.

His dark eyes burned into hers, hurting her even from four feet away. He clenched and unclenched his fists. His dark complexion was flushed and his breathing was labored. He moved toward her and she stepped back, instinctively. Then, seeming to remember their unspoken rules and collecting himself, he looked at the floor, shoulders sagging. "Gone," he said.

CHAPTER FOUR

Charlie eased the Cadillac into the garage, shouldered his messenger bag and walked up the stone path to the front door of his neat little thirty-year-old ranch house. A trio of deer browsed on his lawn, but he left them unharassed—his vegetable garden out back was protected by a high fence, and the fallen pears the girls were munching were useless to him, anyway.

Inside of half an hour, he'd exchanged his shoes for slippers, closed the windows against the night's unseasonable chill, and popped in a Three Tenors CD. His kitchen table was set for one, but he opened a good bottle of Bardolino Bolo and warmed the chicken piccata left over from last night's dinner cooked for visiting friends. Charlie loved good food, but he'd had to learn to make it for himself.

At one time, marriage and a family had seemed inevitable, but as he'd grown from a schoolboy to a young man, the reality of his situation became clear to him. His father's business, which his two older brothers had embraced whole-heartedly, was going to be a hindrance to him even if he had his way and avoided joining them himself. How could he convince a nice girl that he had no ties to the Brooklyn crime family his father and siblings served? For a while, he'd been unsure about whether or not he'd be forced to follow in their footsteps. Studious, and easily the smartest of the three boys, Charlie finally managed to escape conscription by enlisting in the army as soon as he graduated high school and enrolling in college immediately after his tour of duty in Vietnam. Out of affection and respect for Charlie's father's many years of faithful service, Don Tomasso permitted this, but Charlie was never quite sure that the powerful hand wouldn't reach out and claw him into the fold, later on. He decided that having no close ties with a woman would be a good idea. No girlfriend would be endangered or threatened in order to force him to do the Family's bidding. So he'd kept his few relationships brief and impersonal. Too bad, really, since women liked him and he truly liked them back—whether there was a romantic interest there or not.

At the book shop, Al was forever shooting off his sarcastic mouth and committing some foul or another with the female partners, but Charlie's own relationships with the three ladies were smooth as silk. As he plated up his meal and poured a glass of wine he felt the weight of sadness settle on his shoulders. He loved the book store. He loved books and the little worlds they created for him to inhabit when his own reality wasn't so hot. He'd still have his rare books business, but obviously, The Paper Pirate was a better, more professional place to do his thing than this kitchen table. As a retired college professor, Charlie enjoyed a generous pension and a substantial Social Security check each month. He had always lived frugally, and with no children to raise, he'd been able to amass a respectable investment portfolio. He was far better off financially than any of the other partners, but, ever the cautious man, he'd never let that be known.

Charlie hummed along with the tenors as he cleared the table and washed up. Then he dimmed the kitchen lights and ferried the full plastic garbage bag out to the can in the garage. The light by the back door illuminated his path through the twilight. A beautiful sky was overhead, but more forecasted rain showers would make tomorrow a good Sunday to stick close to home and work on his next chapter, which was timely since it would be his turn to submit something at the next writers' group meeting.

Charlie half-noticed what seemed to be a slim shadow across the pathway, but as his foot landed upon it, he felt resistance and sidestepped to take a better look at what lay there. The small corpse and smear of blood made him drop the trash bag and begin shaking violently. Fear and disgust circled his throat like grasping hands cutting off his breath, and his heart thundered, threatening to burst through his shirt and explode. Every vein in his head throbbed, and his eyes were riveted to the spot that he couldn't bear to look at. A squirrel had been disemboweled and mutilated by another animal.

Charlie finally forced himself to walk away and circle the yard, arms wrapped around himself, battling hard to regain composure. "Steady, soldier," he murmured, aloud. "It's just a squirrel." It took three turns around the vegetable garden before he was able to make himself fetch a shovel and a pair of sturdy gloves and deposit the unfortunate beast in the trash can with the kitchen scraps. Inside the house once again, he stripped off his clothes, kicked them down the cellar stairs and hurried to stand in a steaming shower for far too long. *Wasteful*, Charlie scolded himself, but it couldn't be helped. He tried not to notice the tears seeping out of his eyes as he scrubbed the incident—and the memories—away.

* * *

Rick walked toward the puffy recliner where Nina sat in a pool of yellow light from a 1980's style floor lamp. She looked up when he took the book from her hands, noticed the title, and dropped it back into her lap as he turned his steps toward the couch.

"Useless," he muttered, and she didn't waste time wondering whether he meant her or *The Chart Room*.

Nina shrugged, casually, taking up the book again, although anger was rising within her. "Well, I bought it. I might as well read it."

Rick scoffed, shaking out his New York Times and refolding it.

"I don't suppose you've realized yet that I would be more helpful to you if I was better informed," she said. "I had given you credit for being smarter than that." Bravely, she didn't look up to see his reaction to her words.

Rick grunted, and let the newspaper fall to the cushions. "All right, I'll tell you what I know."

He's certainly in a mellow mood, Nina thought, although she was well aware that he would never tell her all that he knew.

"A gentleman sought me out a few months ago. He needed to avail himself of the expertise of the best rare books dealer in New York City. He's very wealthy. He wanted to buy a book—one specific volume of Benjamin Conway's *The Stargazer at Dawn*. It isn't the story itself he's interested in, nor the author, but the fact that someone in fear of his life wrote down some information in the blank spaces, one desperate evening decades ago—before the turn of the last century, in fact."

Nina's interest was piqued. She set down her book and turned a little toward him, wrapping her flannel robe more tightly around herself. A fire burned in the hearth but didn't dispel the chill in the room.

"My client, a Mr. Emil Zoloty, is the great-grandson of this mysterious hunted man. They come from a small country between Ukraine and Russia, on the Black Sea. Zoloty now lives in London, but he still loves his homeland, and they're going through difficult times just now. They'll be holding elections soon, and the front runner is an admirer of a former leader, the very same man who persecuted Zoloty's ancestors and many more of his people. He was a brutal man, a dictator, but many of his crimes were carried out in secret. He maintained—what's that phrase we use now—*plausible deniability*—and he remained popular with many of his countrymen. Naturally, all of these crimes have largely been forgotten by history and by the modern citizens.

"Anyway, Zoloty's great-grandfather was some sort of right-hand man to the head of the opposition to this dictator. He knew of the specific atrocities committed, and had information that would prove the old leader's guilt. Many of the opposition were imprisoned and their leader was killed, and the old Mr. Zoloty barely escaped to America, to New York. He was followed, of course, and chased into the countryside—to northeastern Pennsylvania."

"That's why we're here?"

"Yes. He took refuge in the rectory of an Eastern Orthodox Church that was here at the time, and when he realized that he might not escape again, he pulled a book off one of the shelves when he had a moment alone, and wrote all the proof that he knew existed in the blank pages. He put the book back where he found it, penned a letter to his family telling what he had done, and tucked it in with the priest's outgoing mail. Then apparently he left the rectory and was caught and killed."

Nina was conscious that her eyes were stretched open as wide as they would go, her breathing was shallow and she clutched the folds of her robe so tightly that her fingers were beginning to ache.

Looking pleased with the effect his tale was having on her, Rick smiled a little as he continued, “Supposedly, the letter reached home and was passed down through the family members, but for one reason or another, no one came to America in search of the proof against this dictator. Eventually it became a moot point. The country was taken over by the Soviets, then later in this century regained its independence—a common story in that region. The priest at the church here in Pennsylvania must not have known about the clues written in one of his books, and I was told that at some point it was donated or sold and probably wound up in one of the local bookstores or antiques shops. The Mr. Zoloty that I spoke with wants to be sure that his countrymen know the real story about the man this current candidate is eager to emulate. That’s all I remember, and really, I don’t care to know more. My only interest is in the $500,000.00 he has offered me if I deliver the book to him. The very book,” he added, drily, “that you yourself held in your hands a few weeks ago before you foolishly discarded it in favor of that piece of trash in your lap. Now that you know, you must do everything you can to help me recover it.”

Nina was indignant. “If you’d only confided in me earlier, that book would be in our possession. Maybe you should stop blaming me and recover it yourself.”

Rick shot her a menacing look, but she stretched her legs out on the footrest, letting her robe slip open to show them better, and gave an alluring little smile, letting her gaze sweep him from head to foot and back again. He softened his expression and leaned forward a bit, staring into her eyes. “That diamond solitaire pendant you’ve been admiring in the jewelry store on Lexington would look lovely around your neck," he said, softly.

Nina's hand fluttered to the spot where the pendant would sit, and she smiled absently, pretending to consider the offer. Then she rose and drifted toward the couch, shrugging off the flannel robe and letting it drop to the floor, exposing a short, pretty nightgown. "I suppose it would."

CHAPTER FIVE

Lavinia Holcomb carried a tray up the narrow stairs that led to her attic studio and set her breakfast down on the least-cluttered spot on her desk. The tray immediately started to slide. Grabbing it before the mug of coffee spilled, she pushed aside some of the papers underneath to level them a bit and tried again. *Perfect.* She sat down facing the twin windows and moved a pile of bills off of her laptop, opened the lid and powered it up. Clad in yoga pants and an oversized sweater, her below-shoulder-length blonde hair twisted up in one of those messy buns the young girls favored, she was ready for literary brilliance to pour forth.

At first, she dabbled at editing the last chapter she'd worked on, then started a fresh one, but pretty soon she was opening up earlier chapters that she'd workshopped and was already happy with and was simply wasting time reading. She wasn't sure why she'd thought that sex with Harry Knox last night would somehow inspire her writing this morning. It might have helped if she had been writing about sex, but she never wrote intimate scenes. Way too personal—she wouldn't want strangers assuming they knew what she herself considered a turn-on. But honestly, she reasoned, it wasn't possible to return to pre-1900 Boston and have a look around for inspiration, while it was simplicity itself to turn up at the Dockside Grill on Clam Night wearing an attractive outfit. Professor Knox invariably would be there, and he was handsome, intelligent and *discreet*, a quality privacy-loving Vinnie greatly appreciated. To add to his attributes, he rarely spent the night, didn't expect her to stay over at his place, and, at nine years her junior, he'd always assumed they were about the same age.

The breakfast tray slid precariously this time, and her empty plate and spoon clattered onto the faded needlepoint rug, but she was able to snatch the half-full mug of coffee and settle it in a safer place. She half-stood and reached forward to open one of the windows, enjoying the vintage rattling of the chain that held the dangling sash weights in place. Vinnie actually liked the research phase of writing and normally was meticulous about getting her details right, but the prep work for this historical novel was getting on her nerves. There was electric service at the time her story took place, but, wait, would there have been in the country setting she had chosen? And if not, was there still gas lighting or had there never been gas piping in that rural area? What about those personal gas-generating plants that some resources said wealthy families had? Were they actually common, or some kind of oddity that should be commented upon by her characters? And who gave a shit now, anyway? Wasn't the real story more important? Vinnie sighed deeply, and slouched in her chair, knowing that getting all the background details right was essential to the mood. It had to seem effortless. If only she could vacation in both Boston and her fictitious country town for a couple of weeks in the mid-1890's.

Flinging her arms out in weary petulance, her right hand

landed on an old volume that had slid from its place when one of the bookends on the edge of her workstation had toppled. She glanced over at the book and stroked it gently, much as she had caressed Harry Knox last evening. Her fingertips tingled, and although she tried to pull her hand back, it was drawn to the cover again. Sitting upright, she snatched up the book and opened it impulsively. Then, angry with herself, she snapped it shut and deposited it on the long, narrow table to her right. She faced forward with great determination and clicked on the window that held the chapter she was supposed to be working on.

Now, where was I?

But, although long dead, author Benjamin Conway whispered to her and laid a hand lightly on her shoulder. Vinnie turned and eyed the old book again. He had never achieved the fame he had no doubt desired, and this tale was an obscure early offering that wasn't even available from Amazon. But for some reason, Vinnie imagined that he had loved it, and would welcome a second chance for it to reach the public at last. She lifted the book and opened it, cradling it gently in one graceful, long-fingered hand, resting the bottom edge on her belly. Pity that some Neanderthal had covered nearly all the empty pages between chapters with scribbling in some foreign language. But, no matter; nothing dimmed its attraction for her.

Inspired.

That was it.

She was *inspired* by the story, and if she wrote a similar—well, *very* similar tale, fixing it up here and there, of course, to suit her own taste, she wouldn't exactly be plagiarizing, would she? After all, the story was now in the public domain. She could give the long-gone author credit. She could change the love interest and give her more spirit—who the hell was she kidding?

Vinnie closed the book more gently and propped it upright against the bindings of her collection of style guides, dictionaries, and thesauruses. She coveted this story. It was precisely what she wanted to write, set in the perfect time period, and it so beautifully evoked the plight of a man facing death too early that it made her breathless. She felt that she simply must possess it, as-is.

Vinnie groaned, softly. This wouldn't do. She had plenty of talent of her own. Certainly more than Felicia, the queen of overly-sweet love stories, or Al, who really should have stuck with nonfiction, which he did quite well. One or another of her writers' group partners often commented on her elegant style and her way with words. If only she'd never seen this copy of *The Stargazer at Dawn*. Why on earth had she gotten so ambitious when it was her turn to clean a few days ago? God knew her own house wasn't tidy, and at work she usually wielded the duster—she even called it Felicia's duster—in a most casual manner for intervals as brief as possible. But something had prompted her to drag out the step ladder and check out the highest shelves in the used section that day. It had been Al's fault, she remembered. She'd been sick of his sarcasm and had left him stranded with a couple of whiny customers while she escaped upstairs. Tackling the dustiest upper shelves that customers rarely perused, she'd come across this jewel angled across the empty space between it and a volume of poetry, and she'd been compelled to open the cover and peer inside. She'd been smitten immediately, and had spirited the book home in her tote bag in order to investigate further. Appropriately enough, she'd been curled up in bed when the seduction had been completed.

Now, Vinnie drained her coffee mug and forcibly returned her attention to her current chapter. Ben Conway was not tempting her across space and time, and he certainly wouldn't want anyone stealing his work. She'd desperately been seeking a comeback ever since the promised sequel to her single novel, published under a pen name, had withered on the vine nearly thirty years ago and she'd been forced to return her advance—best not to even think about that. None of her present colleagues knew about either of those books nor would they understand. Any comeback would have to be an original effort, and she'd better hustle. Starting Memorial Day weekend, three weeks away, they'd switch to summer hours at The Paper Pirate, open seven days a week, with extra shifts for each partner until the end of September.

A chill rattled Vinnie when the phrase "If we're still in business" crossed her mind. Despite the drivel she'd spouted at the last business meeting about being reasonable and facing facts, she was desperate to keep The Paper Pirate open. Her heartbeat quickened and she felt a strangling sensation that made her rise and circle the small garret room, drawing in deep breaths and forcing herself to believe that calmness was returning. The business simply couldn't fold. There was nowhere for her to go if it did.

The others would fare better. Sweet and warm, Felicia would fit into any office setting, and Al could always work at the Agway Farm Store or Petals nursery. Lenora was sharp, computer savvy, and still young. Charlie seemed more than comfortable, and he could continue his rare books side business to fill in any gaps.

Vinnie knew she would not survive for long working for someone else, even though she had the education to land a good position. She had hated every "day job" she'd ever been forced to suffer through. Even on her best day, among those companions least likely to disgust her, Vinnie was not a people person. And the rules, regulations, office politics, petty gossip—the very thought made her shudder. Salaries were pretty low in Wayne

County, to boot. She'd grown up comfortably well off, in the ritzy Village of Cove Neck, on Oyster Bay, Long Island. Selling her mother's old home and buying this modest Victorian cottage in working class Brookdale had allowed her to invest a bit of money, which now provided her with a little income, but not enough to live on. Nor would it support her in real retirement, when she'd be collecting full benefits, and that was three years down the road. Paychecks were bigger down in the Scranton area, but the long commute would leave so little time for writing.

Despite the fact that she was often plagued by writers' block, Vinnie *wrote* every day, sometimes for hours. Even if the product of all that effort turned out to be worthless at times, she simply had to create it. She was a *novelist,* although she'd only successfully completed and published one book. Every cell, every fiber, every atom of her was this and nothing else. Whenever she'd tried to pretend to be something different, she'd been miserable, even when rewarded with a good salary.

Now, semi-retired at last, the thought of being kept from writing for eight or nine hours, five days a week, was terrifying, and the idea of being forced to commune with people who did not love books, who quite possibly didn't even enjoy reading, was suffocating. Only The Paper Pirate had been a satisfying work experience, a close and comforting part-time career, and a business she actually partly *owned.* The bookstore must not fail. But how to save it?

Vinnie covered her face with her hands and actually felt a dampness about the eyes that was highly unusual for her. She parted her fingers and peeked out at the old volume on her desk. *Benjamin Conway*, she thought, dreamily. He would have been tall—well, taller than she was, maybe—and his author's hands would have been soft and gentle as he brushed tendrils of hair off her cheek and drew her close against his shoulder.

He'd understand her passion to string words together and he'd whisper encouragement to her. Vinnie uncovered her face and drifted toward her chair, lowering herself into it while lifting *Stargazer* once again. Benjamin was a *novelist*.

He would get it.

Perhaps he would help her.

CHAPTER SIX

Lenora puttered happily in her boyfriend Jason's kitchen on Sunday morning, starting the coffee machine brewing and prepping English muffins to be toasted, since he had said he didn't feel like going out for breakfast. Lenora wasn't big on cooking and adored breakfast out on a Sunday morning, but the truth was, she could enjoy anything shared with Jason. While he showered, she unloaded the dishwasher and watered the lone plant on his windowsill as if she was completely at home in the condo. In reality, this was the first time she had spent the night at his place. Although he had seemed a bit distracted and nervous last night, she nevertheless viewed this as a big step in their relationship. They'd been dating for six months and every romantic encounter before last night's had taken place at her house or at that lovely inn at the Cape.

Obviously, he was becoming more comfortable with her, trusting her—could loving her be far off? She certainly loved him—he was handsome, charming, sexy, and had a way with words that drew people to him. He was a natural as a salesman of wood stoves across his three-state territory. A man who was a mix of endearing, boyish traits and brash confidence with a hint of danger thrown in was irresistible to Lenora—always had been. She'd spent the last six months telling herself that Jason was nothing like her ex-husband. There was no danger of going down that wrong road twice. Well, actually, it would be four times, but. . .

When Lenora heard the water shut off she began opening cupboard doors, looking for plates and mugs. She wasn't trying to impress him with her domestic skills, she told herself as she set their places at the granite breakfast bar—that had never been her style. She was simply being a good, helpful houseguest, one who definitely wanted to be invited back multiple times.

Jason appeared in the kitchen in stylish jeans and an expensive sweater—a sharp dresser had always impressed Lenora as well—and she paused her table-setting to beam a hopefully beautiful smile in his direction. Her heart skipped just like it always did when she looked at him—his tall athlete's body, barely-tamed crop of sandy curls and exquisite blue eyes. . .but he wasn't smiling back.

He moved toward her and gave her a kiss, and murmured his thanks for the breakfast prep, but obviously, he was not feeling as delighted as she was. He had once told her he'd really had a rough time with his ex-wife. It probably was going to take a long time for him to completely recover. Lenora had decided months ago that she was prepared to be patient and understanding. Jason was worth it.

"Go on, sit," she offered, hurrying to switch on the toaster and lift the carafe from the coffeemaker. She filled two mugs and coaxed him back to his stool when he stood to fetch the creamer from the fridge. "I've got it. Oh, you remembered I love hazelnut," she said, and a slightly embarrassed expression flitted across his features, not quite disguised by his smile. A nagging thought reminded Lenora that Jason also preferred hazelnut creamer and might not have bought it especially for her. But, no matter. They were together for the weekend and although it was a bit of a rainy Sunday, she'd make the most of what time she had with him. Jason was so busy with work and the activities of his two children that she wasn't able to see him as often as she would have liked. She was eager to meet his kids and get to know them, but that hadn't happened yet. Felicia said that after six months, it was about time for those introductions, but Lenora wasn't going to push things.

"I hope you have a full Netflix queue," Lenora said, spreading jam on her steaming muffin. "Doesn't look like a day for a walk in the park. Or maybe I should say I hope you *don't* have anything in the queue," she added mischievously.

Jason's mug of coffee stalled just in front of his lips. Then he recovered, and took a sip. "Actually, um, I hope you don't mind, but I have a lot of reports to catch up on, and my expenses to record and turn in first thing tomorrow. Last night was great." He flashed the winning smile and laid a warm hand on her thigh. "And I'm really looking forward to dinner at Gordy's on Thursday."

Lenora knew she looked crestfallen, so she glanced away and lifted her own mug to help mask her expression. She wasn't going to get to spend the weekend with him after all. Well, come to think of it, Jason hadn't promised the weekend, but she had assumed, which was always wrong. And it'd only be a few days until they got together again. For dinner. Thursday night. At Gordy's, just a mile down the road from her place. Which meant they'd be going back to meeting there on Thursdays, as usual. Tears stung Lenora's eyes, but she worked hard at blinking them back and sounding casual when she replied. "No problem. I've got a ton of catching up to do at home, too."

She was giving him an out, like she often did, but this time he didn't just accept it gracefully and turn the conversation to something fun. Instead, he attempted a soulful, almost tortured expression and said, "I know it's asking a lot for you to understand why I'm more comfortable at your place, but sometimes I worry about my ex and the kids dropping by."

Lenora stared at him. *Seriously?* "Well, surely your ex knows that you date," she said calmly. "You've been divorced for six years."

"Oh, honey, I'm sorry," Jason rushed to gather her into his arms and nuzzle her neck. "I should've gotten all this stupid work shit out of the way in the evenings, but with the extra soccer practice and the big push to get that account in New Jersey, I just didn't get to it. Now all the reports and expenses are due and I've got to hustle. I'm an idiot. I'll make it up to you. I promise." Without waiting to see if those words had comforted her or not, he moved right ahead with a passionate kiss.

Well, Lenora thought, *that's one way to end a conversation we really should be having.* She kissed him back, though, and let her feelings appear to be smoothed over, and, for good measure, pretended to remember some important errand of her own that necessitated her hurrying out shortly after breakfast. She even tried to convince herself that he hadn't looked relieved as he stood on the balcony and waved goodbye. Lenora blew a kiss, and squeezed back the tears until she was far enough out in the parking lot that Jason wouldn't see them. Inside her car she sniffled hard and rummaged through her pockets and purse until she found a tissue.

Was she a fool?

Was Jason afraid his usual Sunday date might turn up while she was there?

Was this why Felicia always looked so fretful when Lenora tried to share a story about their relationship?

She started the little BMW and headed toward the IGA. Might as well pick up a nice steak or some shrimp for the dinner she would now be eating alone. The heart-wrenching drama of romance that shc had thrived on as a teenager and young woman was simply painful now, and becoming tiresome. She'd just turned forty-six, and longed for stability and comfort. Maybe it was a bit too late for a baby of her own, but she could be content with becoming the perfect, hip stepmother. Lenora grimaced. She'd have to *meet* the damn kids first.

At the supermarket, she found a parking slot and hurried inside without checking her face in the mirror. When one of the Lakeside Bakery's clerks, exiting with her cart, spotted Lenora, and approached with a smile that quickly veered toward a sympathetic frown, Lenora knew her eyes must be a bit red from crying. *Shit*.

The young woman approached, reaching out to squeeze both of Lenora's hands. "Oh, you poor thing. Don't worry. The town will stand behind you guys and everything will be all right. I know my boss is planning on donating way more stuff to next weekend's bake sale than she promised," she confided.

Lenora sniffled and smiled, feeling more than ever like crying now that she'd been reminded of The Paper Pirate's troubles. "We're really grateful. And so touched to hear so many good wishes already."

"I just love your store. My kids were lukewarm on books from the library because they had to give them back. But being able to own them has really sold them on reading. I'll never forget that."

Choked up, Lenora could only nod vigorously.

"And you've kind of gotten everyone's militant juices flowing, you know? Preserve print books and the brick and mortar stores." She mimed waving some sort of sign at a pretend protest march.

"Well, we're going to try our damnedest to keep the place open. I can't imagine what I'd do without the store."

"What kind of career did you have in New York?"

"Advertising," Lenora said, dabbing at her eyes with a tissue. "I've always done a bit of freelance work for my old employer, on the side. But, although I really enjoy that stuff, it won't bring in enough to pay the bills unless I do it full time."

Everyone in Brookdale and its environs knew that she'd made out very well with her divorce settlement from the philandering scion of one of the Pocono's biggest home building families. The sprawling, lakeside house was hers free and clear, and she had wisely invested the handsome lump sum of cash that Mike had reluctantly handed over to her. But property taxes and upkeep weren't cheap.

"You just keep your chin up," the bakery clerk advised, patting her arm and then rolling her cart toward a minivan.

Lenora nodded, and promised that she would.

* * *

Nina's breathing quickened and she stood ramrod straight with her arms stiff at her sides, hands clenched into tight fists. "I will not stay here," she said, enraged by the taunting smile playing across Rick's lips. He leaned over the bed and zipped his small suitcase slowly, deliberately.

"You'll do what I tell you to do."

"I have a salon appointment on Tuesday," she said, sounding ridiculous even to herself.

He tossed off a little shrug. "I don't give a shit. Half a

million dollars is at stake. You'll stay here and keep an eye on the book store, and do a little discreet survey of the shelves, without drawing attention to yourself. I might suggest the Salvation Army as a good source of disguises. You will not leave the house for any other reason. There should be enough food here until next weekend."

"I will not be forced to stay here for a week," Nina nearly screamed, rushing to the bed and flopping the top down on her own suitcase. Her hands were trembling with rage, along with the rest of her body, and she struggled with the zipper.

Rick uttered a bit of a low growl, and lunged forward, wrenching the suitcase from her hands. He held it above her head and shook it hard, showering a furious Nina with her own clothing.

"You can't do this to me. I won't let you abandon me here," she whined, cursing herself for losing her temper. If she hadn't, a coaxing smile and the offer of a blow job—with more to follow in New York—might have done the trick. Now, however, she was doomed. Rick flung the case across the room and grabbed her by her slender shoulders. Nina fought back the tears she couldn't bear to let him see as he leaned in close to whisper to her.

"You fucked up, Nina. You had my book, my half million dollars, in your pretty little hands. And stupidly, you returned it to the shelf. You'll do whatever you must to help me get it back. And I won't tolerate any whining."

She must have looked as shocked and frightened as she felt. His scowl twisted into a leer and he grabbed at her breasts and kissed her roughly. Nina cursed and tried to shove him away. Even the biggest diamond necklace wouldn't be worth this—she cried out as she felt the room sway.

He'd half-lifted her and thrown her onto the bed, where she landed awkwardly, the wind knocked out of her. Gasping for breath, Nina raised herself on one elbow and cast a tearful glance across the room. Rick stood in the bedroom doorway, holding his suitcase. The sickly yellowish light from the hallway turned him into a frightening silhouette. "Don't contact me. I'll call if I have any further orders for you."

With that, he was gone.

CHAPTER SEVEN

The screen door banged shut—a nagging reminder that Al was supposed to have fixed it long ago. The new closer was in its open box somewhere on the cluttered kitchen counter, so maybe he'd get to that today. Maybe. Al clomped down the wooden steps and scanned the sky over the tops of his backyard trees. An old landscaper's habit, although he had already practiced the old landscaper's habit of consulting the morning news weatherman, a national website and the National Weather Service forecast via the little wind-up radio kept on hand for power outages. This Monday morning, everything was in sync—the night-time rain showers had, indeed, beaten a retreat and a golden light touched the tops of his maples. The backdrop to his private world was a cloudless, pale blue.

Al's two story farmhouse, sturdy but in need of a paint job, sat just outside Brookdale, a bit beyond what could be called the edge of town. He owned three acres and half of it was wooded. In a couple more weeks, he would no longer be able to see the neighbor to his right, and the house to the left was so far off that it already was hidden by the flush of new spring green. Sloshing through the wet grass in his Wellies, he made his way to the ramshackle greenhouse. He glanced at the recently tilled vegetable garden, reaching out a hand to brush each fence post with his fingertips as he passed, breathing in one of the best scents on the planet—moist earth warmed by the sun.

The cold-hardy pea plants were awake, making a fine show with their paired, waterproof leaves and a riot of tendrils flailing about, grasping for the dry branches Al used for supports, the sturdy stalks of nearby garlic, and each other. He might try getting the cabbage in today, but no one in his right mind planted any warm-weather crops in the ground until the end of May, a month away. Al had scoffed at the young idiot of a meteorologist this morning as he "advised" gardeners to cover their flowers tonight, calling a plot of pansies growing on the television station's rooftop deck petunias. As far as Al was concerned, anyone living in northeast Pennsylvania who was stupid enough to plant anything anywhere other than in containers that could be whisked inside when necessary deserved to lose his plants. Usually, Al felt worse about the dead plants than he did about the careless owners and their squandered dollars.

Gravel crunched under Al's boots as he turned his steps. Last night's soaker had been the afterthought, the tail end of a storm system that had produced some wild weather in the southeast late last week and a handful of devastating tornadoes in Texas and Arkansas just before that. As usual, when he heard reports of dangerous weather in the Lone Star State, he'd grabbed his cell phone or tablet to find out how close the damaged towns were to his daughter's home in Austin. This time, a twister had come so close that he wasn't immediately certain that she was okay.

"How're Alice and the kids?" Lenora had asked the next

day at work, grasping his arm and turning him to face her as soon as she stepped through the door to the back room.

Thank goodness his ex-wife Barbara had emailed him early that morning to tell him everything was fine. Her occasional updates were the only reason Al was able to keep up appearances of filial contact.

"It was a pretty close call, but the worst she got was half a neighbor's tree on her garage," he had said, with all the authority of a man who had actually spoken to his child. That rarely happened; actually, it never did. Although she dutifully sent off a Christmas card every December and insisted that young Greg and Emma send written thank-yous in response to their grandfather's gifts, Alice basically ignored him. She told her mother that she wasn't still angry about her parents' ten-year-old divorce, and that she didn't hate her father, but something was up—she certainly had no use for him. Indifference, Al had once heard, was the true opposite of love.

The greenhouse at the back of the property was an odd son-of-a-bitch, as he often described it. The cinder block building probably had begun service as an oversize garage of some sort, and one still entered through an impossibly heavy overhead door. At some point before Al's ownership, a fire had destroyed the roof, and several courses of damaged block had been removed, making three of the walls only a shade taller than the gardener himself. A previous resident had replaced the upper wall section and the roof with a metal frame and glass panels. Evidently, that person had used the structure for its proper purpose, because Al had found growing benches, fans, heaters, and watering apparatus in place when he'd moved from Sullivan County, New York twelve years ago.

Before leaving the house this morning, he had cranked open the old brass shut-off valve in the cellar—he'd really have to get that replaced someday soon—and once inside the greenhouse, he beat back a winter season's worth of cobwebs and tried the spigot. There was a mournful groaning, followed by a nasty hiss, and finally the faucet splattered him first with a rusty sludge, then with clear water.

"You bastard," Al said, although it was a ritual that happened every spring.

Turning his back to the wall, he surveyed the lacy handiwork of what seemed like a thousand spiders, although he knew it was only an industrious few. He had shut and locked the door in mid-November, and there had been plenty of time for diligent weaving between that time and this last weekend of April. Al wielded an old push broom, waving it this way and that above his head, then down, beside his legs, in a rowing motion, as he made his way up and down the two aisles. He started his vegetable plants from seeds, but those were still snug in his basement, beside the boiler, and under a fluorescent light setup. His lawn tractor and garden tools lived in the garage. This greenhouse was used solely for his marijuana crop.

The peculiar building lent itself perfectly to the task. Not only were the solid walls about six feet high, but Al kept the glass above that point covered in horticultural whitewash that blocked out the view for any terrestrial prying eyes. He didn't expect to be, and never had been, troubled by anything as ridiculous as helicopters hovering overhead. If any of his neighbors took up drone-flying, he could whitewash the roof panels as well. He grew only a few plants for personal use, and an upstanding, business-owning, otherwise-law-abiding citizen such as himself wasn't likely to be suspected of doing anything particularly wrong. He didn't even smoke the stuff often—growing it was a blend of nostalgia for times gone by, and a discreet way to thumb his nose at authority while appearing to have conformed to the system.

An hour later, the building had been cleared of webs, the

concrete floor had been hosed down, and the raised bed in the center of the room had been refreshed with a few bags of top soil and Al's finished compost from last year. Nothing more to do for a few weeks, when it was warm enough for his seedlings, nestled now between the hot peppers and the basil, under the flicker and hum of his fluorescent tubes. Time to move on to other yard projects.

Al was kneeling in the dirt beside the stone wall at the front of the property, hacking away at last year's dead growth of ornamental grass. Chipmunks skittered in and out of chinks in the sides of the wall, and blue jays scolded him from the branches of the pink flowering crabapple.

"Well, hello there, young man," a familiar voice boomed, and Al looked up.

"Hey, Preston," he said, standing with some difficulty and plopping an armload of dead stalks into his waiting wheelbarrow.

David Preston, the neighbor to the right, between Al and Brookdale, strode slowly forward. He used a cane, but in a jaunty way, like a Victorian gentleman out for a stroll, almost like he actually enjoyed its company. He lifted his John Deere cap, briefly displaying a thick crop of short, steel-grey hair, then settled it snugly in place again.

"Great morning. It's going to be a great day."

Al smiled wryly. "They're all great days to you."

"Well, I woke up, nothing hurts any more than it did yesterday, and I don't have to go to work." He shrugged. "What could be better?"

Al grinned. They'd been through this a hundred times before. Preston had a good twelve years on him, so Al treated him with a bit of respect—just a little, being careful not to cross the line into patronizing territory. "Not much."

Preston tapped the ground with his cane. "Hear you chased

my grandson out of your yard last weekend," he said without malice.

"I chased him out of the *vegetable garden*," Al corrected. "I offered to pay him to help me cut up that tree that fell over the winter, but he wasn't in a particularly capitalistic mood. So I sent him packing." He faced Preston, hands on his hips. "Okay, I'm a curmudgeon."

Preston shrugged again. "Nah, he's a pain in the ass."

"Is he mad at me?"

"No, he just called you a curmudgeon." They grinned at one another.

The boy was twelve, just like young Greg, the grandson Al would only ever see on Facebook. At times he wanted to like Preston's grandkid, and at others he didn't want him around, silently reminding Al that he wasn't Greg. Al shook himself out of his silly reverie. *I'm getting as bad as the women I work with.*

"So how's the money-raising going? The Come Help Me thing, or whatever?"

"Go Fund Me is started, and the open house and bake sale is set for this Saturday afternoon. Thank-you for your donation, by the way. Charlie is making noises about a fancy dinner dance at The Maples, but they'd have to agree to give us the space for free, so I don't know. It's all going to be pocket change, really. I mean, it will feel good to be supported by the community, but let's face it, it's not a rich community. We need a ton of cash."

Preston nodded, considering. "I'd hate to see you close down."

"Me, too."

"I'm a newspaper and magazine reader. I'll admit that I don't read many books. But real bookstores are just one more damn thing from the past that I don't want to go away. Every day there's something familiar disappearing. If all the shit people call 'old fashioned' now was really so bad, how come it was good enough for us?"

Al smiled, wistfully. They'd covered this subject before, too.

"Like no phone in the house," Preston ranted. "When I was young, not having a phone in the house spelled out *poverty*. Okay, I have a cell now, too, but I'll be damned if I ever disconnect the real one."

Al agreed, while making a mental note to figure out just how much he'd save a year if he ditched his own landline. Might as well get started with the belt-tightening. He had a nice portfolio of stocks and bonds, but he was too young to stop working and start depleting those funds trying to make up for lost Social Security dollars. What an ass he'd been—oh, well, time to stop with the recriminations. If he could hang onto the bookstore, or find another decent part-time job for just another twelve or thirteen years, he'd probably be able to quit work and garden for the rest of his life. He'd be about Preston's age then *—oh, God.*

Preston was wound up on a tirade.

"Mind you, I'm not saying I'm against all Republicans," Preston was waving his cane, "but you'd like to have someone in that office that you can respect."

"Preaching to the choir, Preston," Al said, grateful for the hint to catch him back up on the conversation. Preston seemed pleased.

"Well, I'd best be getting along before my wife sends Phoebe out looking for me. Damned stupid dog always heads right for the poison ivy whenever she's off-leash."

"Take it easy, buddy," Al said, returning to his shearing and hacking. He'd stop before he reached the end of the wall and do something less strenuous until it was time for lunch. He could always finish up along the stone wall this afternoon, and still be able to stand up straight when he got out of bed tomorrow morning. "Pace Yourself" was the new motto. He wasn't getting paid for this shit anymore.

Back in his kitchen, Al switched on the little TV in the corner to catch the noon news while he waited for the microwave to reheat his leftover chili. He checked his phone—it was finished charging so he lifted it off the top of the toaster oven and scrolled through his email. There was a message about a Facebook post from Karen, a woman he dated on and off. They came in handy for one another from time to time during their "on" periods, but this was an "off" period and that was okay, too. Al liked the fact that he still sort of had a woman in his life, but the plain fact was that he'd never been happy being half of a couple, and likely never would be.

A news story caught his ear, and he looked toward the television screen. Some sort of protest somewhere nearby. . .the clean-cut crowd was up in arms about a medical marijuana facility seeking a permit to operate in the extreme southern portion of his county.

"Not in my backyard," a bespectacled matron insisted, while her peers jostled to enter the camera's view with their misspelled signs. Al rolled his eyes. Still. . .

Hmm. . .

What would be involved in setting up one of those growing operations?

Probably a huge outlay of cash, he thought, ruefully, glancing back down at his phone for a second. A message from Barbara; Emma was trying out for "cheer"—what the hell, weren't girls supposed to be *playing* sports now instead of cheering boys on?

And Greg's team won a science contest at school and they were moving on to "regionals," whatever that was. Al's mouth curled into a wry half-smile when he read the title of the successful entry: *Hybrid Hydroponics—Growing lettuce plants in clay pebbles and organic liquid plant food.* He shook his head slightly, and closed his eyes for a moment. The microwave dinged and he put the phone down, pushing it far away from him before getting a lone bowl out of the cupboard and sitting down to his meal.

CHAPTER EIGHT

Felicia bustled into the back room out of breath and slid into an empty chair, grabbing up someone's chapter to fan herself. She'd just closed the shop a few minutes late because she hadn't wanted to hurry the last customer out of the store. With things the way they were now, she doubted if even Al did that anymore. "I have to say, we've been busy since word of our troubles got out. I hope that's a good sign for Saturday's fundraiser."

"It was the same yesterday," Lenora said, reaching for a mini half bagel with pizza toppings.

Hearty snacks usually accompanied writers' group meetings, which were held two Wednesday evenings per month, beginning at the close of business and lasting about two hours. Although it was assumed that members would then fix themselves late dinners at home, Al normally loaded his plate so as to dispense with that chore, and Felicia smiled in amusement as he did that now, deliberately avoiding Vinnie's scornful gaze.

"All sorts of people," Lenora continued. "Mostly regulars,

but some complete strangers, which is unusual this early in the month, and, you know, in the middle of the week."

"It's true," Vinnie said, arranging three separate chapters beside each other in front of her. "I had an odd experience. I could swear I saw the same woman Monday and again today, but in what appeared to be two different. . .I don't know. . . outfits? Disguises would be more like it. I swear it was the same person but wearing completely different style clothes, with dark hair one day and red the next. She even appeared to be heavier on Monday. She spent an awful lot of time in the used section, but didn't buy anything on either trip."

"That's the woman you pointed out to me," Felicia said.

"Yes. Something about her seemed similar on both days, but I can't put my finger on what it was."

"That's why you're not a mystery writer," Al said, slurping his soda.

"I'll tell you one thing, she smelled like mothballs and old perfume," Felicia said, remembering. "Sort of like Salvation Army stuff before you wash it."

Vinnie shrugged. "You know, you're right about that. Anyway, let's get started, shall we? Does anyone need anything else? Al? Leg of lamb? Loaves and fishes?"

Still chewing, Al shook his head and held up a hand signaling that he was okay. Charlie and Lenora chuckled and Vinnie rolled her eyes toward the high tin ceiling.

A selection from Charlie's chapter was read first, and each member offered a critique. Felicia liked the suspense novel he was workshopping. Classy, like everything Charlie did, it nevertheless made her peer nervously into shadows for at least a day after one of his submissions. "I especially like your dialog in this chapter," she told him when her turn to speak came around. "You do conversations between women very well."

"That's thanks to us," Lenora said, with a wink and a grin.

"His reward for having to put up with listening to us all week long."

Charlie demurred graciously, but Al gave a little snort of laughter, and Vinnie glared at him.

"Okay, who's next?" she said. "Felicia?"

Felicia felt her shoulders sag. "Oh, okay. Why not? I'm afraid I just can't get to the next level with this story. I need something to really wrench the lovers apart and I'm just not seeing what it could be."

"Infidelity," Al declared, wiping his mouth with his paper napkin. "Your Lord Philip is away on business and Natasha realizes the gardener is awfully hot." His eyebrows bounced up and down expressively, and Vinnie clasped her head in her hands and shook it from side to side.

Felicia gave him a doubtful look. "Aw, it can't be that, Al. Romance readers want to see the couple devoted to each other, but torn apart by some seemingly insurmountable odds."

Al shrugged and reached for a chicken strip. "Yeah, but maybe the gardener was *really* hot."

"All right," Vinnie intoned. "Shall we start on page one, Felicia? Who would like to read?"

* * *

Felicia caught herself jumping at the rustling sound of leaves in the planting bed beside her front door. She dropped her keys and caught sight of the neighbor's cat when she swooped to pick them up. Chuckling out loud, she scolded herself. "What a sissy. Right, Chester? I'm a big coward."

The tom sniffed the air in her direction and moved on down the front path toward the road. Felicia locked the door behind her, stowed her coat in the hall closet and headed to the kitchen to heat up a bowl of homemade lentil soup. No work tomorrow, so it would be a good day for revisions. Not only on the chapter she'd just workshopped, but on her other project; the one that so far, she had been too shy to tell the group about.

Defiantly, she sat in Dominick Sr.'s old place at the table with her bowl and mug, as was her habit. From time to time, Felicia wished she could have afforded to move to a different house after her husband had died. Try as she might, it was impossible not to remember him in that doorway or this chair, scowling and scolding and acting imperious. For the first few years of the Cocolo family's residence in Brookdale, Dominick Sr. had stayed with relatives while he worked his New York City Department of Transportation job, awaiting an early retirement. Even though he only spent the weekends in Brookdale, he'd claimed the little den behind the front hall as his "office," although he had no real need of one and spent most of his evenings in the living room recliner, watching television.

Because the den was off limits, Felicia had had to haul her portable electric typewriter out of the closet and set it up on the kitchen table whenever she wanted to write. There was no question of getting a computer for her, so edits and re-writes required endless hours of typing, long after word processors had eliminated that drudgery for everyone else. She had actually saved up enough money from her office manager job to be able to afford a basic desk top unit, but *Il Duce* had been adamant about forbidding the presence of one in the house. He'd told her that she wasted enough time with her foolish hobby, and he wasn't about to make it easier for her to waste more.

It was simple meanness, really, she had concluded long ago. None of the household chores had ever been neglected, even though virtually all of those chores belonged to her. If he'd merely been selfish, worried about having a hot dinner or clean clothes, that would have been one thing. If he had resented her writing because he would have preferred her to keep him company, that would have been better. But instead, he had been determined to prevent her from doing anything she loved. What made a person that way? Sixty years old now, and still Felicia didn't know. She hadn't been happy in the marriage, either, but figured they could have stuck it out and found a way to avoid actually hating one another. But while he'd faced an untimely death at sixty-three four years ago, she was still going strong—healthy, happy, and free. Besides, grudges simply weren't her style.

Settling herself at the desk in *her* den-turned-office, Felicia powered up her laptop, checked her email, and scrolled through Facebook a bit, replying to messages from two of her grandchildren. Then she opened up the WORD file containing her latest chapter and made a couple of revisions based upon her partners' suggestions earlier in the evening. Lenora was the only one who actually liked Felicia's romantic stories. Understandably, they weren't the guys' cup of tea, so Al and Charlie generally restricted themselves to comments about style, mechanics, and grammar, which were helpful nonetheless, and appreciated. Vinnie famously detested Romance novels, and most of her comments were vague and reflected the supreme effort she was making not to allow personal opinions to color her critiques. Always respectful of other authors' rights to create what they'd been inspired to write, she'd murmured something tonight about liking the way the manor house was described, then, as if suddenly deciding that she was ravenous, had stuffed a mini pizza into her mouth.

Felicia smiled, sadly, and patted her pages gently. It was okay. She realized that she was trying, over and over again, to create the loving atmosphere she'd been denied her whole married life. There were millions of Romance readers out there, and she knew many of them shared a similar experience. Hopefully one day, she'd get a chance to reach some of them.

* * *

Nina kicked the ill-fitting shoes into a corner of the bedroom and stripped off the ugly, smelly sweater and dress she'd disguised herself in today. She'd laundered the thrift store clothing, but the ancient smells had stubbornly remained. The red wig had been tossed onto the hideous, pseudo-rustic dresser, beside a long blonde one she'd use later in the week. Nina took a long, hot shower and dressed in the leggings and baggy T-shirt she could never have chosen on a night spent with Rick.

Padding to the kitchen in her slippers, she rummaged through the cupboards and pulled out a can of soup. She grimaced. While Rick was, no doubt, dining sumptuously at one of their favorite restaurants, she was listening to the creak of the old manual can opener. Plenty of food left for her until he came back on the weekend, he'd told her. Plenty of cans of shit she could barely tolerate. As if she was a cat or dog. Nina threw the lid into the trash under the sink and slammed the cheap, plywood door shut. She'd be damned if she'd be kept prisoner in this house. Tomorrow, she'd browse all of the antique shops for as long as she liked and maybe even eat lunch at the diner.

A rage began to swell in her chest, and she breathed deeply in order to force it back into its shell. Rick could never truly be controlled, but he could be manipulated if she would only remember to control *herself*. She'd been with him for nearly eight years, and while, for the most part, he knew only the things about her that she chose to reveal, she knew nearly all there was to know about that difficult man.

As a scrappy teenager from the Bronx, he'd taken a part-time job moving furniture for an auction house. A go-getter, and not squeamish about adhering to the letter of the law, he'd attracted the attention of a shady antiques/rare books dealer who had taken him under his wing. Rick, ever the opportunist, had found a career far more lucrative than anything a two-year CUNY degree could ever have afforded him.

Nina's own life, since dropping out of college after a year, had been spent with one handsome, wealthy man after another. Sometimes she'd been a mistress, sometimes a housemate and partner. Never a wife, but that had been her choice. With the exception of a sweet but aimless boy she'd taken up with in her senior year at high school, she had never loved a man, and had always wanted to be free to move on to a superior situation if one presented itself.

Rick wasn't handsome, but he was a better bed partner than most had been, and wealthy enough. In his business—and life—he skirted the boundaries of the law, pausing to dip his toe over the line now and again, and for some reason that had always excited her.

She scowled bitterly, remembering Sunday night's humiliation. And a stab of fear quickened her heartbeat when the memory of being lifted off of her feet and flung like a ragdoll returned unbidden. It had been Rick's first physically violent act, outside of a sharp tug on the arm now and again, which she dismissed, and a bit of rough sex, which she had to admit she encouraged. Although she had convinced herself that she'd preserved a shred of dignity in this relationship, she had tolerated so much abuse from this unpleasant man without leaving him.

What if, in his zeal to possess that ridiculously valuable book, he forgot the slim volume of rules they'd tacitly agreed to? What if the violence escalated? Would she leave if he hit her?

Locked her up somewhere? Nina shivered. Then her expression hardened, as she rose to bring her bowl and glass to the sink. There was no dishwasher, and she'd be forced to wash them by hand, while Rick relaxed in their—well, *his*—comfortable West Side apartment. Without a man, Nina would be stuck in a rag-tag furnished studio somewhere, and Rick would make sure she left him with no more than a suitcase or two of clothing and odds and ends he didn't want anyway. Why start all over again with a new man?

Eventually, he would find that goddamned book. Perhaps she would be of considerable help with the search. Then he would be a half million dollars richer. The stress of pursuing the reward would be over, and he'd mellow. Nina fluffed her drying hair; a slight smile lifted the corners of her mouth. Although he'd never give her a portion of the money, she certainly could persuade him to share the benefits with her. That necklace, for a start, maybe earrings to match, a nice trip or two. . .and all she had to do was remain on task and keep her emotions under control.

You can do this, Nina. She drifted toward the living room.

Don't get stubborn in your old age.

CHAPTER NINE

Lenora set the last tray of homemade cookies on the counter with the other treats just as Al unlocked The Paper Pirate's front door. Slightly frazzled but pleasantly excited, she fussed with her spiky bangs and smiled at the first few customers as they streamed in. Probably a dozen people stood on the sidewalk, having waited there for the start of the fund raising bake sale. She'd planned carefully and worked hard at putting the event together, but now was the time to simply coast, and see what fortune would bring them.

"Good day for this." She felt a nudge by one of the proprietors of the Lakeside Bakery. "Overcast, threatening a drizzle at any time."

Lenora nodded. "Bad day at the lake is always a good day for places like us. Thanks for, like, the fifteenth time for all the stuff you donated."

The woman waved the statement away. "You guys are constantly promoting our business. Besides, bookstores and libraries have always been magical places for me." She squeezed Lenora's arm and scooted off to the back room, because loyal customers were pressing forward to view the pastries for sale and help themselves to free coffee.

Within an hour, about a quarter of the bake sale items had been snapped up, seven books had been purchased, and four people had told Lenora that she looked pretty in her flowery spring dress. She was disappointed that Jason hadn't shown up yet, but he'd promised, so he'd probably make an appearance shortly. A very tall woman edged toward her with a slim volume of poetry that she wanted to take home.

"I hate to ask if you'll wrap it on a day like this. . ."

"No problem. What's the occasion?"

"Niece's birthday."

Lenora completed the sale and stepped over to the side table, choosing a girly patterned paper from the rolls standing in an old two-gallon crock. "How old is she?"

"Just fourteen, but she's showing an interest in verse and I want to encourage it. We all need some beauty in our lives and I'm afraid she doesn't have a lot."

"Aww. . . well, I hope she loves it and keeps wanting more." Lenora handed over the wrapped book.

"Thank you so much. I'm really rooting for you guys. I work in Scranton, but I copied one of your fliers and urged all my office friends to take a ride up or visit the GoFundMe page."

"That's great. We really appreciate it. It's nice to know print books and physical bookstores are still needed."

"I buy books online, too, but mostly when I know exactly what I want—say, someone has recommended a novel they loved. But browsing that way is so difficult. I mean, who has time to view four-hundred-some results?"

"Tell me about it," Lenora said, and a little light flickered on in her head.

"It's much more pleasant nosing around in here. I often find something I didn't know I was looking for."

After her customer had gone, Lenora quickly gathered her other scattered partners behind the counter for a quick word. "What do you guys think of this: once we start our readings, we invite audience members to stand up and tell us what they love about book stores. Maybe share a story about a memorable experience they've had in one. Not just ours, but any book store."

"I like it," Charlie said. "Someone just mentioned to me last week that his parents had gotten engaged in The Paper Pirate back when it still belonged to the old owners."

"Exactly. Stuff like that. You guys think it's okay?"

Everyone but Vinnie agreed heartily, but that didn't bother Lenora. She well knew that Vinnie always appeared to take her time supporting a good idea she hadn't thought of herself.

"Speaking of readings," Felicia said, "we're supposed to start soon. This is so exciting. We've never had this big an audience for our regular ones."

Al glanced around the sales floor. "I have to admit, I'm impressed. I didn't expect quite this kind of turn out. I guess folks don't know how much they like something until they realize they could lose it."

"Shall I introduce the readings, or would you like to?" Charlie wisely inquired of Vinnie.

"I suppose I'll do it. Al, tuck in your shirt," she added with a haughty tilt of her chin.

"I never tuck in my shirt."

"You look like a slob." Vinnie brushed between Al and Lenora, clutching a volume of Edith Wharton bristling with colorful sticky flags.

"You just don't know how much you'd miss me if you lost me," Al said, with a wink for Lenora, who grinned.

Vinnie's icy comment drifted back to them over the heads of the crowd: "I can but dream of finding out."

They watched her thread her way through the crowded sales floor and station herself behind the antique walnut podium in the corner by the stairs. "Good morning, everyone," she said. Heads turned toward her and the chattering subsided. "Five years ago, my colleagues and I bought The Paper Pirate with the intention of doing nothing more than making a simple living for ourselves. We were mindful of the fact that a bookstore had operated here for over thirty years and of course we wanted to continue that tradition. But I don't think we had any idea how much we would come to love doing business with all of you, locals and summer residents alike, and I'm certain that I speak for all of us when I say that we never expected to experience the love and devotion that we're seeing demonstrated here today. I don't think it's possible to say 'thank you' often enough."

There was a smattering of applause. Behind the counter, Felicia dabbed at a tear and Lenora gave her shoulders a squeeze.

Vinnie read a selection from *Age of Innocence* and closed the volume when she was finished. "Yesterday was Independent Bookstore Day. In honor of that, before I introduce the next reader, I'd like to ask if any of you would care to step forward and tell us about an experience that made you love books, or bookstores, or libraries. . ."

One of the Brookdale Library staff members raised her hand and bounced a bit on the balls of her feet. Vinnie nodded in her direction.

"I loved reading even as a young child, but there wasn't a lot of money for books of our own. And I have to say, my parents didn't feel that books were a priority. I was a fixture in both the school library and the public one—I was the kid they had to usher out when it was time to close. I remember an essay about my local library that I wrote for a contest in sixth grade. The subject was so dear to me that I did a wonderful job and won my first award ever. Not only did I discover dozens, no, hundreds of wonderful worlds on those shelves, but I found a career I truly love."

Vinnie thanked her and introduced Charlie as the next reader. He had chosen a selection from the thriller he was working on, and Lenora was pleased to hear murmurs of appreciation from a few audience members and more than one gasp at the nerve-wracking final paragraph, which featured the hero and a surprise villain struggling at the edge of a tall building.

"Okay, who's next?" He smiled at the crowd. "Who loves bookstores?" A roar of "I do's" was the reply. "Why do you love them?"

A tall, powerfully built young man with dark curly hair and a bad complexion stepped forward shyly, glancing repeatedly to his left and right, looking like he hoped someone else would speak first.

"I was. . .well, I guess I'll just say I was in trouble a lot when I was a kid back home in New Jersey. I ran into a building one day to escape a beating, and it was a bookstore. I must've looked pretty rough—dangerous, maybe even—but the man at the counter talked to me like I was his best regular customer, and took me right away to the back of the store while, um, the guys I didn't want to deal with ran right by the front window. The man acted like he had no idea that he was helping me, and he asked what I liked to read, and what my budget was, and all that stuff. I really didn't like reading much, but I liked sports, so he made sure I went home with a used copy of a Michael Jordan biography. The book was like, two bucks, but I didn't even have that, and he acted like it was a pretty hot book, that one, so I'd better take it before someone else bought it and just come back tomorrow with the money. Okay, so I guess you guys know where all this is going. So, I went back the next day and paid up, and bought more books, and I stayed out of trouble after that."

"Outstanding," Charlie said, clapping a little for him. "Next up is Felicia, who also will be reading from a work in progress."

Felicia cast a nervous glance at Lenora, but Lenora patted her on the back and gave her a gentle push forward. She wished she could somehow give Felicia more confidence. There were thousands of Romance fans out there; it simply wasn't second-rate literature. She was glad to see Felicia owning the spotlight, projecting proudly and remembering not to say anything dismissive of her own work. *Good girl*, Lenora thought, clapping for her at the end.

"I must admit that I'm a sucker for a happy ending," Felicia said. "Thank you all for helping us maybe find one for The Paper Pirate. Who else wants to say why they love bookstores?"

A tall, sharply dressed man poked a finger in the air and took a step forward. "I'm an author—no, no one famous, but I make a decent living at writing and I have done so for nearly twenty-seven years. I've raised two children, and been able to afford my wife the freedom to work part time so she can devote her energies to her art. So, I guess I'm saying, I love book stores and I'm *grateful* that you do, too."

The man was rewarded with few inquiries about his titles as he resumed his place back by the window.

Al was up next, reading from the first of his two traditionally published gardening books. *Thank goodness*, Lenora thought. They really were quite good, but that novel he was working on now was just not ready for public consumption. He didn't do dialog well, but for some reason insisted on filling pages with his awkward attempts, hoping he'd learn by doing.

Today's chosen selection was well received, and three people had gardening questions for him that he seemed delighted to answer.

"Okay, I love books," he said, getting back on track. "I don't care if they're in a library or a bookstore, or in a dirty box at a flea market. I like the way they smell, the way they feel in your hands. I enjoy my Kindle, too, because I can make the font big enough, and I *love* the dictionary." A few giggles. Lenora watched as Vinnie sighed and folded her arms tightly. "Anyway, a book represents months or years of someone's life. It's the best of his talent and hard work, and it's his *dream*. Or maybe he's putting his kids through school because you bought and read his book, like our author gentleman over there, and like me, too. Who else wants to tell us why they love book stores? Come on, come on. . ."

A middle-aged woman wearing large spectacles spoke up. "Books were my escape when I was a lonely kid. The characters were my friends, their adventures were my adventures when I wasn't allowed to have any of my own. I started out getting my fix in libraries, but as I grew up and could afford to build a collection of my own I began haunting book stores, and I've just never stopped. My life has been rich because of books. My life has been a joy because of books."

Felicia started clapping and blew the woman a kiss. She smiled shyly, then bent her head to whisper to her companion.

Lenora scanned the crowd one more time before stepping up to the podium to take her turn reading. No Jason. Sure, he'd probably come, but she would have liked him to hear her read. He never showed interest in her writing, but this was a special day, and he knew how important it was to her. Oh, well, best to put on a bright smile and get out there and charm everybody who *was* there to listen.

Lenora's essay was well-received, and the patron she chose

at the end of it told a poignant tale of having avoided a neglectful situation at home by holing up in his local bookstore back in Brooklyn. He'd also met his wife at The Strand in Manhattan and they actually had gotten married there. Lenora thanked the man and encouraged everyone to enjoy the refreshments. As she made her way back to join the other partners, someone else complimented her on her summery dress.

"I really like that piece," Felicia said, indicating the papers in Lenora's hand. "I'm glad you chose it."

"Thanks," Lenora said, sounding, even to her own ears, like her heart just wasn't in it.

"What's the matter, honey?"

Lenora sighed and gave her head a little shake. "Jason promised he'd be here." She was saddened but not surprised when a wry expression flitted across Felicia's face before she wiped it away with a sweet smile and hugged Lenora's arm.

"Such a busy man, Mr. Jason. He'll be late, but he'll be here."

Lenora watched as Al's sometimes-girlfriend Karen sidled up to him and slipped a check into his shirt pocket. Al turned from his chat with Charlie, smiled broadly and gave her a hug and a kiss. "I'm sure you're right."

"Excuse me," a middle-aged woman said. She positioned herself between the two small clusters of owners, glancing between them, which had the effect of collecting them all into a circle in front of her. "I'd like to add this envelope to the box, but I have another offer, as well. I'm Debbie Newsome. I doubt you know my name, but my parents were Walter and Dorothy Ott. You might be more familiar with them."

Lenora was scrolling through her memory banks when Charlie's face lit up and he moved forward a step, to take the donation.

"Local royalty," he said, and the woman brushed him off,

with a modest smile. "Bronze plaque on the hospital's new wing, donated the band shell in the park, scholarships all over the place." He stuck out a hand. "It's a pleasure to meet you."

"You're too kind. But they *were* wonderful people, and avid readers. I inherited their impressive personal library some years ago when my mother passed. My husband and I live in a more modest home than the one I grew up in, and I'm afraid that once I chose my favorite books, I left the others to languish in a storage facility. It's quite wrong—books belong in human hands. My mother assured me that she would understand if I sold some of them, but I never had the heart. Right now, I really can't think of a better use for them than to help you folks keep this bookstore open. If you're all agreeable, I'd like to gift them to you, to sell as part of your fund-raising efforts."

"Oh, that's wonderful," Felicia clapped her hands together.

"How kind of you," Vinnie said. "Are you sure?"

"I'm quite sure. I've always loved this place, as did my parents. Many of the volumes will remember these shelves. My family has been shopping here as long as this was a bookstore."

"Thank you so much," Al said, reaching out a hand.

"Yes, this is a wonderful donation." Charlie beamed.

Lenora realized that she was staring stupidly with a washed-out smile on her face. She remedied that and thanked the woman properly. Arrangements were made to discuss the transfer of the book collection on Monday, and Mrs. Newsome was joined by two young women who looked as if they might be her daughters, whose arms were full of cakes and cookies.

Vinnie hurried to the register to ring up the sales.

"What a generous offer," Karen whispered, her arm linked through Al's.

"I'm speechless," Charlie admitted. "All of this. It's amazing."

"Maybe we can move some of the duds in the used section to the basement to make room for her books," Felicia said.

"Sure. I'll help you with that on Monday," Al offered.

Lenora knew she should be just as happy as they were and just as excited about planning the marketing of the Ott books, but her heart couldn't be lifted. She turned to seek the quiet of the back room, until Felicia caught her by the arm and turned her to face an approaching couple.

Oh, God, Lenora thought. Mike the ex and his new wife, Rochelle, dolled up in preppy yachting gear, heading toward her with big smiles plastered on their faces. *Okay, be pleasant. Say hi.*

"What a fabulous turn-out," Rochelle gushed.

"Yes, it is," Lenora said. After a nasty divorce, she and Mike had settled into an awkwardly amicable relationship, and his second wife had always been nice to her. Weird, sort of, but then, she was not the woman who helped Mike cheat on Lenora–she'd been the one with whom he'd cheated on *that* bitch.

"Listen." Mike cleared his throat and reached into the inside pocket of his very expensive looking Gore-tex rain jacket and plucked out a check, which he held out to Lenora. "We just want to do our part. Good luck to you guys."

Stunned, Lenora stood like a statue as he bent forward and kissed her cheek. Her partners rallied around and made the big fuss she knew Mike would want made of him, as she smiled absently and nodded once in a while until the nautical pair made their exit. Using the need to tuck the check safely away as an excuse, Lenora went into the back room, hoping it would be empty. Two Lakeside Bakery employees and a teenaged daughter belonging to one of them were sipping and chatting around the coffee maker. Lenora slipped into the tiny bathroom and leaned her back against the closed door. She unfolded

Mike's check and took a peek. Five hundred dollars. *Wow*. Tears welled up in her eyes and she dabbed at them with toilet tissue. Then she did some practiced deep breathing and willed herself not to cry. Why ruin her make-up? Yes, it was still early, but why waste the day waiting and hoping? *Just get back out there and have fun, damn it. Jason's not going to show.*

CHAPTER TEN

"I love flea markets. I've been trying to find serving pieces to match my old dishes for ages." Felicia said as she helped Lenora slide a cardboard box into the hatch of Felicia's car. "And that picture frame will look great in your dining room."

"Yep, we scored," Lenora agreed, pulling the door shut and dusting off her hands. "Do you mind if we take another swing past that stall with the old galvanized milk cans and barn finials before lunch? I think I've decided on one of the cans."

"Of course not," Felicia said. "Best to be a little late to the lunch tent, anyway. See, the line's going down already."

Lenora turned in the direction of Felicia's pointed finger and nodded. They stepped out of the parking lot and skirted a stall filled with antique oak furniture and another brimming with calico curtains and embroidered table linens.

"This is so much bigger than the flea markets in Wayne County. And such cool stuff. It was worth the two-hour trip to Allentown."

"I thought you'd enjoy it," Felicia said, fingering a tag on a cane-seated chair before catching up with her friend. "It's a beautiful Sunday for a drive."

"You know how I usually complain a little bit about more hours in the summer months? Well, I'm not doing that this year. How foolish. It's much better than losing the store."

"Absolutely."

Lenora was grateful for the invitation to join Felicia and had been trying to keep up a cheerful attitude all day. But their predicament was never far from her thoughts, even after yesterday's spectacular display of Brookdale's love and support. "Do you really think we can pull this off? I mean, okay, the bake sale turned out to be awesome. Everyone loves bookstores in general and ours in particular. But, we have to come up with a lot more money to qualify for that loan. And the clock is ticking. September first isn't that far away."

"To tell the truth," Felicia said, "I don't know. I'm just going on faith. But I'm not really the Polyanna Vinnie insists that I am. I admit I've been checking the want ads and the employment websites."

"Have you, really?" Lenora was shocked. "I've asked my old boss about the possibility of more freelance assignments, too. I could probably build up enough of a clientele to help pay the bills, but I'd have to work more hours than I do at the store." She sighed as they approached the stall she had wanted to revisit. "I like advertising work, but I don't love it. I guess I'm spoiled, right?"

Felicia was hefting one of the huge metal finials that once graced the peak of a barn's cupola. "I don't love secretarial work, either, but I did it for enough years and I certainly could do it again." She called Lenora's attention to the stall's proprietor, who was making his way over to them with a big smile on his face. "Maybe we should be believing one hundred percent in the saving of the store, but a girl's gotta have a plan B, right?"

"May I help you ladies with something?" the ruddy-faced antiques dealer said.

Lenora tried to perk herself up for the encounter. "Yes. Can you do any better on this one?"

"How about seventy-five? One less thing to pack up and take home."

Lenora smiled. "Done."

* * *

Lenora's mood was considerably improved by the purchase of the milk can. After eating, she and Felicia laughed and gabbed as they made one more round of the stalls before heading back to Felicia's car for the ride home.

"I'll drive to the rest stop and then you take over?" Felicia asked and Lenora agreed. She'd have been happy to bring her car and do all the driving but the little BMW wouldn't have had room for many treasures.

Felicia popped in an old Fleetwood Mac CD she'd purchased from one of the vendors and the two women sang along and shared their memories of the eighties on the way through town to the Turnpike entrance. Lenora turned to look out the passenger side window as they were rolling past a Tucked Inn. She was admiring the pretty display of late spring tulips when her gaze was arrested by the sight of a familiar face. Jason—and a tall, attractive woman with long sandy-blonde hair—emerged from the restaurant at the front of the building, smiling and chatting. Lenora's heartbeat and breathing halted for a brief moment. Turning in her seat, she watched them as long as she could. They walked to a white Toyota and appeared to say their goodbyes. He opened the driver's door for her, then watched her back out of the parking slot. Lenora scanned what she could see of the parking lot for his car, but there wasn't time Felicia had driven on.

Well. . .okay. Lenora faced front again and tried to regroup. Most likely a business lunch. Allentown was part of Jason's territory. Maybe the woman was an owner or buyer for a local lumberyard or other such business that sold his line of fireplaces. Sure, it was Sunday, but maybe she'd been too busy during the week. They had appeared to be enjoying each other's company, but they hadn't touched or kissed. Of course, an illicit couple wouldn't, in a parking lot, but they probably wouldn't dine in such a public place, either. Lenora pulled in one more deep, calming breath and let it out slowly.

"You okay, Hon?"

"I'm sorry, Felicia, what were you saying?"

"Just that I'm enjoying the eighties a lot more now, talking about them with you, than I actually did at the time. You sure you're feeling okay?"

Lenora reached out and squeezed her friend's arm. "Of course I am. I was just thinking the same thing."

* * *

Vinnie twisted the key and let herself into The Paper Pirate through the back door. The meeting room/kitchenette was lit only by a couple of small nightlights, but instead of flipping the switch, she paused to let her eyes adjust to the dimness. It wasn't likely that anyone would notice someone moving about in any of the shut-up Main Street stores on a Sunday evening, but she wanted to be absolutely sure that her errand was kept secret. Leaving on the glasses that she usually needed only for driving helped her navigate around the table and find the swinging door that led into the sales space. Here, white mini holiday lights illuminated the display window at the street entrance and the front of the sales counter year-round. Vinnie made use of their soft illumination to snake between the tables and easy chairs and make her way to the staircase.

The fact that Harry Knox liked Vinnie's writing had been a lovely surprise that still delighted her. Of course, he couldn't make an appearance at the bake sale yesterday. They didn't exactly hide their relationship, but they certainly didn't advertise it, either, even after nearly three years of dating. Virtually all of her partners knew she was involved with a man, and one or two probably knew who he was, but they hadn't heard the information from Vinnie. Although there was no need whatsoever for secrecy, she was fiercely protective of her privacy. Harry seemed to enjoy that bit of harmless intrigue and gladly went along with it. When she returned home after the shop closed yesterday, she'd found him sitting in her porch rocker, partially veiled by the trumpet creeper that clambered up one of the support posts. After a kiss, he'd inquired about the success of the bake sale and tucked a check of his own into her hand. He listened attentively to her account of the readings and the generous gift of the many books by Mr. and Mrs. Ott's daughter as they ate dinner. Vinnie found it vaguely quaint that he had remained so considerate and charming after all their time together. She had trouble admitting to herself that his kindness and interest in the things she cared about were due in any measure to affection. She was glad of his desire for her because she wanted him, too. But if he loved her. . .well, it was just easier to keep things as they were.

Relaxing among the pillows and blankets a bit later, Harry surprised Vinnie by expressing interest in hearing what she had read at the fundraiser.

"Um, I left the book at the store," Vinnie said, with a puzzled frown, pushing her long hair off of her forehead and propping herself on an elbow. "I don't think I have a copy here."

"So much the better," Harry said with a mischievous smile. "Then read me something of your own."

Astonished, she pulled on her robe and padded barefoot up to her studio and returned with the first pages she had laid hands on, a short story—careful to have not picked up the product of her "collaboration" with Ben Conway. Nestled back against the pillows, she read her work to Harry for the first time and he liked it. He hadn't just claimed to like it. She could read the pleasure on his face quite plainly, and his comments made it obvious that he understood what she was trying to portray and how she was going about getting to her conclusion. *Son of a gun.* She was sorry she'd gently avoided this moment for so long.

A satisfied smile spread across Vinnie's face even now, as she tripped on the last step and fumbled about in the shadows for the little stool. She lifted *The Stargazer at Dawn* out of her purse and gave the cover a farewell glance before tucking the book back into its place on the dusty top shelf. "It's been nice flirting with you, Benjamin," she murmured, aloud, "but Harry's a lot more fun. And he likes my work."

CHAPTER ELEVEN

Al burst through the back door of the shop, yanked off his jacket and impaled it on one of the wall hooks, noticing that everyone else's wrap was hung up already. "Sorry I'm late," he hollered, but in fact, he wasn't sorry at all. Since the bake sale on Saturday, he and Karen were "on" again, and she'd only left for home at the same time he'd headed to The Paper Pirate. He wasn't on sales duty today, but every partner had agreed to help clear out the duds that had been in the used section for eons to make room for the donated Ott books, which would begin making their appearance bright and early tomorrow.

"I'm down here." Charlie's muffled voice floated up the cellar stairs and through the open doorway. "Come and help."

"You got it, buddy." Al's heavy steps created thunder on the wooden treads. Charlie was slitting open one of the boxes that held ready-to-assemble wire shelving units. By Al's calculations, they'd been ready for the better part of two years. "Where're the girls?"

Charlie nodded toward the ceiling. "Up in used. Boxing up and making room. And I'm making room down here."

"There's probably enough shelf space here already—" Al began.

Charlie interrupted him. "Vinnie has spoken. Besides, it's high time we got these out of their cartons." He stooped and snatched at a strip of paper. "Ah. The instructions."

"We don't need those," Al brushed him off, grabbing one of the uprights.

Charlie sighed patiently. "Humor me."

Al smiled, fondly. Everything his meticulous partner did ended up looking right, working well, and deserving compliments. He handed the support piece to Charlie and opened the instruction sheet, smoothing the folded paper against the leg of his jeans.

In spite of the fact that they were quite different, they enjoyed a shared background that most working-class men could claim they'd been brought up to tinker and create things with their hands. Al settled into the supporting role, partly out of respect for Charlie's skill, but mostly because Charlie never insisted upon it. They worked well together, and the pair of shelving units were assembled and secured to the wall in short order. Al noticed the look of quiet pleasure on Charlie's face and grinned

"Looks good," he said.

Charlie stood facing him with his hands on his hips. "That's what we do, Al. That's what men do. We build, we fix, we protect. And just because we're not the only ones who can do those things hasn't stopped us yet."

* * *

Nina tugged at the blonde wig—who knew these damn things came in sizes? This one was a little too big for her and slipped around uncomfortably. She covered the half block between her and the shop quickly, then grasped the door handle and pulled. Two men younger than she was gladly let her hold it open while they sauntered out of The Paper Pirate. Nina glowered. But, she told herself, their lack of manners was the fault of the frumpy outfit. When dressed as herself, wearing her own hair and a little make-up, men of all ages scurried to hold doors, lift boxes, and generally ingratiate themselves to her even when it was obvious that their only reward would be her smile. *So, this is a good thing*, she reminded herself. *The disguise is working.*

Rick had returned to her country house prison early on Saturday, and had been furious with her for failing to locate *Stargazer*. "You'll stay away from that store, now. I don't want you to become obvious," he had growled. This Monday morning, she was slipping inside the bookstore instead of hustling off to do the grocery shopping as she was ordered to do, while Rick took a walk to clear his head. Although a little anger on Rick's part just about ensured exciting encounters in bed, too much was a bad thing. It made him distant instead, harsher, and scary. Forbidden or not, Nina was determined to take one more shot at finding the damned book and redeeming herself so that she might bask in the riches that were waiting for them.

The place was buzzing with activity. Six customers browsed, and it looked like all five of the owners were present, arguing in the used section at the top of the stairs and ferrying boxes of books across the sales floor, behind the counter, and into the back room. She had to step quickly out of the way to avoid the little one with the short black hair, who was struggling to keep her smartphone against one ear while she carried a box that was likely too heavy for her. Sounds like muffled hammering seemed to emanate from beneath the old floorboards.

Such a fuss. Nina herself didn't love books. Magazines and newspapers were more to her liking, but she'd always put on a good show for Rick. She feigned interest in a best seller on the table closest to the front window, hoping to escape notice until things quieted down upstairs, so she could carry out her search in peace. She hoped it wouldn't take too long—she really did need to get those groceries before returning to the cabin.

The voice of someone nearly barking orders floated down the stairs—sounded like the tall, blonde woman who'd spooked Nina by observing her a little too closely on Wednesday. Drifting over toward the biographies to conceal herself, Nina heard the forced cheerfulness of another woman's reply.

"We have plenty of time, Vinnie. We can do this. Let's not get upset with one another."

Suddenly, two youngsters burst out of the children's section, running carelessly, and flushing her out of hiding and into the center of the sales floor. The third female owner, the slightly chubby one with the thick brown hair was instantly upon her and they collided. The woman must've had her head turned back toward the stairs as she uttered the last of the platitudes likely intended to calm her testy partner. She offered Nina a sweet smile, and a "sorry, hon," then gave a little shriek when she noticed that the overstuffed box of books she had been carrying had tilted precariously, and at least a half dozen volumes were beginning an almost slow-motion slide toward the floor.

Pissed off and wary of discovery, Nina stifled a reply, adjusted her wig and considered the shelter of the biographies section again when the wayward children made another pass, followed by their angry mother, causing Nina to swerve and face the book shop owner again. The woman was desperately trying to rescue the sliders, still clutching the heavy box. One by one the books flopped onto the carpet. Rapid fire images hit Nina one by one: a cookbook, a biography, a volume of landscape photos and then—she gasped audibly. The vintage treasure she'd cradled in her hands a week ago. Although she hadn't the slightest intention of helping the floundering saleswoman at first, Nina dashed forward and stuck out her hand to grasp *The Stargazer at Dawn*. Her thoughts raced. She'd catch it, scoop up the other fallen books while she was at it, return the rest, then turn *Stargazer* over a bit and say, "Well, maybe I'll take this one," nonchalantly. *Yes. Sweet victory!*

However, the two giggling tots returned to circle her, trying to tag one another, as the book bounced onto the rug, spreading its pages at exactly a spot that showed the long-dead Mr. Zoloty's writing in a foreign hand. Breathless, Nina dove forward, willing to land on her knees if she had to, but one of the children yanked on the hem of her jacket and forced her to turn for a split second. When she lurched toward the prize again, she saw an older man scooping up all the books, sliding them back into the box he had taken from the woman.

"I've got this, Felicia," he said kindly. "If you'd like, you can just stuff the boxes, and Al and I will carry them down to the basement."

Nina's pounding heart nearly stopped. Her head swam and her throat was parched. She barely heard Felicia coo, "Aw, Charlie, you're such a gentleman," as she headed back to the stairs, pausing to help the frazzled mother collect her children. Aghast, Nina felt the world go dim and her knees begin to buckle. She gulped a lungful of air and fled the store so she wouldn't pass out.

* * *

Nina abandoned the car and dashed up to the cabin door. The keys she clutched in her trembling hand slithered out of her grasp and clattered about on the welcome mat. Cursing, she knelt and groped for them, accidentally knocking them into the shrubbery. The weathered door swung open just as she dug them out of last fall's dried leaves. Rick stood glaring and opened his mouth to speak. The words died in his throat as she shoved him back into the hallway and slammed the door shut.

"It's there," she croaked, her chest heaving as she struggled for breath and calmness.

Obviously astonished, he gaped at her. "What's there? Where the hell are the groceries?"

"*Fuck* the groceries," Nina said. "The book. The *Stargazer*. It's still at The Paper Pirate."

"But I thought—"

Nina stepped up to him and clutched at the front of his fleece sweater. "Rick, I swear to you, it was nowhere in that store last week. I positively scoured the shelves. I don't know where it's been, but I saw it there today." Without dropping her eyes from his, she snatched the crooked blonde wig from her head and gave it a toss in the direction of the sofa.

"You're sure it's the one?"

"Of course I'm sure. How many copies of that book do you expect are floating around? Besides, I saw the handwritten notes. It was the one. It's there." Dropping her purse and shedding her jacket, she began to pace the length of the living room, between the fake stone fireplace and front entryway where Rick stood, too stunned to speak. "They were boxing up books in the used section and carrying them to the basement for some reason. It fell onto the floor no more than a few feet away from me. I would have had it in my hand if that little bastard kid hadn't distracted me." Nina's wild eyes darted around the room before she covered her face with her hands and let out a tortured wail.

"All right," Rick said, stunning her with his quiet tone, approaching carefully and settling his heavy hands on her shoulders. "Let's sit a minute. We'll think."

Nodding gratefully, Nina grabbed her purse and sank onto the sofa. She extracted a small brush and tried to put her matted hair to rights while Rick assumed a meditative posture beside her, elbows on knees, chin in his hands. At last, she gave up the styling attempt and twisted it into a careless knot instead, which was really all her trembling hands could manage.

"If they're storing it in the basement, for whatever reason, neither of us is going to be able to buy it. We can't risk marching in there and asking for it point blank, can we? Or *can* we?"

Rick pulled himself up straighter, head swaying from side to side, as if he hadn't yet committed to a shake or a nod. "I'd rather not. Besides, they probably don't even know they have it. It's a book practically no one's ever heard of. Most likely, they'll just say that they can't help us."

Settling down, Nina struggled to collect her thoughts. "We're doing nothing wrong by asking to purchase a book. We could even say one of us saw it in the store earlier, and ask if they'd recently moved any stock to the basement."

Rick looked doubtful. "Technically, we could do that. Technically." He locked eyes with hers. "But of course, we can't."

"Why not? It's just another lousy two dollar used book to those people," Nina sniffled, wiping at her eyes with her sleeve.

Rick sighed deeply. "Charlie Santorelli. One of the owners. He was vaguely familiar to me, so I checked him out. He's a rare books dealer like me. If we go in there asking for an obscure book, and he notices the writing inside—and trust me, he will notice—he'll deny having it, do a little investigating of his own and easily learn about Mr. Zoloty. Zoloty approached several New York dealers before coming to me. I was the first man to agree to make this extensive search. And after two months of hard work on my part, my competitor will be the one to reap the reward." Rick shook his head firmly. "It can't happen that way."

Nina raised her tear-streaked face to his. "We can go on a day when he's not working."

"No. My guess is that any of them will be suspicious enough to check the book out with Santorelli first. We can't risk it. However," Rick settled back against the cushions. "There is another way. I'll offer to buy the store," he said, and a grin spread across his face, no doubt in response to her jaw dropping open. "We've heard the local gossip. They're in financial trouble. I have the money for a down payment on a new loan, which they lack. They've got to have been considering the possibility of having to sell the place. I could make them an offer. I'd have the book, sell it for $500,000.00, and then," he shrugged, casually, "If I can't find a buyer for the shop right away, I can hire a small staff to run it for a while, until I can. Either way, I really can't lose. Now, which alias shall I trot out? How about Paul the accountant?"

He looked inordinately proud of himself, Nina thought, fighting off an anxiety attack. She nodded cautiously. Buying the book would bring too much scrutiny. Buying a cash-strapped store would be...well, American.

Who knows? It might work.

CHAPTER TWELVE

The sound of brass bells jangling announced the arrival of a customer, making Vinnie look up from the Excel spreadsheet on her laptop. Those deplorable bells; she thought she had stuffed them safely out of sight, but obviously, Felicia had found them and returned them to the knob.

Vinnie and Charlie were sitting beside each other behind the sales counter, but the eyes of the swarthy-looking man who approached them were fixed on her partner, and the man extended a hand to Charlie alone.

"Good day, sir," he said. "My name is Paul Gronsky."

Charlie rose and nodded, gripping the man's well-manicured hand. "Carlo Santorelli. What can we help you with today?"

"I'm here to discuss a business matter concerning your bookstore. I have an offer to propose, and I believe it might be of considerable interest to you."

Vinnie got to her feet and folded her arms, thoroughly pissed. The man was very obviously ignoring her. "What about the bookstore?"

Gronsky glanced at her only briefly, impatiently, as he might've done if she was a child who had no business interrupting the conversation. Eyes riveted on Charlie again, he continued. "I've noticed the flyers around town, the fundraising efforts. I'm a huge fan of brick-and-mortar bookstores, and I'd hate to see Brookdale lose this treasure. I'm a silent partner to a very successful bookseller in New York, and I have a vacation home near here. I'm approaching retirement age but can't imagine giving up working entirely. A shop like this would be the perfect solution. When I heard about your financial difficulties, I couldn't help wondering if you might consider selling The Paper Pirate to me?"

"The business isn't on the market," Vinnie said, coolly, earning her a quick glance from the oily patron. The bells clattered again, and a mother with two small children entered the store.

Gronsky leaned toward Charlie and lowered his voice. "Mr. Santorelli, I hope we can meet privately to discuss this matter further. I've done a little research on comparables and I'm prepared to make an offer of $275,000. on the building, the business, the whole package. I believe that's a bit more than you owe."

Vinnie scowled. *Asshole.* Even if they were forced to sell, there was no way she would allow this jerk to bid.

"Might we set up a time and place—"

Charlie held up a hand. "Mr. Gronsky." His voice was soft and dignified. "Please be aware of something. This store is owned by five partners, and three of them are women. If we were to consider your offer—and that's a pretty big 'if'—you'd have to deal with *all* of us."

Vinnie stifled a triumphant grin. *God bless you, Charlie.*

Gronsky deigned to give her a longer look this time. He frowned at the bold challenge in her eyes but his expression softened as his gaze traveled southward, then eased into a phony smile as he forced his gaze upwards again. Vinnie stopped herself from refolding her arms to cover her breasts, sticking her hands on her hips defiantly instead. *Yes, here they are, jackass. And this is about as close as you'll ever get to them.*

"Of course," he said, in a conciliatory tone, glancing between the two partners. He extracted a crisp business card from his wallet and although instinctively he began to hand it to Charlie, he must have thought better because he placed it flat on the counter instead. "I hope to hear from you soon." With a nod, Gronsky turned and left the shop.

"What an absolute jerk," Vinnie said, in a hushed tone the other patrons wouldn't overhear.

Charlie picked up the card gingerly, as though it reeked, and moved it back and forth until he obviously found the spot at which he could read it without glasses. "He's certainly a page out of the past."

Vinnie leaned over to see for herself. "He's an accountant?"

"That's what it says. And evidently a silent partner in some sort of bookstore in Manhattan."

Vinnie snorted a little. "Not silent enough for me."

* * *

"No, Mom, that's wrong," Lenora said, tucking her legs under her. "We don't *always* meet on Thursdays. It just seems like it to you because that's a convenient day for both Jason and me. As a matter of fact, I just spent a weekend at his place." She had been curled up with a book on the window seat in the box bay window facing the lake when her cell phone had rung, and she shifted position now so she could focus on the calming view of the water dotted with a few small craft.

"All right," her mother replied, gently, but sounding a bit

weary. She'd just reported on the progress of the community vegetable garden before broaching the subject of Lenora's romantic relationship, so she was probably sitting in her favorite chair by the window in her north Bronx apartment. "The last thing I want to do is argue with you. It's just that no matter what our age, we get a bit short-sighted when we think we when we love someone."

Lenora frowned. *Think?* "I know that happens, Mom, but it's not what's going on here." Good thing she had settled down after the odd Jason-sighting on Sunday and realized that of course she had witnessed a business lunch that couldn't have been squeezed in during business hours. She felt she could listen patiently to her mother's fussing and not start an argument.

"I believe you," her mother said, her voice wavering a bit too much. "Look, Lenora, I would love it if you found a man to care for you. You're still young enough for an adopted family, if you want one, and nothing would make me happier than seeing you settled. You're a grown woman and smart, and I know you can take care of yourself. But I can't shake the feeling that you seem determined to sabotage yourself. Maybe because of Eric. . ."

"Mom, *please*."

"Okay, that sounds like a little too much drama, but you know what I mean. Sometimes it's like you seem to think you don't deserve the best—which you do. What happened truly was not your fault."

Lenora straightened herself and held up her chin, even though her mother couldn't see her. "Mom, let's agree to let go of Eric, please, shall we? It was in another lifetime and I was just a kid and no, I *don't* blame myself."

"It's just that I. . ."

"Mom, I love you, but I don't want you to become a helicopter parent at this late stage. We've had our difficulties, but we've forged a good relationship, and I really want to hang onto that. I'm sorry, Mom, I have to go now, but I'll call during the week. I want you to come up and stay for a weekend before we get into our busy season at the shop, okay?"

Her mother hung up after sounding like someone surrendering her position for the sake of peace, not like a woman convinced that her daughter was perfectly okay. Restless now, Lenora set the cell phone down on the window-seat cushions and got up to walk the length of the big ranch house to the kitchen for a cup of tea she didn't really want. Anger rose inside her and she tried to turn the gas down before the pot boiled over. Her mother had turned eighty early in the year, and although she was basically healthy and still mostly independent, she did have a lot of time to sit around and ponder things that made her worry—particularly about her children—when there was no pressing need.

Eric, indeed. Why couldn't her mother let that sad memory go? Her high school boyfriend's face drifted across her mind and Lenora shivered, involuntarily. *Just a chill*, she insisted to herself, deciding she did need a warm cup of tea after all.

* * *

"Fool." The sound of Rick swatting the kitchen table with the folded newspaper startled Nina, and she turned quickly from the sink, where she had been rinsing a coffee mug. "Santorelli is a fool to let that pushy bitch control him."

"Oh?" Nina forced her tone to sound like she barely had any interest in his rant.

"She stuck her pretty nose in and had the nerve to interrupt me."

Nina nodded, absently. "This was the tall, blonde one?"

"Yes," Rick growled. "Although I doubt any of them know their place."

The pig. Nina shrugged. "Well, she *is* an owner. I guess she's concerned about the store."

Rick dragged out a kitchen chair and sat down heavily. "What kind of a man gets himself tangled up in business with women? And defends one of them when she makes an ass of me?"

A gentleman? Nina wisely kept that to herself, beginning to like this Charlie Santorelli guy.

"A *fool,* that's who," Rick thundered, slapping the table with the flat of his meaty hand.

"Maybe they'll discuss your offer and take you up on it anyway. They're in trouble, as we both know. If they need to sell, it won't matter if you all like each other or not."

Rick sneered, and seemed to begin to settle down. Nina sashayed over to the table and made sure to rub up against him slightly as she feigned interest in the local news headlines. She had developed a knack for sensing just the right level of his anger and agitation that would produce an interesting evening without risking any bruises to herself. She didn't have to like or respect him in order to use his money or enjoy his company in bed, and appearing to take his side would earn her valuable points that she needed. Rick leered up at her, pulled her onto his lap and pushed his hands up under her sweater. She nearly always guessed right, and tonight proved to be no exception.

CHAPTER THIRTEEN

"It's just so sudden," Felicia said. She glanced around the table at the faces of her partners, all summoned for an emergency meeting in the back room of The Paper Pirate on Wednesday evening. "I know we were saying that we might have to consider selling the store, but the fundraising is going so well and I thought we were all feeling optimistic."

"We were," Charlie said, gently. "But this man's offer came out of the blue and it's only right that we discuss it."

"I know how Felicia feels," Al said. "I kind of thought it would be our decision. Like, if we really did need to sell, we'd vote on it, pick the realtor, choose an asking price. I mean, that's usually how this goes."

"I think we all felt that way," Vinnie said. "And to add to that, I'd hoped that we'd have some kind of say about who carried on running the store. I mean, we've seen how much affection the town has for us. Don't we owe it to them to see to it that if someone else must take over, it's the right person? This Gronsky character is disgusting."

"Maybe he's a good businessman," Charlie said, a distressed frown creasing his normally serene brow. "I Googled him. He seems to have been a CPA in the city for a number of years. Maybe he'd know enough to hire staff more friendly and respectful than he is to actually man the sales desk."

"Well, we're running very short on time, so I guess we need to take a hard look at where we stand right now, financially," Lenora said, "so we'll know if selling is something we have to consider. You guys have to admit, we've all been in denial about the possibility."

Vinnie turned a disdainful look upon their young partner, but Felicia had to admit Lenora was right.

"Okay, let's get it all out in the open," Al said, rubbing his forehead.

Felicia listened attentively as Vinnie laid out the hard facts each partner already had on his or her copy of the report. Having been the Cocolo family accountant, Felicia was accustomed to dealing with figures. Yet now, the numbers seemed to swim around in her brain as soon as they slipped in through her ears: $243,596. owed to the bank on September first, to pay off the balloon mortgage; the need to put down 20 per percent now, rather than the ten they'd scraped together initially, simply to keep their monthly payments in a range they'd be able to afford. $48,719.—the figure was uttered with cool detachment by Vinnie, but the sound of it made Felicia transfer the tissue she'd slipped into her skirt pocket—just in case—to one of the hands she held in front of her on the table. It was one hell of a lot of money.

On the plus side, Vinnie related, they had a little over five thousand of their business savings to contribute, they'd gotten that small business grant for $3,500, and the Go Fund Me page, remarkably, had netted them $4,700. so far. They could keep it running for a while, but admittedly, donations had begun to taper off sharply. Remembering that the bake sale fundraiser had brought in $2,800 made Felicia raise the tissue to the corner of an eye. *Amazing*. How sweet and generous the wonderful townspeople were. The partners might or might not get the $5,000 grant that was still pending. Without it, the down payment needed by September 1 would be $32,619.20.

"We should hear the final decision about the five thousand dollar grant sometime next week," Vinnie said, closing the lid of her laptop. "Personally, I feel we ought to operate on the assumption that we're *not* going to get it. Of course, I hope I'm wrong."

Al sighed. "Point is, either way, we're far from the goal. Scary far."

"Even if we decide to put the place on the market, it could be a long process," Lenora said softly, drawing imaginary curlicues on the tabletop with her fingertip. "It could take more months than we have left to find a buyer."

"And here's an offer that just fell into our laps," Al said. That hung in the air for quite a while before anyone else spoke.

Felicia sniffled and blew her nose. To hell with Vinnie if she didn't want to see anyone get emotional. Charlie turned a warm smile on her, and, after she'd stuffed the tissue back into her pocket, he reached out and squeezed her fingers gently.

"Let's take a really quick, absolutely preliminary vote on what we might possibly do about Mr. Gronsky's offer," he said. "Right now, I vote no."

"Absolutely no," Vinnie said. "And that's a 'no' having nothing to do with the fact that he's a slimy chauvinist."

"Uh. . .I don't know," Al said, looking guilty. "Maybe. Okay, I don't want a jerk like that saving our hides, but, well. . .a bird in the hand. . .we wouldn't ever have to see him again and like

Charlie said, maybe he'd end up being good for The Paper Pirate."

Although Vinnie shot him a look full of daggers, he didn't look repentant.

Lenora groaned. "I hate myself for saying this, but I'm a 'maybe' also. I'm just so against us *losing* the store, having it taken away from us because we defaulted. I'm sorry, guys," she said, turning to Charlie and Vinnie. "I'm a 'maybe.'"

Felicia's stomach lurched when, as she knew they would, all eyes turned to her. She let out a little wail, and Al grinned, tilting his chair back and reaching over to the counter for the box of tissues, which he slid across the table toward her.

"Thanks, Al," she said, whipping two of them out and waving them around a bit. "My heart says no, of course. But I have never defaulted on any loan in my life. Even though I know our personal finances are separate from the business, I'd be mortified. My parents would roll over in their graves. They'd forgive just about any sin short of murder, but not this."

"Your parents are dead," Vinnie said, dryly. "Where are those rose-colored glasses you're always sporting?"

"Aww, don't be mean, Vinnie," Lenora said, reaching out to pat Felicia's shoulder. "We've always stuck together, no matter what."

"All right, I apologize," she conceded. "I certainly recognize the need to do *that*."

"Look," Charlie said, holding out both his hands, palms out, in a "halt" gesture. "I have an idea. Let's tell him no. Not only will we hear about the second grant pretty soon, but we have that big fancy dinner-dance fundraiser coming up in a month. The tickets are going to be a hundred dollars a couple. There's the potential to make up a big part of the deficit that night. Let's keep our minds open and all options on the table, of course, but let's tell him no tomorrow."

"Deal," Al said. "Hey, he might even come back with a better offer." This too, fell flat, and he sat back dejectedly. "Sorry. What does everyone else say?"

It was unanimous. "Deal." Vinnie was the last to say it, and an unpleasant sneer crept across her pretty face as she did. "I volunteer to be the one to deliver the news."

"Uh, I wonder," Lenora said, looking a bit nervous, "I wonder if maybe one of the guys should tell him. I mean, if he's such a misogynistic jerk, will he really accept the decision from any of *us*?"

"She has a point," Al ventured. "How about we have Charlie tell him? He seems to have some respect for Charlie already."

Vinnie scoffed. "Someone like that has little respect for anyone."

"Who cares what an asshole like that thinks of us, anyway?" Lenora said.

"There's that generational thing, again," Vinnie said. "You came of age after the women's rights movement had caught on. You didn't have to deal with the same amount of crap Felicia and I did."

"I'll do it only if *everyone* agrees," Charlie said. "I think that no matter who is the messenger, we must tread lightly. I'd hate to come onto him with a superior attitude and then be forced to take his offer—or worse yet, seek him out to ask if it's still good—later on."

Felicia beamed at him. He knew just how to say almost anything in the right way. "I'm fine with Charlie turning Mr. Gronsky down."

"Me, too," Lenora said, shooting Vinnie a sweet little "c'mon, how about it?" smile.

Vinnie dragged her chair back, rose, and drew herself up to

her full height. "Very well. This evening has given me a beastly headache. I'll expect to be informed of Gronsky's reaction."

Charlie nodded. "Of course."

* * *

Why is Dominick Jr.'s car in my driveway? Felicia wondered, pulling in behind him. She was feeling vulnerable and in no mood to endure an encounter with her son, who was hard to take even on her most confident days.

"Dominick?" she called out, locking the front door and dumping her purse and sweater on the hall table. "I'm home."

No reply, but when she followed the sound of the television she found her firstborn ensconced in the chair that had been placed in the spot his father's old recliner had once occupied. His feet were up on her nice coffee table, something she hated even though he'd taken his shoes off, and obviously he had helped himself to a plate of leftovers and a bottle of beer. Felicia regarded him sternly, hands on her hips, which was probably what prompted him to place his feet on the floor and turn his eyes from the blaring TV set to her face.

"Hi, Ma."

Felicia aimed the remote at the television and dialed back the volume considerably. "Hi, yourself. To what do I owe the honor?"

Dominick flashed the same phony, unpleasant little smile his father had always used in place of the real thing. "I'm going to have to stay here for a while."

Felicia's shoulders slumped and she eased herself onto the sofa. "What gives?"

Draining the beer, he shrugged and reported, "Rent went up two hundred dollars a month. Can't afford it with my child support payments. I'll have to find another apartment." His guilty gaze slipped back toward the television screen.

"Where are your things?" Felicia almost whined.

"In storage," he said, brightly. "I came with just a couple of suitcases and moved myself into my old room. I didn't want to put you out."

Felicia's hands spread themselves out in midair, mimicking her mother's old gesture of exasperation, without her being fully aware of it. "Dominick. You don't call? You don't ask? You don't say please, Ma? *Dominick*."

He sat forward and straightened up his posture. "Please, Ma. I need help. I really can't do the two hundred more and still have enough money for the kids."

Oh, nice, mister, Felicia thought to herself. He'd started off with a semi-respectful tone, but ended with a guilt trip. She fished the wadded-up tissue out of her pocket and applied a clean corner to her eyes one at a time. She hated showing tears to Dominick Senior or Junior because to them, tears showed weakness, not humanity. But it had been a rough evening, and she couldn't help herself. "How long?" she asked, wearily.

Her son rose and paced the room, snapping, "Jesus, Ma, I don't know. I've been online already and I'm hooked up with a realtor who's looking for me. It'll be as short a stay as I can manage. I don't fucking want to be here anymore than you want me here."

Felicia looked up, wounded, defeated, exhausted. "You have to be him, don't you? You're half me, but you always, always have to be him."

To her surprise, those soft dignified words must have gotten to her son because he ended up at her side, kissing her forehead before gathering up his dirty dishes and heading toward the kitchen.

Felicia sighed deeply, lifted herself from the couch with

some difficulty and drifted toward the stairs. His kiss still felt cold upon her skin. It was her house, and he needed a place to stay for free. He'd backed off when she'd softened her stance, just like his father had done.

That was all.

CHAPTER FOURTEEN

"All right everyone, let's settle down. You'd think no one had seen food in weeks." Vinnie stood with her hands on her hips, scowling. The others hovered around the kitchenette counter, raiding bags of appetizers Felicia had brought from the Chinese restaurant to accompany their Wednesday night meeting.

"Thanks, Felicia, this was a great idea." Lenora slipped into a seat at the big oak table and popped the top on a can of soda.

"You have to let us chip in," Al said.

"Don't worry about it, just enjoy." Felicia found a seat and arranged her snacks and her chapters in front of her.

"You're too good to us, Felicia," Charlie said. "Come on, get yourself a plate and join us," he said gently to Vinnie, giving her face a closer inspection. She was something besides annoyed. *Worried? Upset?* He didn't have a chance to make up his mind before she turned her back and went to fetch an eggroll for herself.

"Who wants to begin?" Lenora asked. It was an innocent enough question, but Charlie had a feeling it wouldn't sit well with Vinnie, and in fact, it seemed not to. The present group didn't actually have a leader—the woman who started the writers' group each of them had joined years ago had long since moved away, and they'd never felt the need to choose another facilitator. But Vinnie liked to take charge, and despite her prickly, somewhat superior nature, everyone liked Vinnie.

"If I may, I'd like to share something before we start." She stood behind her chair and the seated partners looked up at her. Her lips twisted into a wry expression that she quickly corrected, and delivered her message in an emotionless tone. "I've gotten the email—we weren't the ones selected for the $5,000. small business grant."

"Aw, Geez, I had all my fingers crossed," Felicia said.

"So disappointing." Lenora's shoulders slumped.

"Ah, well, it's not that big a surprise." Al shrugged. "Would have been nice, but it's not like it would have saved us."

"And it's not like we don't have a detestable plan B so we can cash out and run away from what was supposed to be a dream for each of us," Vinnie drawled, throwing a frosty, reproachful look at both Al and Lenora.

"Hey, I didn't say that. You're putting words in my mouth."

"I couldn't if I tried, Al—it's full of food."

Charlie took his cue. "Look, we're all disappointed, but we'll take it in stride, right? Come on, guys, let's start the meeting." For some reason, his words—even when he didn't know what the hell to say—had a noticeably calming and unifying effect on the group. Maybe it was the level and confident tone of a veteran college professor, the fact that he was the oldest, or because he seemed to get more than his share of respect from the other partners. Charlie wasn't sure, but he was flattered, and always tried to live up to the responsibility that came with his assigned role.

They dispensed with Al's chapter in short order. Charlie

wanted to like the story, but frankly, it was a hackneyed attempt to write fiction, like painting by numbers. His friend had gotten hold of a book about using writing formulas to churn out popular genre fiction, and was forging ahead with his plan to create one more grumpy, troubled detective than the literary world actually needed. *Why not another gardening book?* Charlie had typed the words into the written part of his critique, but he'd ended up deleting them. Al's two previous books on the topic were witty and instructive and, hell, not everyone was meant to write fiction. He was a published author, for God's sake. The only one in the group, save for Lenora, whose few poems had made their way into a local anthology. *Write what you know*. Charlie had deleted those words, too, and had instead suggested that he give his detective a unique characteristic to set him apart from all the others out there.

Taking her turn, Lenora commented on Al's skillful creation of the moist and gloomy atmosphere on the waterfront where the main character loitered.

"I can really feel the mist rolling in," Felicia agreed. "And the shadows—makes me feel like the bad guy is hiding in every one. I like that Stoney is lured there by a really convincing ruse. You know, nobody likes when characters blunder into a situation where they're obviously going to get into trouble. I think the phony tip about another case he's working on is very effective. And, I mean, everything seems to fit—he has no idea what's going on until the very end, when it's too late. On another note, I don't really think his girlfriend would've made quite such a big scene in the restaurant. Forty-something women usually don't."

"Yeah, we learn to be much more subtle," Lenora said, with a cute little grin.

"Felicia isn't finished," Vinnie immediately scolded. Everyone looked surprised. "You've had your say."

Lenora looked as dazed as if she'd been slapped. "I'm sorry. I just said . . .I mean, usually we're not that strict. . . it was just one little comment. Go ahead, Felicia, I'm sorry." She patted Felicia's hand, and Felicia waved the whole thing away.

"Oh, no problem. I'm done anyway. It's a great mini-cliff-hanger ending, and I can't wait for chapter seventeen." She handed the marked-up chapter back to Al, and flashed a warm smile around the table, but Charlie noticed it faded when confronted by Vinnie's arctic glare.

"Thank you, Felicia," Al said, theatrically, very purposely ignoring Vinnie, who, of course, bristled.

"Not only would a forty-something woman not carry on like a total ass in a public place," she said, "but no woman who is as smart and confident and professional as you insist upon saying that Lila is would take such ridiculously childish offense at Stoney's brief and incredibly lackluster flirtation with that dopey bitch, Sandy. Lila *knew* Sandy had information that he needed. Of course he would play up to her and pretend to be interested. The whole scene drags the Lila character to a depth of imbecility that rivals even the abysmal 'trying to be a lady lawyer' scene."

Vinnie folded her hands in front of her on the table and appeared to initiate a staring contest. Al seemed more puzzled than angry.

"Well then," he said at last, reaching out to snatch his chapter from under Vinnie's elbow, "I guess I'll cut the restaurant argument scene a bit."

"Who's next?" Charlie said, brightly, wincing when Vinnie's blue eyes speared him. *Oh, shit.* He was just trying to deflect and move on. . .

"Writing's supposed to be fun, guys," Felicia said, in a soft, musical tone, bathing everyone in the warmth of her most motherly smile. "Vinnie, you're up, right? I see you're giving *Riverside Glen* a rest, huh?"

Vinnie appeared to thaw a bit. She shuffled some papers and flipped through her chapter. "Yes. I've started something new. I'd like someone to start from the beginning to the break near the end of page four. Who would like to read?"

No one volunteered. Both Al and Lenora were frowning and not looking at her. "I've got a bit of a scratchy throat," Felicia said, "but I guess I could. . ."

"I'll read," Charlie said, and that seemed to satisfy everyone. He cleared his throat and began. He couldn't help remembering how perplexed he had grown as he'd read the submission to himself at home last week. Vinnie's work was always well-crafted, often beautiful and, at times, masterful. He'd spent eight years in her company wondering why the hell she wasn't published yet. This new, untitled work was excellent, but. . .different. The voice in which it was written was similar to hers but not totally familiar. Of course, all writers experimented—he'd watched each of his fellow group members learn and grow and try out different styles in the eight years they'd been together. But those changes had always happened gradually. Vinnie's last turn was barely a month ago. No one evolved *that* quickly.

When Charlie was done reading, he gave his critique and hoped that he sounded genuine and not in the least puzzled. It was only one chapter. The next selection would probably be pure Vinnie.

Felicia positively gushed about how eloquent, how lovely, how sad the tale seemed like it was going to be, and even though Al and Lenora seemed stung by the queen bee not an hour ago, they both had appreciative and encouraging comments for her.

At about a quarter to seven they began to pack up and clear the table of leftover Chinese food.

"Remember," Vinnie said, above the voices of the others, "next time we'll expect a submission from Charlie, Lenora and Felicia."

"Oh, and hey, before we all go, listen up." Lenora dumped a load of paper plates and napkins into the trash can and brushed the palms of her hands together. "I hear the library is trying to put on some sort of a fund-raiser for the county's literacy program. I'd like to tell them that we'll do something, you know, since the town was so supportive of our store, and it's not all about us, etc."

"Sounds good," Al said, pushing in each of the chairs. "Any ideas about what to do?"

"Actually, I have one."

"Of course Lenora has one," Felicia said, proudly.

Their young friend looked bashful. "Well, this time I do. I'd heard about people doing marathon readings of classic works, or any book, really, and I thought that might be fun. We could host it here, charge an entry fee that will go to the literacy program, serve some sort of refreshments, and the five of us could take turns reading a whole book."

"Sounds like fun," Felicia said.

"I'm in," Al said, and disappeared into the staff bathroom.

"I like it," Charlie said. "We'll have to decide what to read."

"Yeah, I'll work on timing, and see how long a book we're going to have to use. It's got to take long enough to be an effort for us, but, you know, not be exhausting. Maybe we can even have volunteers from the audience come up and read a few pages for an extra big donation. I don't know, the idea needs fleshing out, but it's a start anyway."

The three partners present turned toward Vinnie, and she paused her gathering-up of personal items, seeming to realize that her opinion was being sought. In the brief silence they heard the toilet flush and the water run in the bathroom sink. "Oh, well, of course. It's a great cause and a brilliant idea to continue our support of the community. It sort of feels like making a statement that we're still here, and going to remain here."

Al rejoined them. "What book should we read? I'll look through the box lot I just got from the auction. Looks like lots of cool stuff in there."

"We'll all make suggestions and vote," Lenora said, shutting off the overhead light.

Charlie moved to flip the other light switch, but stopped when his phone rang. He fished it out of his pocket and answered, beginning to wave goodbye to his friends, then quickly holding up a hand in a sharp "stop" gesture when the caller identified himself. The four other partners froze, Al softly shutting the door he'd opened for the ladies. Charlie listened to the unctuous drivel, feeling his face harden into a snarl. The caller was embarrassed to have insulted the partners with his meager first offer, *blah, blah, blah*. The guy was nauseating when he attempted civility. Finally, Charlie heaved a sigh and nodded, briskly, as if he could be seen. "Right. I'll convey the message and we'll get back to you shortly." More blathering, but Charlie cut the man off. He powered down the phone before slipping it back into his pocket, and turned toward the eager faces across the room. "Paul Gronsky," Charlie said, with distaste. "He's upped his offer to $375,000."

CHAPTER FIFTEEN

"*Idiots*." Rick paced the length of the living room, spun awkwardly, and retraced his heavy steps.

Nina's heart picked up the pace and she felt her mouth hanging open. It couldn't be true. "They refused your second offer?"

"Bastards," he growled in reply, pushing roughly past her when she tried to stop him in his tracks. "No, but they're going to think it over. Obviously, they would, but I'm losing patience with them."

"I hope it works this time."

"It will work. It's got to work. I need to think." Rick stopped in front of the fireplace and regarded her with disgust. "It couldn't hurt for you to do some thinking yourself."

Would you even consider an idea of mine? Nina thought, but did not say. She was thoroughly pissed off with the partners. She'd hoped this book drama would be over soon, so she'd be off the hook for screwing up with her choice of Conways, and she and Rick could start enjoying a nice fat payoff. She'd been comforting herself with stealthy glances at images of the diamond solitaire necklace online. Now it seemed to have been snatched from her grasp.

"Morons," Rick blustered, and Nina found her thoughts echoing his words.

"They're sentimental," she said, coldly. She expected a rude rebuke, but he paused his storming around for a moment and seemed to consider.

"Meaning what?"

Nina lifted her shoulder in a slight shrug and settled herself calmly in the easy chair. "They need time to realize that they have to sell and move on. Even the idea of making a profit on the sale doesn't motivate them like it should. You or I would be able to make a quicker decision." She met his gaze and gave a slight smile.

Rick found himself a spot on the sofa and seemed to relax a bit. "Of course. You're right. It's just that I've spoken to Zoloty again and he seems. . .I don't know. Nervous? Agitated in some way. *Anxious*. That's the word. He told some tale of a grass-roots political group back in his home country that's mounted a campaign of sorts against this presidential candidate Zoloty wants defeated."

"Really? So there are others who agree with our client."

Rick nodded, folding and refolding the newspaper in an old subway rider's habit to isolate a story he wanted to read. "They're spreading unflattering information about the old-time dictator that the new candidate idolizes, and trying to show that, if given the power, he would engage in the same dirty deeds. They've dug up a few interesting facts, according to Zoloty, but of course the volume we're after is the treasure trove they need. He's getting antsy. I told him I'd made an offer on the store, which he thought was a brilliant idea." Rick's face eased into a vile, smug expression. "Naturally, I couldn't tell him they'd refused."

"It's just a matter of time, now that you've upped the offer." Nina plucked *The Chart Room* out from behind a cushion then thought better of bringing it out for Rick to see. She actually liked the book and wanted to finish reading it, but there was no reason to remind him of her shameful mistake just now when they were having a rare civil conversation.

"Yes, of course." He seemed to read a bit, then let the paper fall into his lap. "The guy must really be loaded. He said he's already donated thousands to this grassroots organization to fund their 'campaign of inconvenient truth' as he called it."

Nina pursed her lips and wrinkled her brow in thought. "Why does he care so much about what goes on in a country he doesn't even want to live in anymore? It's a pretty dismal place, if you can believe the news stories written about it. Surely he's long ago gotten any relatives out and settled them in London with him."

"A foolish question," Rick said, bluntly, lifting the paper to a reading angle again. "A better one is why should I give a shit why a rich man wants to spend too much money on something he thinks he believes in? Didn't some asshole just bid two hundred dollars on that extra-large cornflake before the website shut down the bidding?"

Nina considered. "I suppose you're right," she purred, and noticed that it brought the usual contented smile to Rick's craggy face. Once he seemed engrossed in the newspaper, she slipped her book out into the open, rested it on her knees to hide the cover, and began to read.

* * *

Al took a swig of beer before turning back to his laptop to continue editing. He'd already toned down the restaurant argument scene between Stoney and Lila, but hadn't totally tamed it. After all, the writing-method book he'd bought insisted that readers liked that kind of drama. What the hell had gotten into Vinnie, anyway, to have acted like such a bitch at the meeting? She could be testy at times, but never cruel, and she'd always taken the idea of respecting each author's work very seriously. Al guessed tonight's performance was caused by the fact that she held his and Lenora's "maybe" votes for selling the store against them. Still, it was no excuse to so flagrantly break the rules of critique.

A tone alerted Al that he'd gotten an email, so he maximized the right window and opened Lenora's new submission. She was trying her hand at Young Adult Fiction, a genre that actually was aimed at older children, probably about the age of her boyfriend's kids. Maybe, he thought, she was trying to reach out to them. She painted a rosy picture of their romance, but evidently Felicia didn't think things were going as well as portrayed. Al hoped Vinnie wouldn't go for Lenora's jugular at the next meeting.

He leaned over to switch on his printer and a movement outside his open window caught his eye. Preston and Phoebe were out for their evening walk. Preston leaned lightly on his cane, pausing to spin it once, like a baton, which made Al grin. *What a pisser*. He thought to call out a greeting, but Preston probably wouldn't connect the voice with the second-floor window of his neighbor's house, so Al turned back to his laptop. His writing space was a small room above the entry hall—too big for a closet, too small for much of anything else. A desk, printer stand, and three bookshelves created a cockpit-like enclosure that allowed everything to be close to hand for a writer in a rolling desk chair.

As the printer chugged and spit out pages of Lenora's chapter, a thought that Al had never entertained popped into his head and actually made him pause his editing, sit back, and consider. Would the group continue to thrive if the bookstore had to be sold? It didn't seem like the decision to sell could ever be a unanimous one, even if selling became unavoidable. Just how acrimonious would their relationships become? Al didn't want the store to fail, but he'd survive if that happened. On the other hand, he sincerely wanted to preserve the writers' group and those four friendships. Could he start another group? Would some of the others? *Shit.* That would hurt as much as Barbara's remarriage had tugged at his heart six years ago. More than the cooling off that accompanied his brother's move to New England. More, in fact—although he hadn't realized it before tonight—than anything other than his estrangement from Alice and her kids.

Al tried to set his mind to finishing the editing of his chapter, but inspiration was out on break. He'd have to do something to prevent the group from falling apart. He'd start with Vinnie. There was that charity reading they were going to do. He'd rummage through that box of old books he'd picked up at the auction and see if there was something she'd love. Virginia Woolf or Evelyn Waugh. Wait maybe something newer, since it had to appeal to the audience. Regardless, he'd find the perfect book, or rather, *suggest* it and let her decide. Al grinned. Finally, he was picking up a few tips from Charlie.

Another alert made him click to see a new message. It was Barbara, faithfully forwarding an email that their grandson Greg had sent to her alone. A photo of leggy, pale green lettuce plants greeted him. Greg's science project, no doubt. "Not bad, buddy," Al murmured. "They should've been closer to the grow lights, though. Lettuce wants to stretch too much." A heavy weight settled on his heart. It was advice he could never offer. "Good job, my man. Good job."

* * *

The breeze that drifted in through the double windows and toyed with the papers on Vinnie's desk was warm and smelled sweet—those pink blossoms from her neighbor's yard, no doubt. A glass of wine sat close at hand as she typed, and when she took a break to re-read her words, she lifted it to her lips. The brittle old volume that she copied from—before adding her own improvements—was held gently open by her eyeglass case. With a soft sigh, Vinnie lifted it and turned a page. She frowned at the coarse scribbling that covered the blank page facing the beginning of the next chapter. *Imbecile.* The wretch had no respect for a masterpiece.

She'd resisted as long as she was able, and told herself she had struggled long enough to concentrate on *Riverside Glen*, as she ought to have done. But the siren's song had reached her ears even from the depths of The Paper Pirate's basement.

"I'll probably regret this, Benjamin," she murmured aloud, swirling the pinot noir in her glass. "But the temptation is just too strong."

CHAPTER SIXTEEN

"Dominick is staying with you?" Lenora poured two cups of coffee, black for herself, Felicia's fixed up just as she liked it, and carried them both to the table.

"Don't ask," Felicia said, rolling her eyes. "Where is everyone? No one's usually late to business meetings."

Lenora shrugged, opening her laptop and angling it so that her partner could see. "Here's a list of book suggestions for the marathon reading. What do you think?"

"Oh, they all sound good. I haven't had much time to come up with any ideas. I hope Vinnie won't be mad. It's not like my son's home a lot, and not like I can't get him to help me around the house a little. It's just that it was more peaceful living alone."

"Hey, I understand. Don't worry about it. There'll be plenty of books to choose from. I've sort of timed these out, and they work out to about twelve hours, if we keep at it, which we should be able to do, with at least five readers. And I really think some of our more colorful customers would be happy to cough up a bigger donation for the literacy program in exchange for being able to read in front of a crowd."

As she and Felicia grinned at each other, Charlie came in through the back door, leaving it open while he found himself a place at the table.

"Mr. Charlie, you were born in a barn?" Felicia mock-scolded, and his eyes twinkled as he smiled at her.

"Nope," he said, "Al is right behind me."

"Hey, folks," Al said, stepping into the back room and slamming the door behind him.

Felicia rolled her eyes. "He's closed it for both of you."

"Where's Vinnie?" Al seemed to pounce on a chair and nearly dropped his laptop and a grocery sack of books on the table. "I think I have a few books she'll like for the marathon reading thing."

"She'll just be a few minutes late," Lenora said. "Dentist appointment. I have some good choices, too, but let's not forget the most important topic for discussion."

That thought seemed to cast a pall on the others, and Lenora watched Al's shoulders slump as Felicia heaved a sigh.

"Let's get it out in the open as soon as we start," Charlie said.

Lenora heard light footsteps on the back stairs and then Vinnie made her entrance. "Sorry I'm late. The dentist had some sort of emergency and it threw off all of his appointments." She took her accustomed place at the head of the table and slipped her MacBook out of its expensive leather messenger bag. "Have we begun?"

"Of course not," Charlie assured her. "We were just saying that we had best start with the most important—and most unpleasant—subject first."

"I agree. We should discuss Mr. Gronsky's new offer straight away." Vinnie fixed each partner with a challenging glance. "And no 'maybe' votes this time. Let's man up—or woman up—shall we?"

"Let's go over the numbers," Lenora said, softly. She admired Vinnie's talent and her breeding and poise, and hated the thought of being at odds with her. She'd just let that comment go.

"Very well. I see you're booted up already, so would you like to take over?"

Lenora nodded, shyly. "Mr. Gronsky's old offer would have gotten us out of hot water, and left us each with a few thousand dollars profit. Honestly, none of us really liked it," she said, glancing quickly at Vinnie and hoping she would get the message. It didn't look like she did. "The new offer of $375,000 would allow us to pay off the balloon mortgage and walk away with something in the neighborhood of $25,000 to $27,000 profit each. Theoretically, that easily would give each of us a year's time to get settled in another part time job, something all of us need." She doubted this was true for Charlie but didn't want to embarrass him needlessly. "So, it's significant, right?"

"It's significant and he knows that," Charlie said. "Obviously, each of his offers was well researched. The first one would have covered our asses and saved him a good bit of money. Now he knows just what to offer to make the figure hard to refuse."

"Oh, he's playing with us, no argument there," Lenora said. "I don't think any of us had any illusions about him dealing respectfully with us."

"Which is really neither here nor there," Al said. Vinnie shot him a lethal look and he winced. "What I mean is, *we* still decide what we do with the store. Anyone can research this stuff on the internet and any good business person *would* do that."

"Right. It's not about do we hate Mr. Gronsky," Felicia said. "It's do we want to sell the store? Period."

"I vote no." Vinnie said it as a challenge issued.

"I vote no, too." Felicia said, softly, but with absolute conviction. Lenora knew that Felicia's financial position was the weakest of them all. She was voting from her heart.

Vinnie stared hard, first at Al, then Lenora, who was very grateful when Charlie intervened.

"I vote no with a condition, or explanation, or whatever you'd like to call it."

"Which is?"

"Which is that we don't have to make a decision two days after the offer is made just because it's our business meeting night. I've spoken to Jim Alexrod from The Maples on the Lake. He's had a wedding cancel Saturday June 4. He said he nearly always refunds deposits when a couple breaks up, but these two were such a pain in the ass, he's keeping theirs. So, we can have the lower level space free of charge, and he's throwing in a bunch of small-plate selections and soft drinks."

Charlie beamed proudly as Al, Felicia, and Lenora responded with expressions of gratitude. Lenora stole a glance at Vinnie, and noticed only a forced smile.

"So, my suggestion is the same as it was last time. Let's wait until after this shindig and see what we collect there. I know it's three weeks from tomorrow, but Gronsky has no reason to be impatient. Time is against *us*, not him. He can retire with or without a bookstore."

"I don't think three weeks is too long to expect him to wait," Al said.

Lenora noticed that Vinnie huffed a bit and folded her arms. "I'm with Charlie," Lenora voted.

Vinnie didn't look impressed. "So we're sticking with that cowardly ruse, are we?"

"Not cowardly," Charlie said gently. "We'll each know exactly which way we want to vote after that last fundraiser. There'll likely be no more money coming to our aid after that party."

Lenora felt a pang of sadness. But he was right. Her mind wandered to the invitation she'd given Jason to the Pirate Ball, but now that there was a firm date, she wondered whether or not he'd come up with a previous engagement.

"Come on, Vinnie, Charlie is right," Felicia said.

Vinnie's aristocratic features twisted into a brief scowl. "So, the 'maybes' have it after all. I'm disgusted, but let's move on."

Al seemed about to say something, so Lenora quickly interrupted. "Um, I have some really cool ideas for books we can read at the marathon for literacy." She maximized her list and turned her computer to face Vinnie, who squinted a bit, rather than dig her glasses out of her purse. Lenora kindly slid the device closer. "I've sort of timed them all out. I think we can do any one of them in about twelve hours, which should be long enough to be marathon-y but not exhausting."

"I like *Storm Shelter*," Felicia said, gleefully. "Lots of drama in that one, and great dialog, which would be good for reading, since we can be a little theatrical and put some emotion into it. Sort of act it out a bit."

"Good point. Here's mine," Charlie turned his laptop around.

"Oooh, *Catcher in the Rye*," Felicia said.

Vinnie had booted up her MacBook by this time and turned its screen toward the partners. "Of course, we'll email these selections to each other and make our choice before the next business meeting so we can begin reacquainting ourselves with the chosen book."

Lenora and the others turned to Al, but instead of spinning his laptop, he pushed his plastic sack of books to the middle of the table with a triumphant expression. "Email away, but I've got the perfect ones right here."

Vinnie looked revolted, but Felicia extracted them and turned them around to inspect the titles while Lenora looked them over eagerly. *A Summer Guest*, *Rafferty's Choice*, and a classic one-hit wonder that Lenora had devoured in high school, *Dauntless,* by Eve White.

"If you want my vote, it's for *Dauntless*," Al said. "It was so well-loved when it came out, but now it's like a friend who moved away and stopped writing. It'd be a real treat to hear again. I don't know anyone who *didn't* read it back in the day. But I'll let you guys decide. And honestly, Vinnie, I kind of think, since you've been so upset about the sell/don't sell question, that you should be the one to decide."

Awww, Lenora thought. He was being so boyish and cute.

"Not *Dauntless*," Vinnie snapped, disappointing Lenora, and obviously Al as well. "I personally don't care which of these others we pick but I detest that book. I didn't know what the bloody fuss was about at the time and I certainly haven't figured it out in the intervening thirty-odd years."

"Whatever," Al said, looking royally pissed. Well, Lenora thought, after all, he did make a supremely nice gesture. "I think they should all stay in the hat and we'll all vote, which is as it should be."

"I wasn't the one to suggest that I should be the sole chooser of the book," Vinnie said. "Don't make me out to be the diva, as is your custom."

"*My* custom? There's no truth to it?"

"I came for a business meeting. Not to be insulted. We have far more important matters to deal with than this ridiculous marathon."

"Well, the book choice isn't a big deal, but the marathon

isn't ridiculous," Lenora said, sounding annoyed despite her effort not to.

"Don't obfuscate. It doesn't suit you."

Lenora was prepared to let the whole matter drop, but Al scowled and threw a fiery look at their patrician friend. "They didn't teach manners at your ivy league alma mater? What the hell's gotten into you? Do you think the book store will survive if the partnership doesn't? Even if someone gives us a million dollars? Think about it, sister."

"Um, Al. . ." Charlie murmured.

Felicia wrung her hands nervously, a little like one of her romantic heroines, Lenora thought.

"I'll thank you to remember your own manners." Vinnie stood abruptly.

"Uh, Vinnie. . ." Charlie attempted.

"I'll not be demoralized any longer. Finish the meeting without me."

"Don't give us orders," Al said. "Sit down and let's work through this."

Vinnie's face reddened and her eyes flashed blue fire. "You're a jackass."

Al looked hurt, and almost like he was going to relent, but then defiance flickered in his eyes. "And you're a freaking bitch."

Vinnie snatched up her belongings and departed in a huff. The guys looked at each other and shrugged, Charlie suggesting a switch to a discussion of the utility bills, but Lenora met Felicia's eyes and Lenora knew they'd both seen the same thing—Vinnie had been on the verge of tears.

CHAPTER SEVENTEEN

Felicia slipped three books into a bag and handed them to a smiling woman who thanked her before leaving the store in a rush. She pulled one of the stools up to the counter. "My poor feet. What a morning, huh, Charlie? Already a good crowd of summer people. Then that woman bringing all her nieces and nephews in to pick something out—they were adorable, weren't they? And the Ott books are really moving off the shelves. I'd say about a third of them have been sold."

"That's probably thanks to all the social media postings. I've had customers come in and ask for them specifically." Charlie looked up from his laptop. "Lenora says we've got a lot more followers now that we're trying to save the store. If we make it, that should really help business boom in the future."

Felicia felt a twinge of sadness. *If we make it.* "I'm praying real hard, Charlie."

"Oh, I am too, Felicia. And I'm kind of rusty at that, but it's funny how you can remember stuff you were raised with when you need to."

"What're you so busy with over there?" Felicia leaned over until the stool nearly tipped.

"The revised work schedule. I shouldn't have to do this, but it's better than all the last-minute scrambling to get someone to sub so Al and Vinnie don't have to work together. I'm not going to add to the drama, but I was pretty pissed off that I had to work five days last week. This was supposed to be a part time gig."

"Tell me about it. It's gone on way too long, Charlie. What are we going to do? I tried to talk to Vinnie but she insists that Al owes her an apology, and she wouldn't even listen to anything I had to say. She's never been this unreasonable before. She's been pretty cool to Lenora, too, although, thank Heaven, Lenora's just ignoring it, so far."

"And Al feels like he's just taken enough from her over the years and that it's finally time for her to apologize for something."

"This feud is wearing everybody down. Have you noticed we've all been getting more testy with each other? How can we go on if nobody but you and me'll work together?"

Charlie sat back, a stern frown creasing his brow. "I'm pinning all my hopes on the dinner dance this weekend, Felicia. I think that we'll make a good bit of money there, and that should improve everyone's morale. There's something like sixty tickets sold already. And Jim Axelrod from The Maples on the Lake is promoting us like crazy. They're the ritziest place for miles around, with some pretty wealthy regulars. Who knows, maybe some of them love to read and will take an interest in us."

Felicia reached out to straighten a stack of brochures. "Lenora and I went to Scranton to check out the sales racks for new dresses. It was such a strange feeling having to decide whether or not to ask Vinnie to go with us."

"Did you?"

"Of course." Felicia's shoulders slumped. "She said no."

Charlie shook his head, sadly, and returned his attention to the laptop screen.

Felicia rose and wandered out onto the sales floor. "We need a psychology book, huh, Charlie? So we can figure these two out and find a solution."

He chuckled. "Good luck with that one. I was an English major."

"Well, how about poor me with a two-year business degree?" she called from the Non-Fiction section.

"You're a woman, so you're a step ahead of me."

"Oh, I wish, Charlie. The best I can do is think that they both backed themselves into corners and don't know how to come out of it and still save face. You know what I mean?" She wasn't sure he could still hear her, as she'd drifted to the far corner of the store.

"See, that's what I said. You're a step ahead of me."

Felicia smiled a little, running her fingertips over the spines of the psychology books. Nice, but she still didn't know how to fix the mess. A trio of identical volumes caught her eye and she slipped one off the shelf and examined the cover. *Everyday Fixes*. She pried the book open carefully and read the flyleaf. Something about empowering ourselves to overcome the stuff that brings us down and damages our relationships. "Oooh." And it was written by that pretty Genevieve Garvey, one of Felicia's favorite movie stars, who had studied psychology in her youth. Felicia must not have been on duty when these were unpacked, because she hadn't realized they were here. But, no matter. *Can't hurt*. The bells on the doorknob jangled and Felicia tucked the book under her arm and strode to the middle of the sales floor to greet the new customer.

* * *

"It doesn't really matter who's right or wrong," Karen said gently, peering at Al over the tops of her reading glasses. "Either one of you can make it right."

Al sighed, and let his tablet rest on his knees. The night was cool and breezy, and they had traded the porch rockers for the comfort of Karen's bed. "I texted her." He said.

Karen's smile was a little crooked and her nose was wrinkled up a bit. "You did, huh?"

"Yeah, about store stuff, you know, the balance sheet or whatever."

"Hmm." Karen set her e-reader aside. "You two had a big blow up nearly three weeks ago, and you *texted* her about store stuff as if nothing had happened?"

Al felt his face flush. "Yeah. Okay, that was shitty of me. But, what was I going to say?"

"Um, how about, 'I'm sorry for what I said and I figured you were too. Let's have coffee and talk.'"

Al grimaced. *Well, that was just about perfect.* "Women are better at this stuff."

"A lame excuse, and incorrect, anyway, since I'm assuming Vinnie didn't say something similar to you."

"She didn't answer at all."

Karen nodded slightly, and returned her attention to her book. Al stole a sideways glance at her. She probably was going to let the matter drop, unless he continued the discussion. She was pretty damned cool, really, and he was lucky to have her. But it was kind of late to take her advice about Vinnie now, wasn't it?

He glanced back at his tablet. There was a new Facebook post from Barbara. She had shared something about their grandson, which grabbed his attention right away. Young Greg had posted a photo of an ancient Christmas cactus obviously on its last legs. Al recognized it immediately as one Barbara's mother had given her; the same one Barbara had sent to live with Alice when she'd moved to Austin, as a good luck token. The beloved ancestral plant was dying and Greg, the budding botanist—*wow, that was a hell of a pun*—was going to try to root some cuttings so that it would live on. Al scrolled and shook his head sadly at the sight of the next photo. Greg had clipped branches more than six inches long and set them in fresh soil in smaller pots.

"Look at this." Al nudged Karen and she took the tablet he offered her. "Poor kid. Sounds so confident. And most Christmas cactuses *do* root right away, but not this bastard. I remember the tough time I had rooting cuttings for Barbara before she sent this one south with Alice. Not to brag, but I have ten green fingers and it took me months. Three tries before I got a plant that lived. Know what the secret was?"

Karen shook her head, handing the tablet back to him.

"Ridiculously small cuttings. Less than two inches tall. And rooting hormone powder, something I never needed on a Christmas cactus before this devil. And a plastic bag over it like a mini-greenhouse. What a pain."

Karen gave him a sly smile. "Why don't you email and tell him that?"

"Oh." Al felt his heart sink into the pit of his stomach. "Well, he's a smart kid. He'll figure it out for himself."

"The mama plant is dying, now," she warned. "Not moving to Texas. How long do you think he has?"

Al stared at the tablet screen, feeling like he was facing a mile high steel curtain at least a foot thick. *Not long*, he thought. Then, something he'd always hated to say, "I can't."

Karen shrugged, and seemed to decide on a diplomatic course involving feigning a ravenous interest in her eBook.

Then she sighed, set it down on the mattress, and reached out a hand to stroke Al's arm. "Too much wasted time," she said, gently. "We're not kids anymore. And even if you live to be a hundred, every day you don't have them in your life is a missed opportunity." She smiled when he looked into her eyes. "It doesn't need a lot of planning or a big fuss, you know. It doesn't have to be done in precisely the right way. You just open an email and say hi and bullshit your way through a little message like you've got all the confidence in the world. Then you cross your fingers and wait. You can do it any day of the week. You can do it now."

Al felt a catch in his throat, so he chuckled a bit, to make an emotional moment lighter. He stared at the little screen. He wouldn't even have to type in an address. Just hit reply to all, and get Barbara in on the conversation, too. It might smooth things over a bit and lead to some private emails between Greg and—*oh, shit*. Who was he kidding? *Wasted time*. Twelve years without Greg, nine and a half without Emma. He twiddled the stylus and noticed that Karen was watching him. But the familiar weight settled on him and suddenly the tablet stung his fingertips. He put it aside and reached for her instead.

* * *

"So, am I invited?" Harry said it with a mischievous gleam in his eye. Vinnie felt her eyebrows arch. "To the Pirate Ball," he said, refilling their wine glasses and twisting the bottle a quarter turn just at the right moment to prevent a drip. The candle flames fluttered in his wake as he drew his arms back and picked up his utensils. It was raining and Vinnie had claimed to have set them out so that a possible power outage wouldn't disturb their meal, but the fact that she looked younger by candlelight was not lost on her.

"Well, of course," she said, patting her lips with her napkin. "I really should have mentioned it sooner. I just assumed. . . but we know how dangerous that can be." She lifted her wine glass and sipped. A horrid notion pierced her thoughts and she reached out to him across the table with her free hand. "This silly little half-intrigue that we play at. . . you know I'm not in the least bit ashamed of you, don't you?"

His melodious laugh reassured her. "Of course I know." He squeezed her fingers gently. "And I'd hoped you realized that I'm not, either. We're not actually hiding, you know. Just not, well, *displaying* the relationship."

Vinnie was delighted and rewarded him with a warm smile. "How well put. That's why you're perfect for me." *Too much*? she wondered. It always was a bit of a dance, deciding on the right words that would convey some of her feelings for him without sounding too much like "I love you."

But Harry looked pleased and carried on cutting up his steak without seeming to have a care in the world, so she must have hit the right mark.

A guttural rumble of thunder made Vinnie flinch. "I wonder when thunderstorms will stop producing an ominous feeling in my heart."

"One year," Harry said with absolute authority before putting his fork into his mouth.

"How amusing. Precisely one year?"

He nodded, and finished chewing before he said, "Yes. On October fourteenth you and your partners will be sitting around that old table of yours, laughing at how worried you'd all been about losing the store."

Vinnie wanted to play along, but felt her spirits drag. "I don't doubt you're right. About the business being saved, that is. But the part of us all sitting around the table together. . ."

She let her voice drift off because she felt a sudden tightness in her throat.

Harry regarded her for a moment, swirling his wine and taking a sip. "Have you tried to talk to Al?"

Vinnie shook her head quickly, and went to work hacking up her steak into bite-sized morsels.

"It's not an easy thing to do," Harry said, softly. "But so much easier with a buddy than a lover, don't you agree?"

"Yes, I'd been thinking the same thing. Had been, anyway. Then I decided I was wrong."

Harry chuckled. "You might just dive in. You know, give him a call about some business matter and get into a discussion about that first."

Vinnie mock-grimaced. "Harry, that's dreadful," she scolded, rolling her eyes. "So like a man."

Harry shrugged. "He's a man. I guarantee he'd respond to that approach."

Of course he would. In fact, he'd already sent a banal email about expenses that she had ignored. She felt her shoulders slouch forward. "The sad truth is that I haven't the nerve. Oh, I know how important our friendships are and I realize that there can be no Paper Pirate without amicable relations between all the partners, but I'm afraid I behaved abominably and I don't know how to. . .to. . ."

"To orchestrate the reconciliation gracefully."

Vinnie raised her glass to him. "Well done. Perhaps you should call him."

"But *I* didn't behave abominably toward him," he replied with a devilish smile.

Vinnie stifled a little giggle. *I do love you. Even though I can't quite say it.* "Well, mediate, then," she suggested, all business.

"I can go and get your phone," he teased, half-rising from his chair.

Vinnie lifted her chin and shot him a calculated look of mild disdain. "Let's not disturb our dinner. I'll call him tomorrow."

"You're a miserable liar, you know." Harry quite leered at her, elbows on the table, no less.

Vinnie attempted a verbal parry but flushed and grinned instead. "Ridiculous. Be a darling and pour me a little more wine."

* * *

Once Rick set his phone down, Nina crept closer and caught his eye. "Was Zoloty angry? It sounded like a tense conversation."

Rick scowled at her. "He tried to pull some shit on me, vaguely threatening to put someone else on this job if I can't produce results, but he won't. He needs me. I'm the one who knows exactly where the book is and of course I've never told him the real name of the store, or the town we're in. He's a spoiled rich boy and I let him have his little tantrum." As he turned to face her, a particularly nasty smile turned up the corners of his mouth. "He ended up apologizing to me. And upping his offer to $600,000."

CHAPTER EIGHTEEN

Charlie straightened his black bow tie—Lenora had been amazed that he actually knew how to tie a real knot—and surveyed the festive scene before him. The Maples on the Lake was an exquisite, late-Victorian structure with stellar views of Wilson Lake—well, actually this banquet room was on the lower level and one could only get a peek at the water through the legs of the teak furniture on the slate patio just outside the windows, but, no matter. The remodeled room was richly decorated in subtle period style, the food was excellent, and Charlie knew that all of the partners shared his gratitude for the owners providing the space gratis and agreeing to host the final fundraiser for The Paper Pirate.

The hundred dollar per couple tickets had been snapped up in astonishingly short order. The room was filled with the local elite, dressed in their finest—black tie for some of the men, Sunday suits on others, and a range of cocktail dresses and even a few gowns on the women. Everyone chatted and laughed and seemed to be enjoying the soft piano music while grazing among the linen covered tables offering a buffet of small plate fare. Charlie kept an eagle eye on the donations box on a table apart from the food. He had long ago lost count of the guests slipping extra bills inside. The only partner without a date for the evening, Charlie had offered to take charge of the box so the others simply could enjoy themselves. He hadn't told them that he'd deliberately avoided asking out any one of a number of ladies who might have accompanied him to the party. He had a job to do and needed to focus on that.

It was seven o'clock; the complimentary wine was gone and the cash bar was doing a brisk business. Soon the desserts would appear, the pianist would retire, and a popular DJ from Scranton, an avid reader who also had donated his time, would take his place so that the dancing could begin. Charlie drifted toward the donations box table so he could thank the ruddy-faced gentleman who was having difficulty stuffing what seemed to be a wad of bills through the narrow slot. That done, his sharp eyes circled the room again, trying to pick his partners out of the crowd.

There was Al, looking fairly dapper in his only suit and his dated tie, laughing with Karen and another couple while chomping on some sort of canape, balancing a tiny plate that was much too full of the food intended for their guests. Charlie had to smile and shake his head in gentle amusement. He himself was decked out in a tux and he'd tried to persuade Al that, as one of the principals, he should consider wearing one, too, but, no dice.

The girls were a special treat to look at—Charlie didn't think he'd ever seen any of them in evening dress before. Obviously, Felicia and Lenora's shopping trip had been successful. Of course, Felicia had chosen something floaty and subtly ruffled, in a pastel color, and had twisted her hair up in a flattering style. Lenora had found a dark dress with a plain front but a dramatic dip in the back, showcasing the scattering of little butterfly tattoos that seemed to float across her shoulder blades. Her short, angular bob haircut was a little bit more "done" than usual, with some sort of sparkly clip over one ear. Charlie thanked another well-wisher and scanned the room again. Ah, there she was—the real stunner—Vinnie. She had refused to accompany the other ladies to the department stores, but Charlie doubted that any of them would have offered a dress that would've outshone the deceptively simple, slim column of slinky black that clung to her curves tonight. Her longish hair was pinned up, showcasing her graceful neck, which was circled by a dazzling diamond necklace that must have belonged to her wealthy mother and probably rarely left its velvet case. *Wow*. She could be a pain, but Charlie felt very jealous of her handsome college professor boyfriend when she slid across the floor toward him and twined her arm around his, leaning in close to whisper something that made him smile. The young women who drifted around Charlie were a pleasant sight, but it wasn't so easy to do sixty-four like Vinnie did it. Did Al even notice her? Charlie couldn't tell. Their feud actually hurt him, almost as if they were all family. He'd hate to see the store saved financially, only to be threatened by a rift between the partners.

The Maples owner, Jim Axelrod, was notorious for being publicity-hungry, but that was working to the shop owners' benefit tonight. Eager to be seen as a patron of the literary arts and all-around generous guy, he'd made sure to invite the local television news crew to the fund-raising event. A young African American man was circulating through the crowd with a small camera on his shoulder. Earlier in the evening, Jim had posed for him in the gorgeous main lobby to give The Paper Pirate—and himself—a little promotion, and the partners had arrayed themselves around him, smiling politely. Vinnie, of course, had said privately that she found Jim to be distasteful, but Charlie was happy to get assistance for the book store anywhere he could find it.

He gazed out across the crowd again. Thankfully, Jason had come with Lenora. How different she seemed when she was with him, more softly feminine, less like the hip, tech savvy, still very much New York City woman she was even after living in the Brookdale area for 20 years. Felicia had arrived with a neighbor's brother, newly moved to Pennsylvania, a balding, dapper man with a pleasant face. *Good for her.* Even if the man didn't become a regular boyfriend, Felicia deserved to be escorted to a fancy dance by a nice gentleman.

A quick, contemporary song gave way to a slow tune, and Charlie noticed Al setting down an empty dessert plate and leading Karen, a slender woman who vaguely reminded Charlie of Jane Fonda, minus the plastic surgery, out onto the dance floor. Al wasn't a great dancer, but neither was he clumsy. It was amusing to see this other side of him. He still had a touch of that boyish charm thing going for him, and he handled Karen in a gentle but comfortable way that made it clear that they were a romantic couple. About mid-song, Brookdale's mayor tapped Al's shoulder, and he graciously stepped aside so that the man could dance with an obviously delighted Karen. Charlie watched as Al crossed the dance floor diagonally, hands in his pockets, weaving between couples. He appeared to be headed back to the desserts, but something arrested his gaze, and he stopped. Charlie followed the line of Al's sight and noticed Vinnie at the edge of the parquet, still as a statue, drawn up to her full height, chin tilted at an aristocratic angle, cool, gorgeous, hands folded in a ladylike manner at her waist. They stared at one another for quite a while and Charlie crossed his fingers and then crossed his wrists behind his back for good measure. *Come on, buddy. Be the man and apologize.*

Al moved slowly toward Vinnie, head a little bowed, but still holding her gaze, a wistful smile on his—thankfully—clean shaven face, and when he was only feet away from her he extended his hand and nodded toward the waltzers. Vinnie glanced away, petulantly, but only for a moment. When she looked at Al again, he was still standing there, still smiling, still holding a hand out, the offer of a dance obviously still open. One step would be all she needed to take. *Come on, Vinnie,* Charlie tried to will her to respond. *One step and reach out that pretty hand.*

She made a quick little glance around her as if hoping for a distraction, but thank goodness, her date was dancing with Felicia over by the windows. Finally, Vinnie hesitantly reached out a hand, jerked it back slightly, then appeared to draw a breath and make a decision. She stepped forward and gripped Al's fingers lightly with her own, and he pulled her smoothly onto the floor and wrapped an arm politely around her waist. *Lucky bastard.* Charlie grinned. *Maybe I'll try to get into a fight with her next time.* His spirits soared as he watched them talking, nodding, swaying comfortably together. Finally, Al coaxed a smile out of Vinnie, then a little chuckle when he mis-stepped. When the song was over, they drifted toward Harry and Felicia, and Charlie was thrilled to see the four of them chatting amiably. He stole a glance at the ceiling. *Thank you, God.*

Presently, Jim and his pretty, pudgy wife approached him, Mrs. Axelrod with the offer of a dance, and Jim with a promise to watch the donations box for a while. Elated at the reconciliation between his friends, Charlie accepted gladly, and, in fact, spun a few other women around the dance floor as well before dutifully returning to his post.

At the end of the evening, each of the partners—and Jim Axelrod—addressed the party-goers with heartfelt thanks, and gradually, the couples drifted out the door.

"I'm going to stop by the store and lock this in the safe," Charlie said, nodding at the box held snugly under his arm. "You guys finish your evenings, and we'll meet there tomorrow morning to open it and count the money together. Say, about nine-thirty? That'll give us a half hour before we open."

"Oh, that sounds like fun," Felicia said. "I'll bring bagels and breakfast stuff."

"Bagels? Cool. I'll be there," Al said and Charlie noticed that Vinnie gave him an amused little smile rather than her usual scowl.

"Thanks, Charlie." Lenora hugged his free arm and pecked his cheek before slipping off with Jason.

When the others had departed, he shook Jim Axelrod's hand warmly. "Thank you, my friend."

"It was our pleasure to help." Jim nodded toward the box. "Hope you did extremely well tonight."

Charlie shrugged. "I have a good feeling," he said.

* * *

Alone in the private office at The Paper Pirate, Charlie set the donations box on the desk, put his black briefcase beside it and opened the clasps to reveal many stacks of bills nestled inside. Pulling up the chair, he set to work stuffing them, one and two at a time, through the slot in the gift-paper-wrapped box. He'd spent the morning unpacking those other bills and tucking them in the briefcase.

"Carlo." Charlie almost heard his mother's weak voice again. "Tommy. Julius. *Vene*." She had motioned them over to her bed. He and his brothers had gathered around her. "Closer.

Before the others come." She had begun to cough a little, but had waved away the offer of a glass of water. "When I'm gone, you'll want to remodel the house a little. You know, make nice for the buyers." She'd sat up with an effort and looked intently at each of them in turn. "You'll want to start with the rec room. Take down that ugly paneling. Maybe start with the wall with your grandfather's picture on it." The three brothers had exchanged puzzled glances. Mama had settled back against her pillows and drew a shaky breath. "Whatever he was," she'd continued, her eyes resting on Charlie in particular, "your father loved me and he loved his children. Do what I tell you. You'll find something he wanted you boys to share."

It was scarcely a month later when they had met at the empty house and pried off the knotty pine boards to discover three shallow metal boxes packed tightly with small bills. Although he despised the idea of dirty money, Charlie had been unable to rebuff his father's final gesture of affection. Stashing rather than spending the cash somehow made keeping it feel less wrong.

Last fall, he'd been sorely tempted to use his share to help with repairs to The Paper Pirate, but that would have been too obvious. Possessing so many bills of 1960's and early 70's vintage might have drawn suspicion of some sort, and Charlie was ever the cautious man. But since that time, he'd been spending them gradually for very small purchases and saving the change he received in newer bills that one day could pass for donations. He had hoped that someone else would suggest fund raisers, and thankfully, Lenora had.

Charlie tested the new weight of the donations box and smiled before settling it in his safe and locking up. Then he snapped his briefcase shut and left the office, heading for the back door. He paused with his hand on the knob and turned his steps to the sales floor for a quick glance around. The room smelled of new books and furniture polish and the little white holiday lights left burning overnight cast interesting shadows everywhere.

"Thanks, Pop," Charlie said, gruffly, before he turned and left for home.

CHAPTER NINETEEN

"Oh, Charlie, count it again," Felicia said, clapping her hands together like a little girl.

Vinnie smiled indulgently. While Felicia and Al leaned over his shoulders, she and Lenora sat on either side of Charlie at the back room table. The money from the donation box was stacked neatly in front of them. So many piles! A warm wave of joy and feeling of security enveloped her.

Charlie laughed. "Felicia, I've counted it three times. It's not going to change. I admit my hands are shaking, but you've all been counting right along with me. It's $28,625. Added to the $4,900. ticket money, it's more than enough to push us over the top. We can call the bank tomorrow and arrange the refinancing."

"And," Vinnie added, "tell that swine, Gronsky, that there will be no deal."

Al let out a whoop and grabbed Charlie and hugged him hard. In various states of giggles or tears, the other partners followed suit, not settling down until everyone had hugged everyone else at least twice.

Mopping her wet face, Felicia produced a bottle of sparkling grape juice from her tote bag and held it out toward the group. "I brought this to toast whatever the outcome. I figured we'd be closer to our goal, but never, ever did I expect this."

Al took the bottle from her while Vinnie retrieved five glasses from the cupboard above the sink.

"What on earth do you think happened?" Lenora stood in the midst of the activity, holding her hands on either side of her head like she needed to keep it from floating away.

"A rich benefactor," Al said, handing her a bubbling glass.

"More like several," Vinnie said, not being able to imagine any one person stuffing that much money into the box. "I suppose it doesn't matter. I'm beyond delighted."

"There were a lot of well-to-do people there last night," Felicia said, sipping. "I say we don't look cross-eyed at this wonderful good fortune and just run with it."

Laughing, the others raised their glasses and clinked them together.

"This means that we can dust off all those tentative plans we had for events," Lenora said. "We can host that book signing and extend the kids' program and give a definite answer about joining in the winter festival."

"Yes, ma'am." Al smeared cream cheese on a bagel. "We're back to business as usual."

Vinnie glanced at her watch. 9:50. Speaking of business as usual. . . She left the others to their breakfast and went to boot up the register, unlock the door, and display the "open" sign. She'd call Harry with the good news at some point—probably tonight, once she'd settled down and could deliver the message in an appropriately dignified manner. Her present state of giddy excitement and gratitude just might make her chatter on and reveal more of her feelings than was wise.

"God is good," Felicia was saying, as Vinnie slipped back behind the counter. She wouldn't have been able to utter those words herself, but she dipped her chin and closed her eyes for a second, just the same. The life she loved would continue as if this dreadful scare hadn't happened. Her status as a self-employed business owner was secure, her relationship with her handsome, younger man was running smoothly, and her new novel was taking shape nicely. Well, she did seem to have fallen into the distasteful habit of using more and more of Ben Conway's descriptions verbatim, but she was countering that with an artful reworking of the Julia character and a clever tweak of the plot here and there.

Wasn't she?

Hmm...

A new burst of joyful laughter erupted in the back room. Vinnie shook off the unpleasant notion and rejoined the others.

* * *

"Dominick?"

"In here, Ma," he called, in a rough and grouchy voice.

Felicia dropped her purse in the hallway and hurried to the kitchen, where she found her son slouched at the table, hair wet from the shower, dressed haphazardly in shorts and a T-shirt, clutching a mug of coffee with both hands. "There's my boy," she gushed, throwing her arms around him and giving his forehead a big kiss.

"Maaa," he whined, trying to pull away.

Felicia giggled and thrust a paper sack into his arms. "I brought you something, Mr. Sleepy. Your favorite bagel with cream cheese, and even better, some really good news." She pulled up a chair and watched him peer cautiously into the bag, then smile as he extracted the treat.

"What's the news?" he asked, taking a bite.

"We had a really good night last night. I mean, insanely good. We now have enough money to arrange the new loan and keep the store." A little thrill of joy rushed through her and Felicia couldn't help giggling again. "Isn't that wonderful?"

Dominick swallowed and sipped his coffee. "Wow, yeah. Kind of surprising, though, isn't it? You guys were way short of your goal."

"I know." Elbows on the table, Felicia folded her hands together as if in prayer. "We have a benefactor. Or several. I'm just over the moon about this and I really can't explain what happened, but it happened, and we're just going to take the money to the bank and get our new loan."

Dominick nodded his approval. "That's great, Ma. You need the income."

"Well, sure, I need the money, but more importantly, I love the store." She rose and spread her arms wide. "I love my partners, I love the town, I love the whole world, and I love my baby boy." She wrapped him in another hug, and although he made a half-hearted protest, he chuckled, set the bagel down and hugged her back.

* * *

Al walked briskly down the lane and turned in at the long slate path that led to his neighbor's house. *Good*, there was Preston sitting on his front porch.

"Hey," Al called out, and the old guy looked up from his newspaper.

"What's going on?" Preston flopped the paper into his lap and removed his reading glasses. Al climbed the steps and scratched the dog's ears when she stood and waddled up to him.

"I've got great news." Al slipped into the chair Preston offered. The retriever sneezed on his shoes then sat down at his feet. "We made a killing at the party last night. Don't ask how it happened, but the donations box was stuffed with money. We have enough to arrange the new loan tomorrow."

Preston's bushy grey eyebrows shot upward. "No shit?"

"No shit. I called Karen, and she's thrilled for me, but she's on a day-trip with her girlfriends, so we'll have to celebrate another time. Then I emailed my brother and Barbara, but I really felt like telling somebody in person."

Preston nodded. "Well, you're a lucky bastard. I'm happy for you. Can't figure it out, though. Sounded like you needed thousands."

"Yes, sir, we did. The tickets were a hundred dollars a couple, so we didn't expect to get more than another thousand in the donations box, but it was packed to the gills."

Preston wrinkled his brow and appeared to be thinking hard. Finally, he brightened and slapped his knee triumphantly. "I've got it. Did you see that Jorgensen guy at the fund raiser? You know, the one they say is a multi-millionaire but has the same little bungalow on the lake that his parents brought him to as a boy. The one that drives a beat-up 12-year-old Volvo and uses all the coupons at the market."

"I'm not sure. We tried to greet everyone personally, but I didn't speak to him myself."

"I'll bet he was there." Preston seemed convinced, and for Al it was as good an explanation as any. "Maybe he loves books."

Al smiled. "Or lost causes. Tell you what, I don't really care. I'm just so goddamned thrilled."

"Me too. Listen, the wife's out and I think there's two beers left in the fridge. Let's celebrate."

* * *

Stuffed with bagels and warmed by gratitude over The Paper Pirate's good fortune, Lenora drove home feeling content. Jason had spent the night and she'd hated to leave him, even for a couple of hours, but he'd said he understood her desire to be at the official counting of the donations. She couldn't wait to tell him the great news in person. The sky was a clear, deep blue and the day promised to be fine. They could picnic on her little dock down by the lake and maybe even drive over to look at the rowboat that someone was selling on the opposite shore, down by the dam. It'd be fun to take excursions along the shore with Jason—and hopefully the kids. Maybe they'd even venture out to explore one of the small islands that dotted Wilson Lake.

Lenora's sweeping front lawn was wide open, except for a couple of specimen trees, so she could see clearly that Jason's car was gone even before she turned into her driveway. A twinge of panic stabbed her and she neglected to brake, skidding a bit before lurching up toward the garage. *Easy, girl*, she scolded herself, but still couldn't help jogging up the path to the breezeway and dropping her keys as she fumbled to open the lock. Rushing into the kitchen, she stupidly called Jason's name before the little slip of yellow paper on the table stopped her short.

Lenora's brow furrowed as she reached to pick it up. He'd left her a handwritten note on the pad she used for her grocery lists. Some rubbish about a minor emergency with his daughter. She dropped heavily into a chair and let her purse slide to the floor.

A note?

Who of their age still scribbled notes? Clearly, he hadn't wanted to have a conversation about this, talk or text. *Probably a load of shit*, she thought, without a bit of guilt. It was highly unlikely that anything was seriously wrong with the girl, but something definitely was not okay with their situation.

The morning's pleasure completely evaporated, Lenora dragged herself to the back deck and curled up in a wicker chair. She could see down across the rolling lawn that sloped to the lake and could just about view the dock where she most certainly wouldn't be having a picnic this afternoon. "I love him," she said, aloud. *Sounds lame. Okay, let's stick to hard facts*. He was handsome and charming when he chose to be and she desired him. Sex was good and she liked having a partner to enjoy nice dinners out with and romantic weekends in Victorian bed-and-breakfasts that simply were no fun alone. She definitely regretted not having made time for a family and had hoped to co-opt a ready-made one now. Sure, those things were possible with someone else, but she truly admired his devotion to his children, his ability to strike up a conversation with anyone and make the person feel at ease, his work ethic, and genuine kindness toward underdogs. She *did* love him. But did he feel the same way? Lenora sighed, deeply, and slouched further down into the soft cushions. She knew the answer, but wasn't ready to admit it.

* * *

Nina crept cautiously toward the kitchen doorway. She'd retreated when Rick, on the phone with one of the Paper Pirate owners, had begun to flush crimson and grip the back of a chair with trembling hands. Ever the superb actor, however, he fascinated her with his convincing performance despite his obvious agitation, and it drew her back again. "I'm so disappointed to hear that, Mr. Santorelli," he purred, nonchalantly. "But of course, I'm happy for you and your partners. I've actually been looking at another store in the Catskills. A bit bigger town and some off-street parking. Might be a better choice for me. Yes, well, thanks, best of luck to you, as well."

Rick set the phone down and drew in a ragged breath. His features were twisted into a frightening snarl, and the sound he uttered before flipping the chair onto its side reminded her of a wounded, enraged beast. Before she could slip off to the bedroom, he caught sight of her in the doorway, and Nina's body went rigid. She forced herself to take a step into the room and remark casually, "Don't tell me those idiots have refused you."

Evidently, she'd hit the sweet spot. Rick controlled his temper and nodded, walking back to the table, and gripping the back of another chair so hard that his knuckles whitened.

Nina's face grew hot. "I hate them," she snarled, and she meant it. What would be Rick's next move? More to the point, what would she be forced to do now?

"Hah. You and me both. Fortunately," he added, seeming to gather his wits further, "I have a plan C."

Nina felt a pang of fear deep in her gut. Knowing his determination and being aware of some of his former exploits allowed her to make a pretty accurate guess. But she raised her eyes expectantly and said softly, "Which is. . .?"

Rick lifted the chair a few inches off the ground and slammed it down again. "I'll take what I need."

Nina jumped, but recovered quickly and forced a sly smile onto her face. "What's the plan?" she asked, with feigned eagerness. "I hope I can help." She certainly had debased herself many times in her years with Rick, but other than making a few dishonest phone calls and picking him up one night in what might be described as a get-away vehicle, she hadn't broken the law. The last thing she wanted was to begin now.

"Maybe," Rick said, with a disgustingly smug expression, "but I'll handle step one myself."

Thank goodness. "That's a pity," she said, with a careless shrug, sauntering over to right the fallen chair. Bending, she felt the wide neck of her top slipping down over one shoulder and subtly helped it along. Might as well take advantage of his just-right state of agitation and bravado. "Let's get comfortable in the living room and I'll pour us a drink." She switched on her alluring smile. "You always plan better when you're relaxed."

Later in the evening, Nina lay awake listening to Rick snoring. The bedroom windows were open and the chanting of the peepers filled her head. Her physical tension was gone, but her agitated mind kept her from joining him in slumber. This most dubious of projects was going off the rails, fast. Where were they headed and what harm might come to Nina herself?

Rick had dealt in stolen books before, but usually, they'd been stolen by someone else. Of course, there were notable exceptions, like the time he'd helped somebody out of a fix by taking a valuable first edition that had been damaged so that its owner could get more money from the insurance company than he could by selling it in its altered condition. And he'd always been happy to help out an estranged husband who needed an expensive volume or antique trinket retrieved from his ex-wife's possession.

Nina had written off those capers with scarcely a thought, but the case of Mr. Cassidy still made her shiver, even on a warm summer night. The man's ne'er-do-well grandson had hired Rick to pilfer a rare first edition that had been promised to him in childhood—a promise later revoked when Granddad disapproved of his flashy, wasteful lifestyle. On the night of the theft, Rick had been holding the book in his gloved hand when he was surprised by Mr. Cassidy. A quick shove toppled the old man, and Rick vanished without a trace. His closest call, and he'd still come out on top, Rick bragged. But the geezer broke his neck in the fall. Watching Rick as he read the newspaper account the next day, Nina had witnessed his fear and desperation for the first—and only—time. Since the "client" could never be found in possession of the book, Rick sold it on the black market and turned the money over to him, minus the agreed-upon fee, threatening to tell the police that the grandson had planned the crime and ordered the attack as well, further insuring his silence. In a remarkably short time, Rick seemed to have gotten over the scare and she'd certainly never had the nerve to mention it again.

She glanced over at her partner now. He looked harmless enough, hair disheveled, tangled in sheets, one hairy leg hanging off the mattress. But he was ruthless. He lied, he stole, and he cared nothing, really, for anyone but himself. And he had killed a man.

CHAPTER TWENTY

Charlie slipped the Cadillac into the one shady slot behind the book shop and whistled an aria from *Tosca* as he climbed the wooden steps to the back door. Earlier, he'd awakened from a harrowing midnight dream that had quickly morphed into a hated PTSD episode, but he'd managed to calm himself enough to get back to sleep and was determined to put the whole thing behind him this morning.

Swinging his keys in a practiced gesture, he aimed the correct one at the lock—and stopped cold. *Why's that light flashing?* The alarm system was unarmed. He inspected the door more closely. Only a couple of small scratches, shallow but long, and to an untrained observer they might look like the marks anyone might make when hurrying to get inside. But nothing missed Charlie's notice and the marks quite simply were not there before.

He stepped back and stood for a moment in the warm breeze, still pointing the key at the door, considering. He hadn't worked yesterday, but Felicia and Vinnie had, which meant that Felicia had opened. She was always early, tidy, careful, unlike Al, who might easily have stabbed at the lock in a careless attempt to get in and open on time. Charlie had closed the day before and there had been no marks then. These were fresh. So was the memory of his panic episode, and his heart began to knock against his ribs.

Steady, soldier. You've got this. After a deep breath he tried the knob. It was fastened, and he twisted the key and listened to the soft squeal of the old hinges as the wooden door swung into the back room. Everything seemed to be in order. The door to the private office was opened wide, showing that the room was unoccupied and his safe was shut as usual. There was probably nothing wrong. *Probably.* Charlie fished his phone out of his pocket, settled his briefcase silently on the table and made the rounds of the lower sales floor, careful to keep his back to a wall, and keep his thumb ready to dial 911. He crept up the stairs to the used books section, but found no one lurking between the shelves or hiding in the public restroom. Retracing his steps to the back room, Charlie approached the staff toilet cautiously.

Should've checked this already, old man.

The door was ajar, and as he reached out a steady hand an old floorboard creaked under his weight. *Shit.* No sound from within, where the floor, he knew, was even more vocal. Emboldened, he gave the door a decisive push, and it tapped the bowl of the small antique sink. The tiny room was empty.

Breathing a bit easier, Charlie hurried into the private office and faced the safe. He reached out instinctively, then curled his fingers into a fist and pulled his hand back to his side. It was closed, all right, but not locked. He was dying to look inside, but knew not to disturb any fingerprints that someone might have left. Charlie cursed again under his breath as he flipped through his mental inventory of the contents, wondering which of the volumes had been taken, and punched

9 1 1 on his phone's keypad. Must have been one of the three first editions on the top shelf. *Bastards. Who the hell even knew they were there?*

"What is your emergency?" a calm female voice asked, and he turned his full attention to the phone.

"This is Carlo Santorelli, proprietor of The Paper Pirate," he said. "I think we have been robbed."

* * *

"Should we open at this hour?" Al checked his watch. "We'd get in most of a day." All five partners were gathered around the oak table in the back room, at loose ends after the departure of the police detective. "The cop said we could."

"Are we up to it?" Felicia glanced around the table at the others. She had been twisting and unwinding the same tissue since she'd arrived. Lenora was clutching a sweater tightly around her, despite the warmth of the room, and Al was wearing out the floorboards with his pacing. Vinnie sat stone-faced, barely speaking, save for having answered the policeman's questions. Charlie's heart went out to all of them. He'd hated having to break the bad news in short bursts, but it was necessary to make four calls before the authorities arrived. *There's trouble. Stay calm, but get down here fast*, was the best he'd been able to do.

Lenora shrugged. "Let's open the door and just hang out for a few hours."

"Remember not to say anything to anyone about the break-in," Vinnie said, as Al left to unlock the front door. Her voice was thin and unsteady.

"I've got to say, this is really scary," Felicia said, rocking a bit. "It wouldn't feel so spooky if they'd found anything missing. Stores get robbed. It happens. And the cop really freaked me out when he told us not to mention the incident, so they could watch the place. I mean, of course they think someone will try again. We've just dodged one problem and here's another one."

Al had returned, and he gave her shoulder a reassuring pat before pulling out an empty chair. "If anything happens again it'll be when no one is here. Nobody's going to come in with guns blazing and try to hurt any of us."

"I was so sure it'd be one of my books," Charlie mused. "But there they all were, lined up just as I'd left them." He shook his head, still dazed by that fact. Whoever had trespassed had opened his safe—Charlie pictured the thief as a movie villain listening for tumblers with a stethoscope—but had shut the door without locking it. Although Vinnie had said she was reasonably sure she had set the alarm the night before, that one detail confirmed that the break-in was genuine—in five years, Charlie had never forgotten to lock the safe.

"It was my first thought, too, of course," Vinnie said, folding her arms tightly. "Or rather, my second thought. My first was that the money would be gone, but no."

"So weird that the cash safe didn't seem to be touched," Lenora said. "What could he or she have been looking for?"

"I haven't a clue," Vinnie said. "I have to admit I felt silly trying to describe that woman who seemed to be coming in a few times a week in various disguises. But maybe it will be of some assistance to the police."

"I guess thieves aren't dumb enough to break into the wrong place, huh?" Felicia looked doubtful.

Al shrugged, sitting down at last. He picked up a pen that lay on the table and began turning it end to end between his fingers. "Some of them are pretty stupid, so I guess it's not out of the question. But the entry was so careful, the whole thing so neat. Seems more like a professional to me."

Maybe it was the same characters who'd been breaking into homes lately, as the policeman had suggested. Charlie had read an article about that in the local paper. But something didn't feel right. He felt himself begin to fidget with the business card left by Detective Lawrence, and frowned. *Enough of this shit. Get moving.* "Look, maybe it was someone after the Honor Newman first edition," he said, pushing his chair back and getting to his feet. "It would've been in the safe had the couple not come for it a week early. That was a pretty valuable book. Let's keep giving it some thought, but without driving ourselves nuts over it."

The others agreed and Vinnie, Felicia, and Lenora, who were not scheduled to work that day, went home. Charlie was grateful for that. Let them relax, now, or maybe even get together and comfort one another. He and Al would handle the store.

Business was as brisk as usual, and the guys patiently explained away the morning's locked door and police activity with a mostly-true story about an attempted break-in by an intruder who was unable to enter and was frightened away by the arrival of Charlie's car. "No sense in having them feel as creeped out as we do about the jerk walking these floors right where they're walking and touching the same books they're picking up," Charlie had said, and Al had agreed wholeheartedly.

"*I* sure as hell am creeped out," he had said, surveying each corner of the room suspiciously.

Before they realized it, lunchtime had come and gone. "I think I'll take the most valuable books out of the safe and bring them over to the bank and put them in the safe deposit box," Charlie said. "I'll stop at the deli on the way back." His first thought had been to bring them home to his other safe, but the detective had advised against it, trying vainly to come up with a polite way to say that a slight, older gentleman seen ferrying valuables from work to home might be putting himself in danger. "You okay to hold the fort for a half hour or so?"

"Absolutely," Al said, with an expression that didn't match the tone of his voice at all. Charlie ducked into the back room and emerged from the private office with the books nestled in his briefcase, but paused on his way to the door. Although it was foolish, he was uneasy about leaving his friend alone.

"I'm glad the writers' group meeting was last night and not today," Al said, and the two men stared at each other for a few seconds before Al stepped aside to let Charlie pass onto the sales floor. "I don't think I could concentrate on critiques tonight."

"Me, either." Charlie took a few steps and then hesitated. "Speaking of that, I'm not sure how to say this, or even if it bears saying, but, do you notice anything odd about Vinnie's new manuscript?"

Al presented him with a blank look. "It's really good."

"Yes, I know it's really good. But does it sound like Vinnie to you?" Again, an uncertain stare from his colleague. Charlie smiled and waved the subject off. "It's me, I guess. I'll get back as soon as I can."

The summer sidewalk was dotted with people, the bank was only three blocks away, and Charlie felt confident that an officer would be watching the store at least for the rest of the day. But he was unable to squelch the nervous feeling in his gut. He hoped that the police would catch the intruder soon, before any of the owners made themselves sick with worry about it. It was a small town—would word get around that the store had, in fact, been rummaged through by a would-be thief? They'd be hosting the book-reading marathon this Saturday, and of course, they all wanted the public to feel safe in The

Paper Pirate. Charlie grimaced. There was nothing he hated more than feeling helpless.

Better do something about that.

* * *

Nina climbed the rear steps of the cabin with a wistful glance over her shoulder. She'd much rather be outdoors, but, as pleasant a change as it was, she was tired of walking and wanted something cold to drink. The sight of Rick and the roar of his voice greeted her all at once. "Where the hell were you?"

Nina paused her step and collected her thoughts. *Okay, be nonchalant but not too independent. For God's sake don't say what's on the tip of your tongue.* "Just out for a walk. I'm bored to tears."

"Can you occupy yourself by making my lunch?" he snarled.

"Of course," she said, with a warm smile. At one time it was hard to make a phony expression look real, but Nina had it down, now, along with a convincing, feminine lilt added to her voice at the right moments. "You came in so late and were still sleeping and it's such a beautiful day, I—"

"Save it," Rick ordered. "The day sucks."

Nina felt a chill. So he hadn't been successful. "May I ask what happened?"

Rick heaved a sigh, dragging out a kitchen chair and dropping into it, running his fingers roughly through his wet hair. "I searched every inch of that fucking store. It wasn't there." The sound of his fist pounding the table made Nina jump. She'd had her back turned, busy with sandwich stuff, and hadn't been prepared.

"Not even in the basement?" she almost whined. This couldn't be happening.

"No," was the clipped answer.

"But if it was in storage in the basement it couldn't have been sold. I don't think anyone would have come in asking for a book like that."

"Not likely. I doubt many people have even heard of it."

"So then what do you—"

"Just get the food, Nina. Don't try to figure anything out. You'll hurt yourself."

She knew enough not even to think of a smart-ass answer. In a few moments, sandwiches were ready and on the table, along with a glass of iced tea for herself and a beer for Rick. Nina's stomach was turning flip flops, but she feigned an interest in her ham and cheese. Thank goodness Rick was stuffing his face. If he'd wanted sex instead of food right now, she might be in for trouble. She stole shy little glances at him between bites, and luckily was looking away from him when he finally spoke.

"One of them must have taken it home. For what reason, who knows? Maybe one of the girls wanted something to read."

"I hope they haven't donated some of the used books that weren't selling." Nina had thought that to be an intelligent observation, spoken softly and carefully enough, but when Rick snorted like an angry bull, she cursed herself, silently. He snatched her wrist and squeezed hard enough to bring tears to her eyes in an instant.

"You'd, better, *hope* they didn't."

Nina's breath came in little gasps. Her face was hot and her hand was growing numb already. "Please. . ." was all that escaped her lips. So far there had been no angry Rick-moods that Nina couldn't handle in one way or another or use to her advantage. But never had six hundred thousand dollars been at stake, and never had she been the reason that something of value had slipped out of his grasp. To her dismay, the tears began to spill down her cheeks. Rick responded with a filthy sneer and released her wrist so roughly that she almost tipped her chair. He'd won, and seemed to be satisfied with that, for now. He lifted his sandwich and shoved it into his mouth. Nina rubbed her wrist. A nagging thought poked at her brain—whether or not he retrieved the prize he wanted, and even if she was able to help in some way, he might not rest until he'd punished her for making the job so hard in the first place.

CHAPTER TWENTY-ONE

Day One post break-in. Charlie wondered grimly how long he'd be counting off the days in that fashion. He and Felicia soldiered through a busy morning, endeavoring not to peer into corners or jump at unexpected sounds—or at least, to prevent customers from picking up on their nervousness.

At every break in the action, Felicia whipped out the duster and bustled about the sales floor, tidying the displays, while he sat behind the counter working on his laptop.

"You can take it easy, you know," Charlie finally told her, gently. "The place looks great."

"Oh, this is therapy," she insisted, cheerily. "This will help me erase the intruder's presence. It's me taking back my store," she added, with a tough-girl snarl he rarely saw on her face.

"Are you indeed? Well, it sounds empowering."

"I've been reading Genevieve Garvey's book," she said.

"Which book is that?"

"*Everyday Fixes*. The one I thought we might need to fix the mess between Al and Vinnie. The author has some really good, practical advice in there. You know, she studied to be a therapist, before her acting career took off."

"Is that so?" He was amused, but hoped that didn't show in his voice. Garvey should have stuck with psychology; she wasn't much of an actress.

"Yep. After the searching thing, I flipped ahead a few chapters, but now I'll be going back to the one about overcoming traumas."

Charlie's head snapped up, but luckily Felicia was puttering and waving at someone through the window, and she didn't see him. So far as he knew, none of his companions, in fact, not a living soul knew about his PTSD. He lowered his eyes to the screen once again.

"She says that you have to face these things squarely. The treatment plan involves exposure. A gradual confrontation with the feared stimuli. I'm trying it with spiders."

Charlie looked up, casually this time, and with a smile "And is it working?"

Felicia shrugged. "I'm not running out of the room when I see one anymore. I'm up to the part where I stay and finish what I was doing and then gently ask my son to deal with it. But hopefully he won't be sticking around for too long, so the next step is to either squash it or do a catch and release outside." She stuck her hands on her hips and faced him with mock sternness. "Don't chuckle, Mr. Courageous. It's a start. I used to dash out of the room and not return for hours, just hoping and praying it would be gone when I went back."

"Okay, so it's working, that's good," Charlie said in as conciliatory a tone as he could manage. "What's the final step?"

"Ah!" Felicia approached the counter, and leaned her elbows on it. "That's me letting a spider walk across my hand and not giving a damn."

"You'd better be sure you don't try that one with a Black

Widow, or something like that," Charlie teased, ducking and laughing when she threw the duster at him.

"Just you wait. I'll make sure you're there to witness my triumph. Now, give me that back, I'm not done out here."

Charlie handed it over, and closed the QuickBooks program he'd been occupied with. "Did you tell your son what happened here at the store?"

"Yeah, only because he'd hear it somehow and then think I was hiding something from him. Not that Mr. Sneaky doesn't hide things from his mother. Listen to this, Charlie. That Realtor he's got looking for an apartment for him couldn't get him on his phone, and I guess he had given her my number as a back-up. Well, yesterday she calls and tells me she's got a pretty good place for him to look at, and—get this—he'd better not drag his feet like he did the last time because it'll be snapped up fast. How do you like *that*? Sounds like she'd already found him a place and he deliberately didn't get back to her."

"Hey, it's free at Casa Mama," Charlie said.

"You got that right." The fierce expression on Felicia's face softened. "What did I do wrong, Charlie? My daughter is a gem. But this guy—"

"Did you ever drop him on his head?" Charlie teased.

"Hah! No, but I'd like to, now."

"He just got more of your late husband's genes than Angelina did. You didn't do anything wrong." She still looked glum. Charlie pointed a finger across the counter at her as the door opened to admit two customers. "Check it out. See if Ms. Garvey has a chapter on parenting."

* * *

Al fidgeted with the assortment of odd items that lived on his kitchen table top. On the other end of the cell-phone airwaves, his ex-wife Barbara was gently coaxing, "Greg's too young to make the first move, but I know he'd like to get to know his grandpa."

Al smiled, wistfully, wishing it were true. "You're sure about that?"

A little sigh, a bit of dithering. "Well, I *think* he would. He's never come out and said it, but it's what I believe." This, with more conviction.

Al found some crumbs among the junk mail, pens, and ticket stubs and herded them all into a small pile. It was likely Barbara's concern for his well-being that made her embellish. He probably shouldn't have replied to her "How've you been?" with the news of the break-in at the store. "Alice isn't trash talking me to them?"

"Oh, no! I know she isn't. She avoids mentioning you, and that's wrong, but no, I've never heard her do that."

You've never heard her do it because she knows it would upset you, Al thought, but politely did not say. "Barb, I've thought about doing this a dozen different ways, but then when it comes down to it, I don't, because I wouldn't want to cause any kind of turbulence between Greg or Emma and their mother. It's not really about me anymore."

"I know," Barbara conceded. "It's just that I hate this so much. Especially with what happened to you guys. I mean, thankfully no one was hurt, but who knows what's in store for any of us? At our age, we don't know what will—well, look, I'm rambling on about something that I know you hate talking about, so I'll let you go and get back to work—my break's over, anyway. Take care of yourself, Al. I'm not going to give up on this, ever."

Al smiled. She was okay, she really was. "Thanks, Barb." He ended the call and pushed the phone aside, rising to take his plate to the sink and get back to his chores in the yard. The marathon book-reading thing was tomorrow, so he'd have to get them out of the way today.

Barbara and her husband had spent last weekend in Austin, a surprise visit on the occasion of Alice's birthday. Al splashed water on his dirty lunch things and headed back outside to avoid the memories of how tiny his little girl looked in her crib when they brought her home, or something equally depressing.

The sun was strong, but so far this summer the humidity hadn't been too awful. Al paused for a brief look at the vegetable garden before hauling open the overhead door on the greenhouse to check on his half-dozen pot plants. Last year's harvest had been scanty, and his stash hadn't lasted past March, but he'd found he hadn't really cared. *Maybe I'm finally growing up,* he thought, soaking the planting bed with water.

What would Greg and Emma think if they knew what he was secretly growing? He replayed Barbara's report of miniature golf, swimming, and baking cookies with the grandkids last weekend. He'd long ago shut down the merry-go-round of wondering, agonizing, trying to make sense of what had gone wrong, but every now and then it all resurfaced to torment him.

As a young girl, Alice was proud of her old man's physical job, the knowledge that allowed him to identify every plant she pointed out, his ability to fix her bike and teach her how to build a fort. She loved him once. Then, she liked him, and, as time passed, tolerated him, leaving him with no clue as to why her feelings toward him cooled. Given the total estrangement that had eventually happened, Al would have settled for being tolerated. Dropping the hose, he twisted the water spigot and stepped outside, letting the heavy, old door close with a crash.

Enough of that shit. Go mow your lawn.

* * *

Vinnie tried to write, tried to garden, tried to interest herself in relaxing on the porch with the new book she'd bought, then attempted to clean up her kitchen. Nothing really took her mind off of the invasion of The Paper Pirate.

Get hold of yourself, old girl, she scolded, hugging herself although the kitchen was warm enough to require the services of the ceiling fan. Leaving the contents of the spice cabinet sprawled across the butcher block counter, she exchanged flip-flops for sneakers and set out on a walk.

She headed left at the end of her driveway, smiled, and greeted the senior couple next door, feigning an interest in the daylilies they puttered among, then rounded the corner at the end of the block and took the county road that would lead her out toward the stream. That route would provide more of a workout and give her more time to think than simply circling the blocks at the edge of Brookdale.

If only, as Felicia had said, it had been a simple robbery. She and her partners could take that in stride, especially after the rough waters they'd just navigated together. But why was nothing taken? What was it that someone—a skillful, particular someone—wanted, and did he find it? What would the person have expected to run across in a small local business like theirs? Less than two hundred dollars in the cash safe on any given night, some adequate electronic equipment, the stock of books, any of which could be borrowed at the library should someone be desperate enough for a good read. Why had the would-be thief opened Charlie's safe and ignored three first editions worth thousands? Obviously their crook wasn't a bibliophile, but that didn't narrow things down enough for Vinnie. Some of the police detective's questions had veered into personal territory—as if he was considering the fact that someone wanted to frighten one of them rather than make off with money or merchandise.

Vinnie sidestepped a pick-up truck traveling in the opposite direction and jogged for a moment to remove herself from the cloud of dust that enveloped her. Try as she might, she couldn't imagine that any one of her partners could have anything sinister in their pasts. Certainly, she didn't. Stalkers, possibly? They normally went after lovely young things, not middle-aged and, frankly, older women, but then one couldn't say that for sure. If that was the answer, the break-in would have to have been an opening salvo, since none of the three female partners had been troubled by anyone in recent memory.

Her train of thought led Vinnie to realize that she was on a country lane alone, out of sight of any neighbors. She turned and retraced her steps back to town. *How about the guys? Couldn't be, could it?* Was some love-crazed woman after Al or Charlie? That petite weirdo in the various get-ups who smelled like a moldy basement?

Vinnie shook her head to clear it and shifted herself into low gear to make it back up the hill to her block. Rather than turn her steps toward home, she walked straight ahead, past the Brookdale Little Theater. Perhaps a circuit of the town would calm her nerves.

* * *

Lenora rolled her chair away from the desk in her home office and stretched her arms over her head. She admired the new logo she'd created on her computer screen. Nice how she'd fashioned the customer's company initials into a backhoe and forklift—two of the products they produced. *Home run.* And it had taken her mind completely off the break-in for over an hour. She emailed the proposed drawing and slogan to her old employer—the one for whom she still did freelance advertising work—and opened the document containing her latest manuscript. As a reward for a job well done, she'd allow herself an hour or two to work on that before tackling her next ad project.

After zipping through four great pages, Lenora's fingers slowed, and a grim sadness settled on her shoulders, making her thoughts grind to a halt. What the hell was up with the store being ransacked? Was it a one-time occurrence or something they needed to worry about? She wished she could have been able to talk the situation over with Jason, would have loved to have him ponder a few theories and offer some comfort. Given their months-long relationship she should be able to expect those things. . . But if she'd called yesterday and told him she needed him, she might not have gotten the answer she wanted. So she'd hung out with Felicia instead, which had worked wonders for both of them. Felicia was a first-class friend.

Lenora put her elbows on her desk and propped her chin in her hands. Of course, she'd mention the incident to Jason when she saw him tomorrow for date night. She'd have her act a bit more together by then and wouldn't appear needy or demanding. *Guess what happened at the store,* she could say. And, *Oh, no, we're fine, but isn't it puzzling? Now we have a mystery novel on our hands.* Lenora sighed, deeply. She wished she had a Romance novel on *her* hands. But, whatever. She minimized the manuscript and returned to her graphics program. It was time to get back to work.

CHAPTER TWENTY-TWO

Vinnie settled herself on her couch with a glass of brandy and the new book she'd been too nervous to begin reading yesterday. She'd thought of going up to her desk and continuing Chapter Twelve of her collaboration with Ben Conway, but it was rather late—the fund-raising book-reading marathon having lasted longer than expected—and she was in more of a mood to relax than to work.

What fun today had been. Such a pleasure to once again be in a secure position, able to donate one's time to help the Brookdale Library rather than scrambling to save one's own skin. Audience and participants alike had seemed to enjoy the day's event immensely. The wryly comic *A Summer Guest* turned out to be the perfect choice. Vinnie could still hear the delighted laughter and see the spectacle their good-natured mayor had created with his silly portrayal of the dainty heiress Violet DeLand. Harry had turned up unexpectedly, bringing a wonderfully generous donation check from the college staff. He'd read a few pages in his melodious baritone, meeting only her eyes whenever he looked up. She smiled, now, thinking that their relationship was becoming a decidedly more public one, and finding it remarkable that she wasn't troubled by that at all.

Jim Axelrod, ever the patron of anything that would put his face and the name of his restaurant in front of the public, donated the platters of sandwiches and snacks that were brought in at lunch and dinner time. The Paper Pirate's book sales were healthy and hopefully the same would be said for the donations to the library.

A light breeze blew in through the open window, carrying with it the sweet fragrance of night blooming flowers from the neighboring garden. Vinnie slipped down into a more comfortable position among the cushions and realized that she no longer missed the smell of the sea that was part of every childhood day near Oyster Bay. Brookdale was a refuge from her old life, but one she'd resented at first. The promise of a part time income as a bookstore owner had been attractive to her, but not so much the prospect of becoming familiar to everyone in the small, working class community. She had, at first, resisted Lenora's marketing efforts, relenting only because she realized the necessity of it all. But she'd never really enjoyed their public performances until recently. What had happened to the outgoing, civic-minded young woman who had tried out for school plays, sung in a college chorus and participated in demonstrations? Had she been quite as fiercely protective of her privacy before the debacle of the failed second novel? Vinnie grimaced and let her book fall back against her knees. She knew she had not. The mortification had changed her completely.

The doorbell startled her. Odd at nearly eleven o'clock. Harry wasn't due until tomorrow. Vinnie shook off a twinge of fear and shuffled into her slippers on the way to the front hall. Peeking through the curlicues in the frosted glass panel, she recognized her guest and opened the door at once. "Felicia.

What on earth?" Her friend was trembling and her face was tear-stained. "Please. Come in."

"Oh, Vinnie," Felicia hurried inside and clutched at Vinnie's hands with both of her own, "my house. Someone. . ." The rest of the words caught in her throat and she fanned herself nervously, as if she was trying to push away her emotions.

"Come and sit down." Vinnie pulled her into the living room, settled her on the couch and fetched the bottle of brandy and another glass. "Have a sip and start from the beginning." She perched on the edge of the sofa, and waited for her friend to relax.

Felicia finally drew a deep, steady breath and let it out slowly, a brandy scented release of tension. "I think someone has been in my house," she whispered, hoarsely.

Vinnie felt her eyebrows pop up. "A thief?"

Felicia shook her head vigorously, which sent her wavy brown hair swishing around her face. "I didn't notice that anything is missing, but. . .Vinnie, I know my house. My son teases me about being OCD, but it's not that, really. For years, I had two full time jobs—one in an office and one at home—and keeping to a strict routine just made it easier for me. Not much clutter meant not as much dusting, and knowing just where to find everything meant less time lost searching. Well, you get the point."

Vinnie's own house was untidy, but it certainly sounded like a practical idea. "Yes, of course."

"I was kind of keyed up after the excitement of the marathon, so I flopped down into my favorite chair and thought I'd see what was on PBS. *Well!* I reached out for the remote. . .and the basket I keep them all in was turned the opposite way. It's just easier to reach in from the side without the handles, and well, anyway, at first I thought, oh, Dominick put the remote in its proper place for once and turned the basket? But then I glanced over at the lamp, and it wasn't in its usual spot. Close, but not quite. Now I'm curious, so I get up and start walking around the room." Felicia straightened her back and pushed her disordered hair behind her shoulders. "Vinnie, I found nine things, throughout the house—and I went through the whole house, believe me—that had been moved slightly. So I'm getting more and more panicked and then I just, I don't know, I just couldn't stand to be in there for another second. Was someone still there? Did I surprise him when I came in and was he hiding in a closet and watching me?" She covered her face with her hands, and Vinnie reached out to pat her shoulder. "So I grabbed my purse and ran out. You're the closest, and I know it's late, but I figured you'd be up and. . ."

"I *was* up. I was only reading. I'm happy to help." Vinnie was surprised that Felicia had chosen her over Lenora, or possibly a neighbor, but she pushed that thought aside. "I hope it's nothing, but you were right to get out of the house, and get your bearings. Now, let's think—it couldn't have been Dominick, could it?"

Sipping her brandy, Felicia shook her head. "I can get him to do the dishes and the laundry, and keep his room fairly neat, but he doesn't ever dust or vacuum. Aside from the remote, the stuff that was out of place wasn't anything he would have touched. And the things were here and there throughout the house. *In every room.* I was petrified."

Vinnie slid a bit closer and lowered her voice. "I imagine you were." Too bad it wasn't really in her to put a comforting arm around her friend.

"Anyway, I don't think Mr. Popular has been home since early today. He showed up at the reading when I texted and said it would be my turn soon, and before he drove off, he told me he'd just left the house and wouldn't be home until super late."

"So he was home all morning until just before lunch. And you're sure he hasn't been back? Maybe looking for something he thought he'd lost?"

Felicia fished a tissue out of her pocket and blotted her eyes before blowing her nose. "I don't think so. He was meeting some girl he's been seeing. She lives about thirty-five minutes away from here. Marie, Mary-something? Ah, who the hell knows? I hope he moves in with her."

Vinnie had to try hard not to grin.

"I tried to call him but his phone's turned off. Big surprise there."

"So you won't be able to ask him about it until tomorrow. Would you like to spend the night here?"

"Oh, I don't know, I didn't bring anything with me."

Vinnie shrugged. "I'm sure I can find you a nightgown. Look, I doubt that anyone is hiding in your shadows waiting to strangle you, but how well do you really think you're going to sleep, alone in that house?"

Felicia sighed, and her lips twitched into a sheepish little smile. "Not very well. I really appreciate this, Vinnie. I know I should've banged on a neighbor's door, but the ones I know best are early-to-bed types and I didn't want to give anyone a heart attack."

"Of course not. You relax and finish your brandy, and I'll run up and see to the guest bedroom." Vinnie rose and smiled down upon Felicia. "I'm sure there's an explanation for this and it'll all sort itself out in the morning," she said, not believing a syllable of her own nonsense. *Every room searched carefully*, she thought, climbing the stairs. Nothing taken, and it was likely that a housekeeper less meticulous than Felicia wouldn't even have noticed a few items placed off-kilter. It sounded ominously familiar.

* * *

On Sunday evening, Charlie clicked the gun case shut and carried it back to the shelf in his bedroom closet. He hadn't used the Glock 9mm in ages, but cleaning it and making sure it was loaded made him feel prepared. He'd kept it in his desk drawer when he lived in New York, because he ran the vintage book business out of his apartment and the volumes that changed hands were often worth thousands. He'd never needed to use it. It had sat neglected on the closet shelf since he'd moved to Brookdale ten years ago. Not only was the town quieter and a bit more friendly, but he met with his clients in the little office at the bookstore. His customers came and went during regular business hours and sometimes left with a pricey first edition in the same common Paper Pirate bag that would be used for any, everyday twenty-dollar purchase—hidden in plain sight.

Charlie closed the closet door and turned his steps toward his home office in the spare bedroom. The gun hadn't even felt familiar to his fingertips. He hadn't been on a range in years. *What do I plan on doing with it, anyway?* Charlie booted up his laptop and shuffled through the stack of chapters beside it, looking for the one that needed revising. Since leaving the Army, he'd only owned one handgun at a time and had viewed each of them as being strictly for protection. There was a shooting range a couple of miles past the lake, but he wasn't sure how well he'd fit in with the local clientele, a group he imagined to be made up of deer hunters and retired cops keeping their skills sharp.

He opened an email from Felicia. Although there was

plenty of time for her to submit her chapter before the next writers' group meeting, she was apologetically warning them that she might not have anything until very late. He felt his brow crease as he read her brief account of a possible intrusion of her home. She really "sounded" scared, even though she'd probably worded that message very carefully to try to avoid worrying them.

Charlie drew in a deep breath and pulled his shoulders up and back. None of them would say it, but he knew they were counting on him.

"Don't worry, folks. I'll try my best. Hope I can fix this."

CHAPTER TWENTY-THREE

N*ot a bad way to start a Monday morning*. Al watched as Karen, who had spent the night, divided up the dinner leftovers. She'd even packed him a lunch. He was always glad to surrender his kitchen to her when she felt like cooking—the meal she'd made last evening had been great.

"I gave you the rest of the pie," she said, putting a plastic sack into his hands. "You can share it at work." She bustled out of the kitchen and returned with her purse and tote bag.

"Thanks for everything, Karen," Al said, giving her a little hug and kiss.

"My pleasure. Hey, do you want to go to that Ballads and Blossoms thing next Saturday?"

Al frowned. "The *what*?"

"It's at the arts center. Poets have submitted some of their work and local floral designers are going to create arrangements inspired by the words. They'll read the poems to the audience and I guess the designers will explain how they interpreted the lines with flowers."

"Sounds dumb," Al said, and instantly was sorry when he saw the look on Karen's face. Not angry, but disappointed, sad, the expression that made him feel the worst.

She heaved a sigh, shouldered her purse and faced him squarely. "And this is why I can stay with you and Barbara couldn't. You wring the joy right out of life sometimes, Al, but I don't have to live here." Luckily, she sounded matter-of-fact, and she stepped up to kiss his cheek before turning toward the door. "I'll go with my sister. Call me. We'll do something else on one of your days off."

* * *

Lenora slit open the boxes and released copies of fresh new books into the world. Al lifted a carton and rested it on the top of the stepstool, pulling them out and slipping them into place beside the older stock. Lenora, sitting cross-legged on the floor, was in a better position to tend to the lower shelves. He pointed that out, and she agreed. Besides, she was young enough to stand up again without assistance, although Al's pride didn't allow him to admit that aloud.

"Did you ever find out if Felicia asked her son about Saturday night?" he asked.

"Uh-huh. She told me that he had left her house in time to come to the reading marathon and didn't get home until one thirty in the morning. He hadn't stopped back, hadn't moved anything in the house, hadn't even realized that she spent the night at Vinnie's. By the time he got up, she had come home, showered and changed, and was working in her study, and he just figured she'd been there all the time."

"I'm kind of surprised she told him what happened. I thought she was afraid he'd think she was nuts." Al reached down for another box.

"Well, I don't think she told him everything. I believe she just asked enough questions to get the information she needed. Apparently he's about as intuitive as a brick."

Al laughed. "Yeah, I met him for the first time at the marathon, and he just rubbed me the wrong way. I mean, it only took him six minutes."

Lenora giggled. "It doesn't get any better after you've met him as many times as I have. Geeze, I can just imagine what the old man was like." She reached out to drag the last box toward her and sliced through the tape with her knife. "You know, I hope there's nothing to worry about, but, well, something weird happened at my house last night, or, at least I think it did."

"Really?" Al looked down at her little pixie face, framed by black wisps of hair angled this way and that. For a moment, she looked like a girl young enough to be his daughter, and he felt a sharp twinge of concern.

"I woke up in the middle of the night, and as I was passing the hall window, on the way to the bathroom, I saw some movement, so I stopped and looked out. Al, I could swear I saw two figures running across the lawn. There wasn't much of a moon, and I wasn't wearing my contacts, but it really didn't look like deer or bears or, well, anything on four feet."

"Not sure those are roaming around in the middle of the night, anyway," Al said. "Do you remember what time it was?"

"When I got back to my room, I looked at the clock. It was a little after two. I was still groggy so I just went back to bed. But this morning, I thought about it some more, and I checked all the locks, sort of made the rounds, you know, because of what happened here, and to Felicia."

"Find anything missing?"

She shook her head. "I checked on everything of value, and it was all okay. The only detail that was a little strange was a plant with a few broken leaves in the sunroom, but I could've done that myself the day before when I was watering. I'm afraid I'm not as good a housekeeper as Felicia. I wouldn't really know if something was where I'd left it or six inches to the left or right." She smiled, sheepishly. "I mean, I couldn't even find my own slippers when I got out of bed this morning."

* * *

Nina stepped out of the shower and dried herself carefully, avoiding the mirror because she didn't want to catch a glimpse of the bruises she knew she'd see. They didn't hurt much, and she certainly couldn't complain about how she'd gotten them—last night had been amazing.

It had started badly, with Nina nervous about being forced to tag along to search the youngest shop-owner's house—Lenora Stern, Rick had called her. Nina had concentrated so hard on not knocking into anything in the darkened house or making any noise that it had been difficult to do any actual searching. But with Rick close by, she'd had to do her best. No copy of *Stargazer* had turned up. The last room to be searched was the woman's bedroom, and Rick had pushed her toward the door. But the owner herself was asleep inside! Nina had panicked, gesturing wildly but silently, trying to make her hands and facial expressions do the arguing for her. Rick had seized her roughly and pulled her close, whispering harshly in her ear.

"*Every* room. We're not coming back here. You can do this."

She'd relaxed a bit, feeling like he actually was trusting her, testing her, and, determined not to fail, she'd slipped through the door, open barely enough to admit her slender frame. She'd somehow managed to poke into every nook and cranny without waking Ms. Stern, until she'd tripped over something on the floor, close to the bed. Slippers, maybe. As the homeowner stirred, the reality of Rick's purpose had flashed through Nina's brain—if this chick slept with a handgun under her pillow, Nina would be the target, not him.

As terrified as she'd been, she'd risked a backward glance at the bed just before slithering out of the room. Lenora had turned over, but wasn't sitting up, looking around, or seeming to be startled in any way. Rushing into the hall, Nina had grabbed Rick by the sleeve as she dashed for the sunroom window that had admitted them to the home. Back at the car, after a run across the wide lawn and clambering through the woods, she had forgotten all the usual cautions and had screamed at Rick for having put her in such danger. To her astonishment, he'd smiled and said,

"That part of the search needed a delicate touch, not someone big and clumsy like me. You did good. You're well on your way to earning your share of the spoils."

She'd been too shocked to speak until they'd returned to the cabin, where a hell of a reward for her bravery awaited her in their bedroom. At first, she'd been alarmed at Rick's ardor, expecting violence rather than passion, but he'd proved her very wrong. Quite to the contrary, he'd seemed to find her more desirable after her little foray across the boundary of legality.

Maybe their relationship could morph into something like a partnership, Nina mused now, dressing herself. Could she embrace a life of crime? Maybe. Yesterday's snooping didn't really seem so difficult now, in the light of day. Why should she care about someone who was standing in the way of something she desperately wanted? And it wasn't like she had much self-respect left to shed. *Hmm. . .don't like the sound of that.* She frowned at herself as she brushed her long, wet hair, until a new thought made a cunning smile spread across her face. *No.* Only a weak woman would view it that way. Rick never considered that his dirty deeds showed a lack of respect for himself. To him they were proof of his power, cleverness, and drive. Maybe there was something to be learned from him after all.

CHAPTER TWENTY-FOUR

Lenora caught a glimpse of Jason's car in the drive as she passed the living room window. She wondered who would be knocking at her door, and seeing it was him left her with conflicting emotions. How great that he'd turned up unexpectedly on a Tuesday, but what unfortunate timing. She'd been in the garden all afternoon, had showered and changed into comfortable but unattractive old clothes, and had not reapplied any makeup whatsoever.

Nevertheless, the sight of her beautiful man on her front porch delighted her and she beamed a big smile and got on her toes to throw her arms around his neck.

Oddly, Jason only nuzzled her cheek briefly and ushered her inside a bit too quickly—as if he didn't want any of the neighbors, distant as they were, to see them. "Hey," he said gently, stepping back from her embrace and shutting the door behind him, "I have to talk to you."

Nodding slightly, chewing her lower lip, Lenora led him to the couch. Jason chose a spot as far away as possible from the one she picked and Lenora felt a chill wash over her. This couldn't possibly be good. He looked pale and nervous. And it probably wasn't some minor bad news or he would have delivered it on the phone. Some small, ridiculous—and doubtful—part of her psyche urged her to keep her spirits up. She perched on the edge of the sofa cushions, fingers threaded together, hands held on her knees.

Jason cleared his throat, adjusted the collar of his shirt, and smoothed back his hair. Finally, a quick little smile, and a big sigh. "There's no easy way to say this, Lenora. I care for you, but I've started to realize that you love me way more than I could ever love you, and I know that keeping this up can only hurt you. I want us to break it off, now, and I want you to know how very sorry I am to have disappointed you so often."

Lenora felt a bowling ball to the gut, and the room shifted a little bit. She reached out a hand toward the back of the sofa to steady herself. Jason was watching her closely, so she fought hard for enough composure to reply calmly. "Oh, wow," was all she managed, in a tiny, strained voice. "I'm so sorry to hear that." Without meaning to, she slid into the corner of the sofa and hugged a pillow tightly against her chest.

What else is there to say?

He already suspected how much she loved him and obviously it simply didn't matter. Begging posed a real temptation, but she knew better than that. There wasn't going to be much dignity salvaged tonight, but better a shred than none. Her eyes filled with tears as she turned them toward his handsome face. "Is there. . . ?"

He hesitated a moment, then got it. "Not like you think. But I really feel that I could be drawn to somebody else and I'd never want to cheat on you. I'm not much of a prince, but I've never done that," he said, very softly. "You deserve better."

Yeah, like that's going to help.

Still, Lenora couldn't summon up anger towards him. He

was sitting there quietly waiting, not running out or trying to jolly up a devastating moment. If only he'd been the jerk her mother thought he was. Then she could produce a little scene, embarrass him, and ruin his next few days with worry and dread. But he was just a guy who didn't love her, one of so many in the world. Why not release him without a fuss? Another scrap of dignity to clutch on an increasingly rotten evening.

"Okay, Jason. I guess I appreciate your honesty, but I'm so sad. I don't have the right words to say."

"Of course not," he said, sort of reaching out, but seeming to decide not to touch her. "Are you okay? Believe me, I know what it feels like right about now."

How ironic that he seemed to care more about her feelings now than in all the months before. Lenora set the pillow aside and sat up straighter. "I will be," she said, evenly.

Jason nodded and rose to his feet. He disappeared for a moment, but she didn't hear the door open or shut. Then he was at her side, offering a glass with a bit of whiskey in it, which she took. He leaned down swiftly and gave her forehead a little kiss, and then he turned away, and was no longer her boyfriend.

This time, she did hear the front door close.

* * *

"Oh, shit." Felicia actually said it out loud when she heard the knock, looking up from her laptop screen. Just when Natasha finally got Lord Philip back into her bed, someone was at the door. Felicia hit "save" and hurried out into the hall. When she pulled open the door, she beheld a red-eyed Lenora in cropped leggings and a big, rumpled T-shirt, with an overnight bag slung carelessly across her skinny shoulders. She managed a weak little smile, then pressed a balled-up tissue to her nose.

"Oh, honey, come in. What happened?" *Hope that sounds like I don't know it's about Jason,* Felicia thought, embracing her friend and drawing her inside.

"Jason broke up with me. I had just about decided to make the move first, but I guess he beat me to it."

"Aw, baby, come into the kitchen, I'll make some herbal tea. Put that bag down anywhere. So was he decent about it at least?"

"Absolutely. More so than he's been many times during the past months. He took all the blame and even handed me a drink and gave me a little kiss on the way out."

Felicia bustled about the sink and stove. "Sit, sit. What did you do?"

"What else?" Lenora dropped into a chair. "I had no choice but to act the same way. Thank goodness for being forty-six. I didn't do such a good job when I was younger. Then I drank the whiskey and bawled my eyes out." She looked up at Felicia with a rueful smile. "Then I figured maybe if I wasn't alone, I could sort it all out better."

"Of course you will," Felicia said, setting out mugs and tea things. "Dominick is out carousing and anyway, if he comes back, we can talk in my room. Or I'll send him to his!"

That actually got a little giggle out of Lenora. "I dread telling my mother. Of course she knew all along that this would happen. I guess you did, too," she added, softly.

Felicia sat beside her and squeezed her hands. "Mama's not going to like being right this time. She'll cut you a break. I guarantee it." Eventually, the kettle screamed and Felicia filled two mugs and set them on the table. Lenora watched the steam curling upward, seeming deep in thought. In another minute, the scent of chamomile mingled with raspberry, and Felicia leaned in carefully for a first sip. "I baked a nut bread. It should be cool enough to cut."

Lenora waved her hand. "It's okay. Tea's enough." Her dark eyes seemed filled with all the pain of every breakup she'd experienced and Felicia felt a sharp pang of sadness.

"You're such a nice girl. I wish you could be happy. But love isn't always happy."

Lenora nodded. "It's not like I didn't recognize the signs. Lately, anyway. Not like I thought he was crazy about me. But I did let myself think it might work out in some way. You know, at our ages, it isn't always like a fairy tale."

"No." Felicia sat quietly, stirring and sipping, and letting her friend gather her thoughts.

"My mother—" Lenora grimaced, "well, my mother thinks I punish myself right from the get-go by picking the wrong men."

Punish yourself?

"Ah, who knows who's the right man until you get to know him?"

"True, but. . .she thinks there's a reason."

Ah-ha.

"Reason?" Felicia leaned back in her chair.

Lenora groaned a little. "This is a long story. And a sad one, at that."

Felicia shrugged. "I'm a writer. I like all sorts of stories."

Lenora smiled, shyly. "When I was seventeen, I had my first real boyfriend. Physically, it was innocent, but emotionally it was love. Eric was gentle and smart and always on my side, always willing to help me out. But he was sad. Sad in a way I didn't understand at the time. I did love him, Felicia, I swear to you, but I was so young and so stupid that I reveled in the newness and fun of having a relationship and never gave a thought to responsibility. He'd try to talk to me about what troubled him, but I would turn the conversation to something fun, or gossipy. I'd tell him everything was going to be fine, and

I really was naive enough to think it would be. I was just echoing empty words. I thought they'd be enough.

"Anyway, one evening he called and said he was at the park and was feeling so down that he knew he couldn't take the pain any longer. It was like, well, like we had a bad connection. Not that I couldn't hear him, but I was too much of an idiot to *hear* him, do you know what I mean?"

Felicia nodded.

Lenora stuck both hands in her hair and gave a quick squeeze, then let them fall gently, palms down, one on either side of her steaming mug. "I remember being slightly annoyed because I was waiting for a call from my cousin about a party, and I just pulled out this string of awful, truly horrible platitudes and rattled them off. I told him he was being silly and that nothing could be so bad that he couldn't fix it if he tried hard enough. I told him if he just went home and went to bed everything would be fine in the morning and, God help me, I think I even talked a little about the damned semi-formal dance that was coming up." Lenora shook her head, her expression bitter. "I ended with something insanely perky, and I guess I did say I loved him. Very, very softly, he said 'I love you, too.' It sounded eerie then, but I still didn't get it through my thick skull. Anyway, you can guess what happened." Lenora locked eyes with Felicia. "He jumped off a highway bridge and was killed."

Felicia reached out quickly for her friend's hands. "Oh, honey, you were—"

"I know, I know. I was just seventeen. I was a happy, normal kid and I didn't understand that kind of torment. But I was a smart girl, Felicia, and I loved him. I could've told him not to do anything just yet, that I wanted to talk to him. I could've told my father to take me down to the park, I could've called his mother, called the police. I didn't have to know how to fix it, but I should have known that it needed to be fixed, and that I needed to get help. Later, after the funeral, his mom hugged me and sobbed and told my mother and me that she had no idea what was going on with him. *But I knew, Felicia,*" she leaned forward, agitated, clutching at Felicia's arms. "Okay, it was only for ten minutes at the very end, but I was the only one who knew, and I didn't do a damned thing."

"Oh, honey." Now it was Felicia's turn not to know what the hell to say.

Lenora seemed to calm herself. She released Felicia's arms and sat back, lifting her mug of herbal tea to her lips. "Of course, I've had therapy, I've been forgiven—or not even blamed—enough times to turn my stomach. But in the end, you have to live with a thing." She crumpled her paper napkin, then began to smooth it flat again. "Do I pick the wrong men because I blame myself for Eric?" She shrugged. "Who the hell knows?"

CHAPTER TWENTY-FIVE

Al fumbled for the front door key. He so often entered through the back that the kitchen door key was much more familiar to his fingers. There it was, at last. Al opened the door and turned for a quick wave to Preston, who stuck a hand out the car window in reply, then rolled away. At least they'd dropped his Jeep off at the shop, where Ted could look at it tomorrow morning, but what the hell was wrong with it now? Al switched on the hall light, shed his jacket and headed to the kitchen for a snack. Charlie would have a theory, which probably would turn out to be right. Al walked through the darkened rooms without bothering to light any lamps—there was a night light in the kitchen and besides, he knew the way.

He plugged his phone in to charge, then rummaged through the fridge, lifting lids, smelling leftovers, then snapping them back on when the contents proved to be edging toward science-experiment status. He made quite a racket, shuffling containers over the metal wire shelving, even knocking over a bottle of salad dressing in pursuit of a limp triangle of yesterday's pizza, but when he finally stepped back and shut the door, the expected silence was broken by a creaking noise coming from the front of the house. Al froze, listening intently with his better ear pointed toward the kitchen doorway. The house was old, but more sturdily-built than most, and he rarely heard any noises other than a creak on the upper landing, and a —there it was! A popping noise about halfway down the stairs.

Leaving the pizza, Al stepped gingerly to the doorway, and was most of the way around the dining room table when he glimpsed a shadow falling onto the rug in the front hallway. He stopped and leaned forward. His mother's old clock ticked faithfully from the mantle, and a gentle grinding noise announced the turning of the hour. The shadow halted, then slid stealthily forward.

Okay, not my imagination. Al slipped into the living room, torn between retreating to the kitchen for his cell phone and rushing into the hall to defend his kingdom. In the next second, the need to make a choice was removed. A dark, stocky figure appeared in the archway between the living room and front hall, and when the intruder jerked to a stop, Al knew he had been seen. "Hey!" he yelled, figuring, *why not?* He crossed the room and was disappointed, but not surprised, to see the dark figure hurtling toward him.

How long had it been since he hit a guy? Freshman year at college? *Oh, well, here goes.* Al led with his right fist, but despite putting everything he still had behind it, the other man barely broke step. Al dodged a left hook, but was not as fortunate when a right jab connected, sending Al sprawling. Counting the stars, he dragged himself up. The man had turned and was headed for the door. Instinct overruled common sense, and Al went after him.

As they grappled, Al judged his assailant to be about his height, probably a bit heavier, certainly with powerful arms, which Al was determined to keep him from using again. The man gave Al a shove, then collected himself, and aimed another punch to the gut, which Al was able to deflect a bit by side stepping. Pissed off now, he hit the intruder again, which appeared to enrage the fellow. Uttering a low growl, he charged Al, sending him crashing backward into a bookcase. A sharp pain at the back of his skull threatened to drop a curtain of blackness over the already dim room. He fought it, but the shroud descended quickly. There was only time to hear running footsteps and a slamming door.

Shit. Bastard. Owww. . .

Darkness.

* * *

"What's your name, sir?" The face of a young EMT came in and out of focus, and the voice sounded calm but worried.

Al blinked hard and looked past the young man to a living room now brightly lit and buzzing with activity. Police officers, another EMT, Preston—*wait, Preston?*

"Sir?"

"Alan Rockleigh," he said, reaching out to raise himself with a hand on either of the guy's shoulders.

"Just rest here a minute, Mr. Rockleigh," the man said, which made Al glance around and notice he was seated on his couch.

"Okay."

"Where are you now?"

"Um, home. My living room."

"What town?"

"Brookdale, Pennsylvania."

"And what day is it?"

"Ah, Thursday. June 16."

"Who is our governor?"

"Tom Wolf."

The EMT seemed pleased, and he and his partner administered a few quick tests of Al's balance and cognitive abilities. Within ten minutes or so, Al was up and walking, gingerly checking out the bandage on the back of his head, and trying to get a look at his face in the little mirror by the window.

Preston stepped up to help out. "You look like shit. What's the matter with you? You forget how to call 911? Good thing you forgot your hat in my car, or you'd still be lying on the rug."

Al tried to smile, but that hurt. "All happened so fast. I was going to call but. . .he rushed me, Preston. The jerk's in *my* house and instead of trying to escape, he charges me. Ow."

"You'd better sit down, buddy," Preston tried to guide him to a chair. "Don't be any more of a dumb ass."

Al grinned, in spite of a split lip and aching jaw. Preston was worried about him. "Nah, I checked out okay. I just want to reorient now, you know? Maybe some fresh air."

A young policeman approached them. "Can I ask you a few questions now, sir? Or would you rather wait for tomorrow morning?"

Geeze, I'm not that old and delicate. "Now's fine," Al said, pleasantly. "I'd sort of like to reclaim a little of my dignity, if you get my drift."

The three of them were joined by another officer and Al recited the events of the evening. At their urging, he walked through his rooms, but found nothing valuable missing.

"Maybe he got here just before you did," the younger officer suggested. "Maybe he heard you before he touched anything, figured he'd get going, then was surprised by you."

Al shrugged. "I guess. I hope he won't come back and try again."

"Doubt it," the other officer said, as the group drifted out onto the front porch and down the steps. "Unless there was something specific he wanted from you, which is unlikely. Probably just wanted to peruse the selection of electronics and jewelry."

"Not much of that here."

"How about checking the outbuildings?" the younger officer suggested, gesturing toward the old greenhouse at the back of the property.

Al hoped the shock he felt didn't show on the outside. His half-dozen pot plants were happily dozing inside, and he really didn't need to have them discovered. "Ah, well, there's nothing back there. I, uh, I don't use that thing at all."

The cops seemed undeterred, but one of Preston's eyebrows shot upwards. "How about the garage?" he suggested, hobbling in that direction and pointing with his cane. "Your new lawn mower, and all those power tools?"

"Oh, yeah, good thinking," Al said, as casually as he could manage, and both officers high-tailed it to the garage, where, thankfully yet maddeningly, everything was in its place. To his great relief, no further mention was made of the greenhouse.

All of officialdom seemed to wrap up its business and head off at roughly the same moment, the EMTs giving Al something to sign and admonishing him to get checked out by his own doctor, because he had refused to be transported to the hospital. He thanked everyone and promised to take care of himself and report any unusual occurrences.

Al and Preston were left alone on the front walk, watching the last of the red tail lights disappear around the bend and listening to the peepers and a far-off barking dog. As the last of the mental fog cleared, Al realized that a few things in his office had been slightly out of place, and he wondered why he hadn't mentioned that, or the other break-ins that resulted in nothing being taken.

"Thanks for your help, buddy," Al said, then gestured

toward the darkened back yard. "For that, too. How, uh, how did you know. . ."

Preston cleared his throat and tapped his cane on the slate. "I don't know shit. I just know you didn't want those cops in that greenhouse." He nodded briskly and appeared to be ready to head for home.

Al reached out and patted the old guy roughly on the back. "Thanks. It's just a mess in there, that's all. Some stuff I think it's high time I got rid of."

Preston nodded, and pushed off with the cane. "Give me a call in the morning, if you need a ride anywhere. I'm old. I'm always home."

CHAPTER TWENTY-SIX

T*rapped!*

Nina felt her fury rising, and she had to fight hard to keep it from spilling out of her lips. "What do you mean we have to wait a week to try the next house?" Her voice sounded strained and her annoyance probably was plain, but, evidently, she hadn't overstepped her boundaries because Rick just shrugged, looking unconcerned, lifting his New York Times again while she paced the living room floor like a panther in a too-small cage.

"We can't be too obvious. With any luck, they don't quite realize what's going on, but we can't be too sure."

"I hate it here," Nina growled. She wanted to kick something—the pseudo-rustic coffee table, the damp-smelling easy chair, Rick himself.

"Patience. There's a lot at stake, and I'm not going to screw it up. Too bad that jerk came home when he did. I was done searching and would've been history in two more minutes."

"Bastard." Nina spat the word out, hoping Rick wouldn't guess which man she was referring to. An old hand at this game, Rick should have found a way to sneak out of the house after he heard the owner return. Why the hell risk a confrontation? Why *invite* one, for God's sake, which was really what he had done? He'd just *had* to use his damn fists. Nina tried a few deep breaths. "I feel like a prisoner here."

"Would you rather be a prisoner in this cabin, or in the county jail? Why don't you go for a walk," Rick suggested, without lifting his eyes from the page. "You have an hour or so before you have to start dinner. But be sure you don't talk to anyone."

Start dinner! Enraged, Nina spun on her heel and made tracks for the back door. She pounded down the steps and lashed out with a kick at a stack of decaying plastic flower pots that lay in a heap next to the walkway, scattering them to the corners of the small yard. She almost wished they were skulls—Rick's, or maybe, the store owners', actually anyone's in this insipid town. Shoving her hands into her pockets, Nina stormed out toward the road. She had to walk clear down to the stream at the edge of town before she calmed down.

* * *

"You think anyone's been buying my story about falling off a ladder?" Al asked on Saturday morning, surveying his battered face in the reflection of a metallic vase full of pens he had picked up from next to the register. He'd only shared his unfortunate experience with his partners and the local police, but it was a small town. Who knew how fast news might travel?

"I don't know, but I agree it's wise not to tell customers that you were nearly robbed, after the store was nearly robbed," Felicia said, straightening out the bills in the cash drawer.

"Do I look any better?" Al moved the vase around, trying to

see his face from different angles, but he knew damn well what he looked like.

"No, sorry, hon, you look worse. Bruises are darkening. But it's only been a couple of days. Do you feel better?"

"Yeah, I do," Al said, setting the cup of pens back down on the counter. "I mean, I got the crap kicked out of me, but at least I fought back. I did the best I could. I'm kind of proud of that, in a silly, macho kind of way."

Felicia shrugged. "Nothing silly about that, at our age. Lenora and I told the police what happened at our places, too. Neither of us felt foolish anymore, after what happened to you."

"That was smart. It might be of some help."

"Not that I want to think this group is being targeted." Felicia surveyed Al's face again and winced like it hurt her, too. "What did your family say when you told them?"

"Well, Karen rushed right over with food and offers to do my laundry and stuff, but I couldn't take advantage of her. She's really cool, and it was nice to know she cared so much. Especially after I just said something stupid when she invited me to a poetry thing she wants to go to. I told Barbara this morning, and she said she's glad I'm okay."

Felicia turned a suspicious, squinty-eyed frown on him. "I kind of meant your daughter and the kids."

Oh, boy. "Ah. Oh, well, um. . ." Barbara hadn't had time to pass along the news, get a reaction and report back. In fact, he wasn't even sure his ex-wife would mention the incident to their daughter. Felicia was looking even more blatantly curious, so Al reluctantly decided to come clean. "Listen, not many people know this, but I don't really, I mean, I. . .oh shit. Felicia, Alice and I don't speak. I mean, like, ever. I don't talk to the kids, either. I send birthday and Christmas cards and I get thank-yous for the gifts. That's all it's been for years."

"Oh, my God, Al, how awful for you." Felicia's expression mirrored the look she'd given him upon first seeing his bruises, and Al felt his throat get tight. "I had no idea."

"I lie about having a relationship with them. It's not something I'm proud of."

She stepped closer and patted his shoulder. "Hey, look, forget about feeling bad for lying—it's okay to keep something like that private. I wish I could do something to help you, though. She's the only kid you've got."

Al pulled up a stool and slid onto it. "Only kid I once had," he said, very softly.

Felicia smiled and nodded at a customer who approached the counter, and Al watched her complete the sale and greet another couple who entered the store. When they climbed the stairs to the used section, Felicia pulled up a second stool to sit beside him. "You don't have to, of course, but. . .do you want to say why?"

"I'm not sure I know why. We were okay when she was little. She was always helping me in the garden, and I went to all of her softball games, music recitals, you name it. We were buddies until she started to get a little older. Then she gravitated more toward her mother. Which was fine. I understood that. She went away to college, so there was the physical separation added to the mix. She moved farther away, to Texas, got married, started her family. I tried to keep in touch as best I could, but we drifted farther apart. When Barbara and I decided to divorce, Alice took her mom's side, big time. I mean, Barb and I were amicable, cooperating. . .but my daughter cut me right the hell off. I was pissed, but I tried to keep some kind of connection going. Barbara even took up the role of go-between. I mean, Greg was a toddler and Emma was an infant—they were the only grandkids I'd ever have. But no dice. She was done with me. Maybe she had wanted to be for years and the divorce was a handy excuse."

"Aw, gee, Al. I can't understand it."

"Me either," he said, with a wistful smile.

Felicia seemed to consider the facts. "Well, your side of the problem isn't apathy, right? You kept trying to reach her."

Al studied his shoes. He'd made a supreme effort to win his daughter back, making a fool of himself time and again, with no good result. She'd been a great kid, fearless and fun, but had morphed into a drama queen as a teen, and had yet to outgrow it. Who the hell knew where she'd gotten that from? Certainly not from him, and not from down-to-earth Barbara, either. But he didn't share any of those thoughts with his partner. It would sound like he was badmouthing his own flesh and blood.

"No, not apathy." Hearing himself say the word flipped a switch in his head. "Not with my daughter, anyway, but. . ." Al and Felicia stared at one another for a moment.

"The little ones." She was the one to say it first. "Have they actually rejected you? Or does the odd family situation maybe just seem normal to them?"

A customer approached the counter, and Felicia hopped off her stool, with a warm smile, to chat and make the sale.

So much time lost. Al scanned the floor—no one else ready to buy just now. He drifted toward the door to the back room, pulled out his phone and opened a new email. Just write anything, Karen had said once. Pretend you have all the confidence in the world. The tiny keys were not friendly to his big, work-worn fingers, but he didn't want to wait until he got home to his laptop. Too much of an opportunity to lose his nerve.

Hi, Greg, he typed, as if he did it all the time. *Grandma said your Christmas cactus cuttings aren't doing so well. That old plant has a death wish. I have a few ideas.*

* * *

Her free Saturday was too hot for her to putter around in the garden, so Lenora leafed through the papers on her desk and tried to get her mind in gear to work on her manuscript. It was time to pick up the threads of her normal activities and start living her single life again. Her mother had offered an observation that had seemed strange at first, but resonated with Lenora more and more each time she remembered it.

"There's something I like better about you when you're not with a man," Mom had said. "Hard to put a finger on it, but you're more yourself. Funnier, more daring, capable, irreverent. Just more of all the things I know and love you for."

Which means I'm less like that when I'm with someone, Lenora thought, ruefully. Less like herself, more –what exactly? It didn't take her long to come up with adjectives: needy, fretful, accommodating. Maybe it was a good idea to stay single for a while, and figure some things out before thinking about another romance.

Every therapist she had spoken to after Eric's suicide had more or less told her that her life would go on, regardless, and that she could choose to make it meaningful, or wallow in misery. But there hadn't been a list of instructions—the path through grief wound a different way for each person traveling it.

Lenora woke the laptop up and opened chapter one of her YA manuscript. She hadn't revisited the first pages in a long while. Writing for tweens and young teens was difficult enough even when the author knew exactly what she wanted to say. There were rules about sentence length and structure to be followed, not to mention vocabulary. Certain curse words were okay, but forcing the average kid to grab a dictionary in order to proceed would cost her readers. On top of all that, Lenora had been told by more than one critique group member that she seemed to be searching for a message.

"That's because I'm searching for a message," Lenora said, wryly, tossing the sheaf of papers aside. She'd been inspired to write for readers the age of Jason's children not only so that she might entertain those two, but because reading popular YA novels herself had intrigued and inspired her. The selections she'd borrowed from the library were just as well written as any mainstream novel, and the subject matter had surprised her. Alcoholism, abuse at the hands of relatives or the clergy, death of loved ones—all handled skillfully and thoughtfully, but handled nonetheless.

Lenora opened the file with her rambling notes for the untitled story and scrolled through to the end, skimming over each line. Her heroine, 14-year-old Lydia, seemed to navigate the same comfortable, boring landscape that Lenora herself had occupied, which was what Vinnie had said while they discussed Lenora's last submission. And the message she'd failed to take away, until now, was that although those little dramas and triumphs had made for a happy real-life childhood, they were not the stuff of great literature.

But I'm not writing about myself.

Still, if one was to write what one knew well. . .how might Lydia cope with a close friend committing suicide? Lenora shivered. It was just too awful. But not a taboo subject for YA, and not something that 14-year-olds—or 17-year-olds—were safe from experiencing, then or now. By the light of the little bulb that flickered on in her head, Lenora began making some revisions.

CHAPTER TWENTY-SEVEN

"Hey, come here," Lenora called out. "The police have caught a couple of robbers that sound like our guys."

"What does it say?" Vinnie said, walking through the doorway from the back room, sandwich in one hand, mug of tea in the other.

Lenora, who already had eaten her lunch, was perched on a stool at the counter, surveying the sales floor between glances at the Monday morning newspaper. "They were apprehended Saturday upon leaving a bungalow in Deer Hollow. The police called them 'remarkably neat' and said that it was hard to tell anyone had been in the house—except for the fact that they had digital cameras and a flat screen TV that didn't belong to them."

Vinnie swallowed her bite of food before replying. "If it's our guys, that would be *such* a relief. I'm beginning to feel like a veritable gypsy. I've spent three nights in as many different houses, and I hate to impose upon people." Lenora, Felicia, and Harry had been most gracious hosts, but that really couldn't have continued for very long. The ladies had their own lives, and as for Harry, she and he were doing very nicely, thank you, and she didn't need to spoil things with too much familiarity.

"I didn't mind. It seemed wise, after what happened to Al. I really felt like our group was being targeted and that you and Charlie might be the next in line."

Vinnie felt a chill. "Yes." She took another bite and chewed thoughtfully, listening to her young partner read the short article in its entirety. A months-long spree targeting absent vacation-home owners and local businesses likely had been brought to a halt. Two seasoned pros were arrested and a cache of stolen merchandise was discovered on property belonging to one of the suspects. *Thank Heaven.* She would celebrate by sleeping in her own bed tonight. For a brief time, Vinnie had thought that only a home security system could put an end to her wanderings—an expensive and cumbersome solution to a temporary problem. She'd moved to Brookdale in order to dispense with that type of thing—to be able to sleep with the windows open and to avoid having to punch a silly keypad every time she ran out for a quart of milk.

"Of course, it doesn't mean for sure that the guys apprehended are connected to the break-in at the store or the assault on Al," Lenora said, laying the paper flat on the counter.

"No, it doesn't. But it certainly sounds promising. Just how many neat and tidy robbers do you think are out there?"

"Exactly."

Vinnie glanced across the sales floor and out the window. "I really must finish my critiques for Wednesday. Shame on me. Felicia said she'd be late and I really ought to have gotten both Al's and Charlie's done before this."

"Speaking of critiques, I'm going in a new direction with the Lydia thing," Lenora said, looking as though it had taken a lot of courage to say that.

"Are you? Well, I look forward to reading it." *Too dismissive. Oh, well, too late to take it back.*

Lenora glanced down. "I think I've finally decided what my message is—what I want to say."

"Have you?" Vinnie felt uncomfortable watching Lenora's obvious case of jitters. What the devil was she going on about, anyway? "Well, you know the rules—don't tell us anything ahead of time. Allow us to discover it in the same way your readers will."

Lenora nodded, a little sadly, rose, and went out onto the floor saying she wanted to check stock.

Vinnie took another bite of her sandwich. *I'm not very good at the empathy thing*, she thought ruefully. The changes Lenora was making to her manuscript obviously were meaningful to her. Vinnie liked the young woman, had just slept in her guest room, and hadn't actually apologized for having been so sharp with her about the question of selling the business. She toyed with a few lines of encouragement, but they all seemed ridiculous, patronizing, or both, so she drained her mug and headed toward the back room to finish her lunch.

* * *

On Tuesday, Lenora helped Charlie clear a spot on one of the front tables to create a special place for a newly released biography of retired Utah governor Cal Schmidt, a firebrand who had been a war hero in Vietnam, and, upon returning, one of its most vocal critics.

Lenora turned a copy over, checking out the front cover, a montage of period photos including a head shot of the stern-looking young lieutenant in uniform, and the back, a grouping of three more recent pictures, including one showcasing Schmidt's unruly shock of white hair and devilish smile. "I never thought much about this guy one way or another, but his book got great reviews. Vinnie sampled it but she wasn't impressed. She says it's not possible to have been a war *hero* in a conflict like Vietnam."

Charlie was silent for a long moment, his fingers busy arranging books. "I suppose a wounded man running through a hail of bullets to save two other soldiers is pretty heroic, regardless what your opinion of the war might be."

"That's true enough. Are you going to read it?"

His slight smile was cryptic. "I read them all. I don't enjoy them, but. . .I read them all."

Lenora felt her heart sink. "Oh, Charlie, I'm sorry, I'm being a jerk. You served, didn't you?"

"That I did. Now, don't think for a minute that I thought America should be involved in Vietnam. When I joined the Army, I was running—ah, removing myself—from a bad situation at home, trying to become my own man, all that stuff. I would much rather have defended my country against attackers and protected our freedom, like they did in World War II. But that was over." He shrugged. "So, I fought the one they sent me to."

"It must've been awful. I shouldn't have said what I did. It was awful, right?"

Charlie squared up a stack of books. "To be truthful, I was one of the lucky ones. I spent most of my tour in a motor pool as a mechanic. Oh, we got the shit scared out of us a few times, but we didn't see the kind of action the governor here did. A surprisingly small number of soldiers suffered the worst of the war." He took the book she held out to him and set it upright on an easel. "I never had to kill another soldier. That means a lot to me."

* * *

"How'd it go at the police station?" Karen asked, as she stepped back and opened her front door wider.

Al shrugged, walking in. "Not so great. Wow, you look good." Leggings and a long, flowing sleeveless something-or-other. "Very pretty." Al was glad to see how much this pleased her. Cute, how she gave him that coy little sideways glance. He hugged and kissed her and let her lead him by the hand toward the living room.

"Let's sit. Our reservation isn't for forty minutes yet." They settled opposite one another and Karen sat forward a little, legs crossed, folded hands on her knees, the picture of attentiveness. "So, tell me what happened."

"I'm afraid it's not an interesting story. I went to the station, looked through the famous two-way mirror—just like on TV—at a line-up of men. I had no clue, Karen. I never saw the skinny one, and three of the five bulky guys they showed me were the right height and build. But, as I told the officers, the jerk wore a stocking over his head. I never saw a face. Didn't hear a voice. Oh, well, they called me in, and I cooperated."

"That's all you could do," Karen said. "Still, I wish we could know for sure that one of the men arrested was the guy who attacked you. I'd feel better knowing he was behind bars."

"You got that right. The cops seemed pretty confident these were the guys involved in all the robberies. It's just that they can't pin my incident on them. I guess that's how it'll stay. Nothing was taken from my place and I'm healing up fine. That may be the end of it."

"'The end' sounds good to me." Karen's cat leapt onto the sofa cushions beside her and sidled up closer for an ear scratch. "Have you heard from Greg?" she asked, more softly.

Al smiled, wistfully, glancing down at his shoes. "Nah. Same story there—I made the effort, and I'll live with whatever happens." Barbara had decided not to tell the kids about Al's injuries, so his curiosity about their reactions would never be satisfied. Would they be upset to know that he'd been bested in a fight with an intruder? Al let himself imagine the kids living nearby, rushing to see him after the attack, Emma running into his arms and gently fingering the bruises on his face, Greg giving him a quick hug, then insisting upon knowing all the gory details. Al could almost see them beam with pride at how well their old grandpa had defended himself.

"You won't try again?"

Al considered. "I wouldn't say that. I just want to give him plenty of time first."

Karen sighed, pulling the cat into her lap and stroking its fur. "I suppose that's wise."

"Hey, it sucks to be the grown-up, sometimes," he observed, and Karen rolled her eyes.

"I'm rooting for you."

"I know. Thanks, babe."

* * *

The target rushed toward Charlie, almost like it was in a hurry to mock him for the lousy job he'd done. He eyed his results with a grim frown, still holding the gun in both hands, pointing it toward the floor. One shot had gone completely wild, most weren't great, one wasn't too bad. Nothing like what he'd aimed for, however. It didn't help that the young attendant strolled over and patted his shoulder, offering an encouraging, "Not bad, sir. Not bad."

Not bad for an old man picking up a new hobby, Charlie thought, attempting a phony smile because the guy probably really did mean well. But not nearly good enough for a former U.S. Army sharpshooter with a marksmanship competition badge. He shook his head slowly. *My shot group is in the same building, at least—just not in the same target.* The word *rusty* didn't even begin to describe his performance. Corroded, crumbling, deteriorated, disgraceful—Charlie stopped while he was ahead. Was an unarmed man worse off than one who couldn't control a weapon? Maybe he should've left the damned thing in its case. He'd read that the police had robbery suspects in custody. They hadn't been charged with the break in at the store or the assault on Al, but it was much too soon for that, anyway. Charlie let his hand, still holding the gun, fall to his side. Would he even need it now?

The young attendant was still standing beside him with an encouraging expression on his face. "Go again?" he asked.

Charlie set his jaw and resumed a shooting stance. "Yes, sir."

CHAPTER TWENTY-EIGHT

"Wow, Felicia, this is *hot!*" Lenora giggled. She put down the typed sheets she'd been reading from and glanced around the table at her fellow writers, who looked as impressed as she felt. "And yet so beautifully written."

"Which is just what erotica ought to be," Vinnie said. "Well done, Felicia."

"The heroine is great," Lenora said. "She's resourceful, and smart, but not beyond realistic for a servant in medieval England. Such devotion she feels toward the young princess—I mean, everybody knows the villain is going to ransack the castle and force her to be his bride, and yet Gillian is willing to trade places with her. Even though she might be killed when the invading prince learns the truth."

"I wavered a minute because the two young women look so much alike, but the writing was so good, you got me past that," Charlie said. "It made sense because the evil prince had only seen her once, years ago, when she was a young teen, and even then at a distance. You're really onto something here. I'm looking forward to hearing more."

"Me, too," Lenora said. "I love this scene that I read—what a great twist." The heroine had been waiting nervously in the princess' chamber, all dolled up by the lady's maids, terrified because the prince was coming to claim her.

"I liked the element of suspense," Vinnie said. "I thought that Gillian was going to be hurt, but the prince fell to his knees before her, bowing his head and kissing her hand."

"So cool," Lenora agreed. Stunned by his gentleness, the character had reached out and touched his hair, and he allowed her to lean down to kiss him first. Positively swoon-worthy. Then the fireworks started. "I mean, he absolutely *worships* her. I vote for a real romance, but with graphic details. What do you guys think?"

"Well," Felicia drawled, evasively.

"Sounds fine to me. But it seems like this chapter comes in the middle of the story." Al waved his set of pages for emphasis. "Are you going to start workshopping it from the beginning?"

"Are we going to hear about Gillian and the princess' history together, so we can understand the character's motivation to save her mistress?" Charlie asked.

Felicia flashed a guilty little smile and spread her hands out flat on the tabletop. "Guys, I have a confession to make. This manuscript is already finished. I was being sneaky, telling you I didn't have anything ready for the meeting, and then just sending this yesterday. But I knew you wouldn't need to spend much time critiquing it because, well, because. . ."

Lenora grinned, watching her friend's face squinch up in an adorable little-girl-with-a-big-secret smile.

". . .both the agent and the editor said it was in great shape, and didn't need much work to get it ready for the public."

"Agent?" Al said.

"Editor?" Charlie looked puzzled. "Do you mean that. . ."

"Yes. Okay, here goes—I've signed a contract with a publisher. It's going to be a book late next spring."

The group erupted with congratulatory comments, spilling together so that Lenora couldn't separate one from another or even hear her own words. She stopped gabbing and got up to hug Felicia instead.

"I've been working on this for over two years. I guess I was too shy to bring it to the group," Felicia said when they'd all settled down. "But every time I'd get a good suggestion for the romance manuscript I'm writing, I tried to apply it to this story as well. I really owe you guys a debt of gratitude."

"I'm glad we could help," Al said, positively beaming. "This is fantastic, Felicia. I'm so damned proud of you."

Lenora noticed that Vinnie got quiet, a somewhat pensive look having replaced the delighted smile of a few moments ago. She brushed aside her curiosity. This wasn't about Vinnie. "Is there a happy ending?"

"Oh, I'm afraid not," Felicia said. "Very sad, in fact. First the prince abandons Gillian, and she takes up with a Robin Hood-style group of dissenters that hangs out in the forest, and another handsome guy, of course. The prince doesn't realize her true identity until the very end, just before he's killed—very dramatic locking of eyes across a field of battle. There's the shock of betrayal for him, the remorse she feels about having had to set up the ambush of a former lover—would be perfect for a climactic movie scene, but the story is a little blue for an R rating, I'll admit. Sorry. I'm rattling on. I'm just so excited about all of this, but I really do feel humbled and grateful. I never thought it would happen for me, and maybe it wouldn't have, with my sweet romances. I'm still nervous, though. I really want it to work out okay."

"That's a good publishing house," Vinnie said softly. "Not some seedy trash-monger. You'll do well with them, I'm sure.

I'm very happy for you." She rose and brought her mug to the sink, where she spent an unusually long time washing and drying it, with her back to the others.

Strange, Lenora thought, although she had to admit that she, too, was feeling small stirrings of jealousy. But her devotion to the group made it impossible for those feelings to flourish. "Of course, we'll have a launch here at the store," she said. "In quiet little Brookdale. It'll be a hoot."

"Maybe we can give out condoms along with the cookies," Al suggested. "Or else, nine months later, there'll be a hell of a lot more Brookdalians than there are now."

The others laughed raucously. Lenora noticed that Vinnie had resumed her seat at the table, and was treating them to a mildly indulgent smile, but not really joining in the fun.

"Are they doing much marketing for you?" Lenora decided a change in topic might be wise. "If you have to do some of it yourself, I'll be your press agent."

Felicia appeared to tear up. "You're a sweetheart. Oh, you guys are just the best. But, look, that's enough about *Wrong Princess*. I don't want to hog the whole meeting. It's Lenora's turn now. You're back to poetry, I see."

Lenora winced. "Yeah, I'm sort of in the middle of a major overhaul of the YA novel, and I just wasn't ready to submit anything new yet, hence the poem. In fact, I'll probably go all the way back to Chapter Four and start workshopping the novel over again. I hope that's okay." She glanced around the circle of faces. Everyone looked expectant and no one looked peevish—not even Vinnie. "I've finally gotten the message some of you have been trying to send me—the plot is way too tame." She drew in a deep breath. "I'm going to add a teen suicide aspect. The main character is going to have a friend who tries to kill herself. I hope. . ." *What do I hope? That I can pull this off? That I can teach some poor kid to do a better job of helping a friend than I did and maybe save someone's life? That I can put the Eric thing to rest at last and move on with my future?* She giggled, nervously. "I hope it won't stink," she said. Her eyes landed on Felicia, who smiled, winked, and nodded.

"Hey, just write it," Al said, with a shrug. "If it stinks, we'll help you fix it."

* * *

At home in her study, Vinnie typed furiously. Her mixed feelings about Felicia's success embarrassed her. She loved the group, and truly was immensely proud of her partner. She'd really have to do a better job of communicating that to Felicia the next time they met. *Exactly what the devil is bothering me? The publishing contract?* She'd had one herself. Two, actually, although the second opportunity had failed disastrously. Vinnie pushed aside those troubling thoughts and hammered away at the keys, finally stopping herself when she realized that while she'd meant to copy a brilliant paragraph of Conway's, she had, instead, re-typed an entire page. She had her answer: The writing in Felicia's chapter was terrific. The best effort she had made in their eight years together. And she had written every bit of it herself, no fishy "collaborations." She *deserved* the contract.

"Arrrgh! Oh, Benjamin, this won't do," Vinnie rose and walked away from the laptop, running her fingers angrily through her hair, giving a tug at the roots for good measure. "I have talent enough to do this on my own," she chanted, aloud, pacing from the front of the garret room to the rear and back again. "I did it before. I had a best seller, for God's sake. You never did. I had what you craved, but didn't have the talent to achieve. So why am I so enamored of this lonely first book of yours?" She stopped in the middle of the room and stood with her hands on her hips. *Because it's precisely the story I want to write. And yet, we never knew one another—in fact, you were dead for over forty years when I was born. And I'm amazed to have stumbled upon it while dusting. How absurd.* She shook her head to clear it, marched back to her desk, plopped into her chair, and highlighted a whole page of words. She drew herself up tall, chin tilted at a regal angle and reached out a finger with great determination.

Delete.

"Hah!"

Now what to do? She'd already decided that *Riverside Glen* was going nowhere. She didn't love it, didn't care what happened to her characters. At least some of the research would be helpful if she were to begin another historical novel, and that one odd chapter that had never seemed to fit in might make a good short story.

Fiddling with the mouse, Vinnie clicked tentatively to open a new document. Peter, Benjamin Conway's *Stargazer* lead character, was exquisite, but from her first peek between the crumbling covers, Vinnie had been curious about the underdeveloped girlfriend character, Julia. Absently, Vinnie typed the name nine times across the top of the page, then deleted them all.

I wonder what became of you after Peter died?

CHAPTER TWENTY-NINE

Al approached the paint-mixing counter at the local hardware store, card of paint chips in hand. *Wasted enough time on this*—Hidden Meadow *it is*. Stupid name but a nice enough green for the kitchen. And anything was better than that shitty beige chosen decades ago by the previous owner.

One clerk, Joyce, stood under the "PAINT" banner, and the other, Frank, leaned on the customer side of the counter, looking morose.

"Ah, it's the same old story," Frank was saying. "Every time I need help with some heavy stuff in the yard or around the house it's my neighbor who comes right over. He's a great kid, but my son should be the one to lend a hand. I just don't get it. His mother and I never ask for favors unless we really can't do something ourselves. And we've been giving and giving for twenty-nine years now. What the hell? Just gets to you sometimes. And it's not the daughter-in-law, either. She's a nice girl. My wife sees more of her than I do of our son. We were pals when he was a boy. I just don't know what happened."

"Hey, guys." Al handed Joyce his card and turned toward Frank. "You okay, buddy?"

"Yeah, just bitching and moaning."

"As usual," Joyce said, prying the lid off of a paint can and sliding it under the pigment-dispensing machine. "Look, Frank, you may never know what happened. And probably, it was nothing in particular. You did all you were supposed to do." She pounded the lid back on the can and put it in the shaker. "Parents hope for life-long love and friendship, but there's no guarantees." She turned from Frank to Al. "Right?"

"Uh, right," he said. Frank didn't look cheered up, but she'd probably meant well. Al jumped and grabbed for his phone when he got a text. He'd been doing that ever since messaging Greg last week. This time, like all the others, the text was from someone else.

"Jeeze, Al, you're like my son," Joyce teased, opening the second can.

"Yeah, I'll have to break myself of that habit," he admitted, sheepishly. *There might never be a reply.*

* * *

Vinnie eyed Felicia warily. They both sat behind the counter taking a rest during a brief lull in a busy summer day. *She's not going to bite. Tell her. Why is this sort of thing so hard for me?* Vinnie cleared her throat. "I'm not sure I've properly congratulated you on your publishing contract," she began. "I'm extremely proud of you."

Felicia beamed at her. "Aw, thanks, Vinnie. That means so much, coming from you. I've always thought you were the most talented of us all." This last was said with a shy little dip of her chin.

"Nonsense. We each have our own style. Literary fiction is

no more worthy of seeing the light of day than paperback romances. There's an audience for all genres."

"Well, I still really appreciate your compliment."

The bells jangled as the door opened to admit the mail carrier, with the bald man from the Chamber of Commerce close on his heels. As the latter walked up to the counter and asked Felicia if he could leave a stack of brochures about the upcoming Fourth of July festivities, Vinnie received a text. A smile curled up the corners of her lips as she read. Harry would be home early. While he was glad that she no longer required a safe alternative to her own home, he missed her. He suggested grilled shrimp for dinner and streaming a vintage movie she adored afterward. *Sounds lovely*, she typed in reply.

* * *

Thirty-five, I miss you, Vinnie thought, wryly, as she was forced to run home to retrieve the loathsome blood pressure meds she'd forgotten to tuck into her overnight bag. Undeterred, Harry had said he'd load the dishwasher and put the kitchen to rights while awaiting her return. Perhaps maturity was attractive in its own way. She'd been charmed by his protective feelings towards her, when there was still a concern that her house might be next on some evil-doer's list. Yet he hadn't allowed her to think for a moment that she was incapable of handling difficulties herself. Harry really was the best sort of man for her, she decided, and she was lucky to have met him.

The lake looked dark and still as she drove past; the only craft plying the waters was the sunset cruise boat, slipping homeward toward the public dock. Main Street was empty at eight-thirty, except for a cluster of people outside the frozen custard shop. Vinnie slowed to glance into The Paper Pirate's darkened window, illuminated only by the small white

Christmas lights Everything looked safe and secure. She turned left at the library and rolled a few blocks down the hill, noticing people seated on their porches chatting amid the flickering lights of their citronella candles. Vinnie smiled and waved to a few. Finally, she braked and turned the wheel. The sweep of her car's headlights illuminated her little patch of front lawn and the black-eyed Susans that volunteered in a strip of dirt next to the drive. She twisted the key and shut the engine. Twilight reclaimed the scene. *Even these long June days draw to a close eventually*, she mused on the way up the walk to her kitchen door. A sliver of moon hung in the sky just above her neighbor's lilac bushes.

Unlocking the side door, Vinnie slipped into the kitchen and headed right toward the corner cabinet—intending only to grab the bottle of pills she knew was there and head back to the cozy comfort of Harry's apartment. As she re-crossed the kitchen floor to depart, a flash of motion in the corner of her vision caught her attention. No, it *couldn't* be! Heart pounding, she turned toward the doorway leading to the dining room, dreading what she might see, but feeling somehow prepared for it.

She was just feet from the side door she'd left open, and her hand had slipped into her purse and already had ferreted out her phone. Nevertheless, Vinnie felt an icy chill wash down her back when she caught sight of a dark figure creeping through her living room. *Let him go*, she thought, urgently. *Get back to your car and call the police.* But the figure paused by her television set, and reached out as if to get hold of it. Although she rarely watched anything other than the evening news program or something on PBS, the thought of a vile stranger perusing the selection of her private property got her hackles up. What might he already have in his pockets? Her mother's jewelry? The emerald ring that had traveled from Europe on an ocean liner with her vacationing great-grandmother? The diamond pendant that had encircled her grandmother's neck while she dined with Lady Astor? They didn't belong in a pawn shop.

Glancing down at the phone just long enough to dial 911, Vinnie crept through the dining room. She was shocked to see how small in stature her burglar was. Emboldened, ignoring the emergency operator's questioning voice, she quick-stepped toward the wall and flipped the light switch.

Bathed in the light, the small figure froze, turned a masked face briefly toward Vinnie, then bolted toward the front door.

"Yes, ma'am, I have an intruder in my home," Vinnie said loudly, hurrying after the fleeing person. She—it could only be a "she"—struggled with the front door lock for a moment, then slipped out onto the front porch. Only half-hearing the dispatcher's soothing words, and for a reason she couldn't begin to fathom, Vinnie began her pursuit.

The dark-clad thief clambered down the front steps, then hooked sharply to the right and led Vinnie on a chase through her own backyard and a small woodlot at the corner of her neighbor's property, heading, it seemed, for the stream and the back road out of town. Thankful for the sneakers she was wearing, Vinnie rode the rising tide of adrenaline, hopping over planting beds, dodging tree branches and ignoring the babbling of her phone until the 911 operator raised her voice nearly to a shout.

"What's happening, Ma'am? Are you okay?"

"Yes, of course," Vinnie responded, panting heavily. The retreating figure was getting hard to keep within her sight.

"You seem to be having trouble breathing."

"Nonsense. I'm running."

"*Running*? Ma'am, you're not going after the intruder, are you? Ma'am, please go back to the house and wait for the police."

Vinnie considered this, but suddenly, the fleeing woman tripped and fell, and Vinnie picked up the pace instead. She managed to close the gap between them to about thirty feet or so before her quarry rose and tore through the bushes that led to the back road. Gamely, she followed, feeling dozens of tiny thorns seize her clothing and scratch her skin. Once out of the thicket and on the pavement, she tried to summon a final burst of strength but. . .what on earth would she do if she caught up to the thief?

"Ma'am, please stop running and return to the house," the emergency response operator commanded, politely but firmly. "The police will be there in a few minutes to assist you. Please do not put yourself in any danger. The intruder might be armed."

This bit of information made Vinnie slacken her stride considerably, and the woman in black, obviously as near to exhaustion as her pursuer, staggered around the bend and disappeared. Heart pounding, breath coming in gasps, Vinnie slowly brought the phone up to her ear. She thought she heard a little yelp coming from the direction of the stream, but the emergency operator's authoritative tones quickly drowned out any other sounds.

"Yes, Miss, I have heard you and I am heading back to the house now." Vinnie sighed, and cast one more longing glance in the direction of her burglar before trudging up the back road toward the intersection with her street. Maybe Mother's treasures were still snug in the hidden wall safe in her bedroom closet. "I only thought to catch a glimpse of the person's face or a vehicle," she murmured, seeking to appease the slightly alarmed woman at the other end of the line. She was probably young—and although she couldn't see Vinnie, she would, no doubt, be appalled at the thought of an older woman giving chase to a fleeing criminal. But, like Al, Vinnie had risen to the challenge of defending her home and property without so much as a thought, just as quickly as a much younger person might have done, and that was that. "Yes, I hear a car and I see some flashing lights," she said into the phone. "Tell them I'm around the corner and it will take me a moment to walk back to the house. I don't relish the thought of returning the way that I came." *I'm lucky I didn't turn an ankle*, she thought, picking a twig out of her hair. "I'm on the county road, just about to round the corner onto Orchard. I'm tall and blonde, in grey yoga pants and a light-colored shirt. I'd rather they didn't fire upon me, if it can be avoided," she added, dryly.

The dispatcher assured Vinnie that she had relayed this identifying information and that the police were patiently awaiting her arrival. Once she stepped within sight of the squad car, the operator signed off, sounding a bit too grateful to be rid of her disobedient charge.

On the lawn, Vinnie and two state policemen faced each other warily. The cops were crisply attired and impeccably groomed. She, on the other hand, was sweating, bleeding slightly from cuts on her arms and face, with hair in disarray and one shoe untied.

"Officers," Vinnie said, squaring her shoulders, lifting her chin and assuming her most aristocratic expression while extending a hand, "I am Lavinia Holcombe. Do come inside."

CHAPTER THIRTY

Nina's little scream sounded strangled and unfamiliar, which frightened her until she realized that the black stocking covering her face had muffled her cry. She ripped it off, along with the knitted beanie that matted her long hair. Strange to have been running at her top speed one moment, then to have both feet slide out from under her the next. She'd felt a dull pain in her hip and thigh when she landed on whatever rocks and twigs littered the slope at the side of the road, but wasn't overly concerned until a hot, slicing sensation in her calf had utterly shocked and terrified her. It felt like she'd suddenly cut herself with a kitchen knife—magnified a dozen times. She reached a hand down and felt a tear in her leggings and a wetness that had to be blood. *Shit.* She pulled herself up, grabbed up the stocking and cap and squinted to see what might have caused the wound. The road was unlit by street lamps and the moon was only a slender crescent, but there was just enough twilight left to help her recognize the long shard of broken beer bottle that had done the deed. Nina picked it up using the stocking and carried it with her down to the stream, throwing it into the moving current as she hobbled across the exposed stones, splashing now and again when she missed her footing.

Her head throbbed and her heart pounded—with each beat she felt more blood ooze out of her wounded leg. She hurried to Rick's car and rummaged through the junk on the back seat, grabbing a sweater to wrap around her calf before starting the engine and rolling through the darkened field without turning on the headlights, until she at last felt the hard-packed dirt road under the tires. Thankfully, no one was about on this warm, humid night that promised rain. The dirt road was unfamiliar to Nina and she willed herself to remember the way back, starting to cry when she felt blood begin to seep into her shoe.

She shut the headlights when she approached a string of bungalows and rolled cautiously toward the rented cabin, slipping almost soundlessly into the drive. Killing the engine, she climbed out and tightened the knot in the sweater around her leg. She'd never be able to clean it, but at least she couldn't see any blood in Rick's car. Walking to the back door produced a return of the sharp pain and increased bleeding. Nina stumbled up the steps and reached for the knob. When the door was yanked open, she lost her balance and tumbled forward, onto the floor.

"Well?" Rick snarled.

Even after eight years of knowing the man and his moods, Nina was aghast. "Can't you see I'm hurt?"

"What happened?" he asked, standing aside while she hauled herself to her feet. A large smear of blood showed where she had lain.

"She came home. She chased me. I fell down the embankment by the stream," Nina rattled on, limping to a chair and dropping into it, twisting her leg around to get a better look at the gash in her calf.

"You idiot," he roared. "Another failure. Why the fuck did I trust you with this?"

Good question. Nina knew the answer—things were heating up and the police might be looking out for trouble even after those men were caught in one of the developments. He'd wanted to be sure she was the one arrested if the search went wrong. But she had been desperate to redeem herself. "I thought you said her car was at the boyfriend's house?"

"It was. How the hell do I know what happened? Maybe they had a fight. Maybe she forgot something. At least we know the old bitch wasn't going home for her birth control," he sneered.

As another "old bitch" who no longer needed birth control, Nina was offended, but she was too alarmed at all the blood on her hands, her shoe, the floor, to waste time on that thought. Her stomach flipped and she shuddered. "I'll have to go to the hospital."

"No. No hospital."

Nina stared, wide-eyed. "This is bad. I'll need stitches."

"Not in this town," Rick growled.

"It was filthy where I fell. I could get an infection."

Rick spread his hands and shrugged. "Go clean yourself up and look in the bathroom cabinet. I think there's a first aid kit." He began to pace the floor, running a hand roughly through his hair.

"First aid kit? Rick, look at this, my leg is split open."

"You're being dramatic. Shut up and let me think. Now that you've left it to me to deal with Santorelli."

Furious, Nina heaved herself out of the chair and made for the door, stooping to pick up the car keys she had dropped when she fell. The blood in her shoe squished as she walked—a sickening sensation. "I'm going to the hospital."

With a meaty hand to her shoulder, Rick sent her staggering and retrieved the ring of keys himself. "You're not going anywhere."

"I need a doctor," she yelled.

Rick advanced on her, then stopped in his tracks when she retreated a step. He glanced down at her leg. "You've broken into a home and tried to steal something. The owner chased you and might know that you fell. Don't you think the police will be checking the hospital and the urgent care places? Maybe all the way down to Scranton? Stupid whore. I don't care what happens to you, but you're not going to lead anyone to me."

Face hot, panting with rage, Nina swallowed hard and tried to grasp a straw of composure. "I'm not worried about getting caught as much as I am about losing my leg to gangrene. And I don't care anymore about your goddamned book. If they arrest me, I'll tell them all about you."

"You wouldn't dare."

Nina shrugged. All bets were off. "I'd be in jail. You couldn't hurt me there."

"Maybe I'll call the police myself. Tell them you came home in a state, and I found out you had tried to burglarize someone's home."

Nina rushed to the door but Rick grabbed her, shook her, then shoved her roughly to the floor. "How'd you like to do without your fancy clothes and hair stylist and dinners out for a few years? I wonder what the minimum sentence is for burglary."

Nina scooted backwards and away from him before struggling to her feet. "Less than it is for murder," she countered, wondering how she'd had the presence of mind to think of that.

A few unbearable seconds ticked by. Rick blanched, so she went in for the kill. "Whether you get caught or not, if you give me up to the police, I'll tell them about every dirty deal of yours over the past eight years, every item with questionable provenance that passed through your hands. Then I'll tell them about Mr. Cassidy." Rick gasped audibly, almost making Nina wish she could reel the words back in.

Rick stared at her for a long moment, ashen, every trace of anger and confidence gone. Nina dug deep and found one last trick in her bag.

"I know you'll try Santorelli's house now that you know the book is probably there," she said, as evenly as she could manage. "You'll have what you want, and you won't have to share. I don't want money, or jewelry. Just give me the keys. I'll drive to an out-of-state ER and make up a good story. If I get caught, I know nothing about your scheme. If they catch you, you just broke into Santorelli's. You know nothing about what happened at Lavinia Holcomb's house."

He appeared to consider this, and she limped closer. As soon as she was within range, she reached for the car keys. Rick's face twisted with rage, and he held them above her head. Desperate, Nina caught hold of him, and they struggled for a moment before he administered a backhanded slap and ran out the door.

"No!" Nina howled, hobbling down the back steps, hearing an engine start and the car skid around in the gravel drive before tearing off with a chirp of tires. "Shit."

Okay, you can stand around bleeding or do something.

She hurried back inside, twisting her hair up and peeling off her sweaty clothing. She took a quick shower and scrubbed the nearly foot-long gash in her calf, which produced a searing pain that then settled down to a more manageable throbbing. She dried off and yanked open the medicine cabinet, hauling out the tiny first aid kit. Resting the foot of her injured leg on the toilet seat, she forced herself to inspect the damage, although the sight made her shudder violently. Half of the wound simply was a nasty cut, but as her weight had pressed down on the broken bottle as she slid, the glass had embedded itself and opened up a gash nearly a half inch deep. It looked like she'd washed out any debris, but knowing that she was seeing the inside of her own leg, watching beads of blood begin to ooze forth again almost made her vomit.

"Okay, easy," she said, softly. "Do the best you can." She emptied the small, no doubt outdated tube of antibacterial ointment and packed the cut full, before using all five Band-Aids to help hold the deepest part closed. For good measure, she wound the miniature roll of gauze around her leg and held it in place with the roll of half-dried out white tape, before dressing herself quickly, and brushing out her hair.

Packing needed only five minutes, and mopping up the blood on the kitchen floor took only a few more. Then Nina shouldered her tote bag, dragged her small rolling suitcase down the back steps, and hurried out to the road. There were hospitals in New York, and she had train fare.

She had no idea where Rick had gone, but he'd probably taken the car far enough away to give her enough time to calm down and remember her place in his life before he returned. *Hopefully*.

Simply walking on the smooth pavement hurt—she didn't have it in her to sneak through the woods dragging a suitcase, and she couldn't leave her bloody clothes and other personal items around to be discovered. An unsettling thought seized her—was there any blood to be found on the ground where she fell? Too late to do anything about it now. Spotting a low stone wall, Nina stopped to rest, pulling out her phone, hoping she wasn't in a damned dead zone. Did they even have Uber out here in the sticks? The frigging local taxi would never take her as far as she needed to go.

Sitting in the back of someone's Toyota fifteen minutes later, Nina silently apologized to the town. They did have Uber service and the driver was willing to take her to the train station in Port Jervis. He was a decent-looking young fellow, and after a couple of failed attempts at conversation, he left her to her troubled thoughts.

Had she cleaned everything in the cabin well enough? Had she left any evidence at Lavinia's home? Nina replayed her moves through each room, willing herself to see every detail again, until she felt panic rising, and forced herself to let it all go. What was done was done. What would Rick do when he returned to an empty house? Mad as he was, he probably wouldn't waste time coming after her when he still had that treasure in his sights. He'd think she would be too afraid to rat on him, and quite probably, he was right. Nina drew a deep breath and leaned on the arm rest, gazing out at the darkened woods that slipped by. Finally, it had begun to rain, and beads of water dotted the glass. For all she knew, the bastard might have dumped her after finding the book and taken up with some young slut. *He's not worth the trouble anymore. There are other rich men in New York.*

Country music was playing softly on the radio, and she felt a drop of blood ooze out from under her make-shift bandage and trickle down toward her ankle. Nina reached quickly to apply pressure, then elevated the leg on the seat for good measure. So much blood. *Did* she leave any of it on the slope by the stream?

A gust of wind tossed the trees lining the road and she noticed the young driver grip the wheel harder. In the next moment, he was switching the wipers from intermittent operation to high gear, attempting to swish away the torrent of rain falling on the little car.

"Wow," the driver said, "that kicked up fast."

A relieved and satisfied smile turned up the corners of Nina's mouth and she relaxed, tilting her head back against the headrest, picturing the run-off from the road completely obliterating all traces of her slide down toward the stream.

"Yes," she said, softly. "It sure did."

CHAPTER THIRTY-ONE

"Dominick, I'm heading over to the store for the business meeting. I started a load of clothes. Can you put them in the dryer when it's time? Dominick?" *Where the hell is he?* His car was in the driveway. Felicia scouted through the downstairs rooms with no luck. Finally deciding to leave anyway, she headed toward the front door. Stealthy as a shadow, her eldest child slipped into view. What had he been doing in her private office? She hadn't even thought to look there. "There you are. Did you hear what I said about the laundry?"

He was grimacing, looking impatient and superior, and he clutched a thick sheaf of papers in his hand. "What's this?"

Felicia frowned a little. She didn't like the idea of him rifling through her manuscripts, but wasn't in a combative mood, so she walked up to him and twisted her head to read the title page from the necessary angle. "What's what?"

Dominick snorted a little and held the manuscript straight out in front of her, clutching it with both hands. "*This.*"

"That's a little too imperious for my taste. And let's see what it is you're shoving *in my face.*" Felicia masked her annoyance with a hint of sing-song-y sweetness. "Oh, that's *Wrong Princess*. It's my—"

"What kind of filth are you writing?" Dominick cut her off and towered over her, morphing into his father.

Felicia's mouth dropped open. "And what kind of nonsense is *this*? Invasion of privacy? You have no business snooping in my office, mister. And that's not filth, it's a tasteful, well-written erotic novel that I've signed a book contact on. Your mom's going to be a traditionally published author. I would've liked to have been able to break the news in a happier way, and I had the crazy idea that you might be proud of me."

Dominick scoffed, shoving the manuscript into her hands so quickly and roughly that Felicia had to snatch it before it fell to the floor. "Proud of *this*? What, you're writing this shit because your regular stuff isn't good enough and you got desperate? Who wants to be published like that?"

Too stunned to speak, Felicia just stood and stared. *Remember, this is the adorable little fellow who picked blooming weeds to bring home to you. Don't reach for the sharp objects just yet.*

Obviously on a self-righteous roll, Dominick paced back and forth in the front hallway and waved his hands about just like his father used to do. "You want your grandchildren reading this crap?"

"Not *now*. It's a genre for adults, you big dummy. They can read it when they're twenty-one."

"I don't want my kids reading porn."

"Well, good, I don't either. This will be just fine for them when they grow up. Did you read the whole thing, Mr. Literary Critic? Or just flip it open to one of the hotsy parts and get all judgmental? Besides, sex is a natural part of life. What do you do with Miss Marie What's-her-face, hmm? And how do you think you got here? Your father and I played pinochle, maybe?"

Dominick whirled around and did something she couldn't stand—pointed a finger right in her face and shook it, in a perfect imitation of his old man. "It's fine to have a little hobby, but you're disgracing yourself and our whole family. It's pitiful. I'm embarrassed for you."

Without so much as a wind-up, Felicia slapped the hand with the pointed finger as hard as she could, almost wishing it was his face. "I don't particularly care what you think of me, Dominick. I hope that comes as a real shock to you. I still love you, but this discussion is *over*. Now, I've got a business meeting to go to, but before I leave, I'm gonna tell you something I should've told your father years ago—get out!" Felicia spun on her heel, plunked the *Princess* down on the hall table with a resounding slap and strutted to the door, slamming it as hard as she could for good measure.

* * *

"It can't be coincidence," Lenora insisted. "Or our imaginations. First, the store is—I guess you'd have to say *searched*—and then the same thing happens at Felicia's house, probably mine, Al's, and now Vinnie's."

Charlie held up both hands. "People, remember this is a business meeting. We're not really done discussing the balance sheet."

"I know, but these are unusual circumstances," Felicia said. "We're all getting nervous here, don't know what the hell's going on, and no one seems to have any answers for us."

"Did those two men who were arrested have another partner who's still out there?" Vinnie said. "Does this even have anything to do with them? I put those questions to the police last night, but they weren't really able to answer me. I'm shaken, I have to admit. I know I chased after the intruder, although I don't really know what possessed me, but that doesn't mean I'm not frightened."

"The two guys who were arrested were stealing electronics and jewelry," Al said. "The police found a stash of stuff in their barn. Sure, they were neat, but they were actually taking something, unlike our guys."

Vinnie shook her head. "Maddening."

"Okay, let's look at the facts," Lenora said. "Whoever it was is skillful. Few, if any, signs of forced entry, nothing that we know of was taken, no damage done—well, except to Al."

"I'll say," he agreed. "But I had the bad luck to have surprised the guy. I might not have noticed anyone had been in the house, otherwise."

"There must be at least two of them," Vinnie said. "The one I chased had to be a woman—she was just a smidge taller than Lenora and slim. Plus, I swear I saw long tendrils of dark hair that had slipped out from under her cap. Al wrestled with a man."

"Definitely," he said.

"At first, I was sure they had to be after one of my books," Charlie mused.

"But what could they possibly be after if *not* a book?" Felicia spread her hands in an exasperated gesture. "There doesn't seem to be another option. Why else search *us*? They started with the store, didn't find what they wanted, and probably figured one of us might have taken it home."

"But if it was one of my books, why wasn't my home the first?" Charlie folded his arms across his chest. That thought had been nagging him from the start.

"Not one of yours, then," Vinnie suggested. "Maybe a seemingly ordinary book that has some special value."

"Great," Al said. "I mean, you may be right, but how could we ever guess which one, or why?"

"It would have to be a used book," Charlie said, tapping a finger on the table top. "But I've touched every pre-owned volume that's come into this store, to be sure we didn't have a hidden treasure. Even the Ott books."

"How about the ones that were in the store when we bought it?" Al said, and all eyes turned toward Charlie. "Well?"

Charlie frowned, searching his memory banks. *Think. They're depending on you.* "I glanced through them," he said at last. "I remember making the effort, but there were a lot of them, and I probably just scanned some of the titles."

"But we bought the place five years ago," Felicia almost whined. "Did someone just realize they wanted the book in the past couple of weeks? And, we're a *store*. Why the hell didn't they just waltz in and buy it?"

"I won't say I lack confidence in the local police, but they seemed thoroughly confounded last night," Vinnie said. "I got the sense that they really thought they had their men."

"I'll bet you're right," Lenora said. "They probably don't know what to make of your break-in."

"I don't like mysteries, unless I'm curled up in my favorite chair and holding it in my hands," Charlie said, shaking his head. "Look, I have an idea. I'll call a buddy of mine in New York, another rare books dealer, and see if anyone has been asking around for a certain book, offering a lot of money. . .I don't know. It's a start."

"Sounds good," Al said, turning back to his laptop screen.

"Be careful." Lenora frowned.

"Yeah, Charlie, I'm worried about you," Felicia said, reaching out to touch his sleeve. "Your house hasn't been searched, um. . . *yet*." She winced, like it hurt to say it, but Charlie took it in stride. He knew that perfectly well.

"I'm aware of that. Thank you, ladies. I promise I'll be careful."

* * *

Charlie was awakened by an ungodly wailing. Even as he slept, the sounds had set off a PTSD episode, and he awoke fully in the grasp of terror, sweat pouring off of him, heart pounding like it would explode, barely able to breathe. He felt himself cowering against the headboard and whimpering. Two battling tomcats ramped it up with another round of screeching and howling, and, now wide awake, Charlie realized what he was hearing and began to talk himself down.

"Steady, soldier," he murmured, sitting up straight and letting the covers fall into his lap. "It's only the neighbors' goddamned cats. Steady, now." He began drawing in breaths as long as he could manage, until he was able to fill and empty his lungs completely. His heart slowed to a merely agitated pace. "Okay, let's try Felicia's new trick from that self-help book that you've been avoiding." He switched on the light and got to his feet, shuffling to the bureau to find a dry T-shirt. Standing tall, he faced himself in the mirror, and replayed that day in his mind.

* * *

Charlie had finished his two years in the army, completed four years of college on Uncle Sam's dime, and was about to begin his first real teaching job in September of the year his father and a few other of Don Tomasso's best men were gunned down on a pier in Brooklyn. Until then, the Don had been as good as his word about letting Charlie choose his own career, and Charlie had never so much as glimpsed him in the distance, until he was summoned, along with his two older brothers, to the Don's lair. Charlie had felt sick at the thought of being forced to replace some junior man who would then be bumped up to replace Pop. But when Don Tomasso got right to the point, he addressed Charlie first, and seemed to set his fears to rest.

"I've honored your father's wishes and allowed you to pursue your own life, and I intend to continue to do so," he said. "But your late father was a prince among men—one of God's finest sons, and his death must be avenged. By all three of you," he added, and Charlie thought he'd shit on the spot. Beside him, his brothers looked more than eager to hear the plan and get started on the hunt.

"Patience," the boss told them, sharply. "Let me plan this properly. You'll get your orders before the week is out." Turning once again to Charlie, the Don's eyes burned into his. Charlie fought to maintain his arrow-straight soldier's stance. "You are required to kill at least one man. Then, you'll go back to your scholarly life, and I'll expect never to hear from you again. Do you understand?"

Charlie had nodded and added a "Yes, sir," in what he hoped was both a polite and a confident tone. As far as he was concerned, his father deserved only a modicum of respect for having helped bring Charlie into the world. But for his freedom, he would do anything that was asked of him.

The April morning had been soft and moist, and cooler by the private Catskills trout stream than it had been back home in the city. The brothers approached soundlessly; the three targets perched on rocks under newly green branches, holding fishing poles, and seeming to whisper softly to one another only occasionally. The Santorellis were within yards of the fishermen and on the verge of a neat, clean job when their passing flushed a rabbit out of hiding. Three heads turned, three rods were dropped, and three weapons quickly drawn. Julius and Tommy fired first, and their silenced bullets sent one of the rivals crumpling to the ground and the other splashing face first into the stream.

Charlie had fired as well, but he hadn't aimed to kill, even though he knew he must. He recovered quickly and got a bead on the last man. One of Charlie's shots had torn into the man's hand and sent his weapon flying into the underbrush, but the son of a bitch, with three holes in him, charged the Santorellis in a final show of defiance, screaming obscenitics until Charlie's bullet tore into the side of his head. Incredibly, even that didn't stop his mad rush, as his hands reached out to clutch Charlie's throat, eyes wild, mouth spitting blood, his words exchanged for an ungodly howl, not human, not animal, but rather like it came from a demon at the bottom of the deepest pit in Hell.

Charlie had never heard such a sound. Would the man never die? Panic rose in him and he fought it back, firing again and again, until the bastard lunged forward and wrapped Charlie in a lifeless, deadweight bear hug. As he slid down his assassin's body and collapsed onto the ground, the dead man's blood and brains oozed onto Charlie's clothing. Charlie dropped the borrowed gun and fell to his knees, vomiting up the remnants of everything he'd eaten all week.

Forty-odd years later, he still remembered every inch of the slow crawl to the stream to rinse out his mouth and dip his head into the icy water. Maybe God would simply hold him under until he was dead, too, Charlie thought. Maybe he'd cooperate, and just get it over with. Just one deep breath while his head was under. . .

Tommy and Julius each grabbed a shoulder and hauled him out of the stream and to his feet. "Okay, so that sucked," Tommy said. "It don't always go down like that, but sometimes it does, so just deal with it. We're not done." He wiggled a finger between the three corpses. "These bodies don't get found."

On the ride home, his brothers were in better spirits and tried to cheer him up, as if that were possible. They became annoyed when it didn't work.

"Come on, man." Julius slapped the side of Charlie's head. "You were a soldier. You're a trained killer."

Charlie knew that he was. But the rest—the disgraceful disposal of human beings once they were no longer a threat—was nothing that the U.S. Army would ever have required of him. Charlie didn't reply, and in fact, he didn't utter a word for several days. He barely spoke to either of his brothers again.

Both were dead now, each having reached his late seventies, honored with a decent Christian burial. Charlie had vowed that when he met them in Hell, he would ignore them still.

Sighing deeply now, he returned to bed, propped himself up on both pillows and opened a book. The trick hadn't worked. Sure, he was calmer now, but he would have been by this time anyway. So much for psycho-mumbo-jumbo. The shame, the torment, would be with him for life, or at least until God was done punishing him.

Which was just what he deserved.

CHAPTER THIRTY-TWO

The steak house was all dark woods and burgundy leather, with polished brass accents gleaming in the low light. The Manhattan sidewalk had been scorching hot, but the dining room was cool and fragrant with the scent of frying onions. Charlie inhaled deeply and smiled. The place had been one of his favorite haunts when he still lived in Brooklyn. He scanned the room and found three pairs of eyes searching for him, and the upraised arm of a well-dressed man about his own age was waving him over to a corner table.

"Charlie, good to see you, my friend." John Roth rose from his seat and gripped his hand warmly.

"Same here. It's been much too long. Clarkson, you old devil," Charlie greeted his other friend.

"Sit, sit. I'd like to introduce you to Manny Howard," John presented the fair-haired man seated beside him and Charlie shook his hand. A waiter stepped over to take Charlie's drink order and hand out heavy, leather-bound menus.

"Of course, I know you by reputation," Manny said to

Charlie, sipping a beer. "John's been telling me about the Honor Newman first edition that you found at a yard sale."

Charlie chuckled. "Yeah, that was too easy. Something that would never have happened if I hadn't moved to Brookdale, Pennsylvania."

"You still like it there, Charlie?" Clarkson asked, with a slight frown. "You know, we miss you here in the city."

"I miss it sometimes, too, but yes, I'm happy there."

"I hear it's not as peaceful as you might like right now," John said, and Charlie nodded.

"Lately, we've had some trouble. That's why I called and asked you to do a little snooping around for me."

"What's going on?" Manny asked, with a frown.

The waiter set a drink before Charlie and the men ordered their meals. Sipping, Charlie organized his thoughts and folded his hands on the table. "Here's the deal: you two know that I own a bookstore with four partners. Business is going well, the town loves us, it's all good until—" he spread his hands and shrugged. "Someone broke in. We think he searched the place, but didn't steal anything. Then, over the course of the next two weeks, the same thing appeared to happen to each of my partners at home. We're stumped. The police have no real answers. So we get our heads together and decide that it must be a book they're after." Charlie shrugged, and sipped his beer again. "So I called John to see if he'll ask around to find out if anyone's been looking for a special book, willing to pay a lot of money for it. Anything that might help us figure this out."

"And it didn't take me long," John said. "A man spoke to three of us. Me, Clarkson, and Manny. So. Here we are."

"I really appreciate you guys being willing to talk to me about this. We're all getting worried."

"Hey, no problem," Manny said. "Who wants to start?"

John cleared his throat. "Back in February, I think it was,

someone comes to my office. Late middle-aged man, tall, thin, with a sort of an indiscernible accent. His name's Emil Zoloty, and he's looking for a book."

"This book," Clarkson said, tossing a worn copy of a Benjamin Conway novel onto the tablecloth. "Well, not this particular one of course, but another copy of this book." He slid the volume across to Charlie, who picked it up and riffled through the pages.

"*The Stargazer at Dawn*. I know a little about Conway, but I've never heard of this one."

Manny snorted. "No one has."

"Let's just say there's a reason why Conway achieved what little fame he did *after* writing this novel," John said.

The men chuckled.

"But Zoloty didn't care about that," Manny said, leaning forward eagerly. He didn't want to read the novel. Some ancestor of his was on the run from a dictator's goons, hid out in an Eastern Orthodox church that used to be up around your neck of the woods, wrote all sorts of incriminating evidence in the margins, and hid the book before he was killed."

Charlie's eyebrows shot upwards. "No shit?"

"No shit," John said. "Zoloty had the notion that the book was still kicking around the northeastern Pennsylvania countryside, even though the church no longer exists. He wanted someone to thoroughly search book stores, antique emporiums, flea markets, what have you. It could have taken months. I turned him down. That's a young man's game. But I wouldn't be at all surprised if someone took him up on his offer."

"I nosed around on the internet a bit and came up with this," Clarkson said, nodding toward the volume in Charlie's hands. "But it wasn't the right one. That's when the details came out."

Everyone moved their drinks and cleared their elbows off the table so that the server could set out their plates.

"The mission sounds like a pain in the ass," Charlie said. "Not to mention possibly a fool's errand."

Manny grinned. "Yeah, but I almost took him up on it. He was offering $500,000."

Charlie let out a low whistle. "*Man.*"

"It was really tempting, but as John said, it could've taken months, and my wife was pregnant. I've got a five-year-old at home—just not doable."

"No one's heard from Zoloty since late winter, so I'm assuming he found a dealer who was willing." John shook out his napkin and let it float onto his lap.

"So, do you think this rich guy found someone to search for the book in Brookdale and he thinks, for some reason, that we have it? I'm pretty sure we don't, by the way."

John shrugged, chewing.

"Could be," Manny said, taking a swig of beer.

"But who? We're a pretty upstanding lot. Who among our colleagues would stoop to stealing?"

Clarkson wiped his mouth with his napkin. "When there's that much money involved, it isn't hard to imagine that someone might. You and I have been in this business for a very long time, but we don't know every other rare books dealer in the city."

"True enough," Charlie conceded, cutting his steak.

"He was a one-hit-wonder, that Conway, wasn't he?" Manny said.

The three older men hooted. "Which was his 'hit,' do you think?" Clarkson teased. "*The Chart Room*? Or *Fountain City*?"

Manny looked suitably chastised. "I was thinking of *The Gallery*. That one's pretty good." He was rewarded with snickers from the other diners. "And he did fairly well with that one."

"My dear young friend," John said, placing a hand on Manny's shoulder, "an author who is a one-hit-wonder is required to have had a bona-fide hit. You know, like Harper Lee's *To Kill A Mockingbird*, J.D. Salinger's *Catcher in the Rye*, Eve White's *Dauntless* or Margaret Mitchell's *Gone with the Wind*."

"Okay, okay, guys," Manny waved them off, good-naturedly.

"Does anybody have this Mr. Zoloty's business card, his number?" Charlie asked, then looked around him at three heads shaking.

"Sorry, old man," Clarkson said. Then he nodded toward the volume on the table. "You can have that, if you're curious. I only paid four dollars for it, and it's of no use to me. Something to read on the train home."

Charlie shrugged. "Sure, why not? Thanks."

* * *

Charlie waved down a cab. His face was burning, one bead of sweat was creeping down his back, another slipped down the side of his face, and his shoes probably were going to melt and stick to the damned sidewalk. Climbing in, he directed the driver to the PATH station and relaxed in the cool air, glancing at the old hardbound book on the seat beside him. He didn't remember seeing another with the same title on The Paper Pirate's shelves. But perhaps it had been part of the stock when he and his partners bought the place, and he'd passed over it while checking out the inventory in the used section, or had forgotten all about it. At seventy-one, his memory was still pretty good but not the steel trap it once was. What a curious story attached to the book! Yet it must have been true if someone was willing to spend such a princely sum to get hold of it.

Another blast of angry summer air greeted Charlie when he switched from cab to station to Hoboken-bound train. He hadn't even gotten a chance to cool off again before having to trot over to the soon-departing New Jersey Transit train to Port Jervis.

Can't wait to get home to Brookdale.

He was briefly engulfed in a swarm of cub scouts that appeared from nowhere, and found himself buffeted about in their wake. A whistle blew and he turned sharply to hurry on. Distracted and rushing, he found himself teetering on the knife's edge of the curb before crashing to the pavement, landing on both hands and one knee.

Shit.

A young couple and a uniformed conductor appeared as he was dusting himself off and surveying the damage. His hands were merely sore and dirty, but his knee was throbbing and there was a tear in his khakis.

"I'm okay, folks. Thank you for your concern."

"Would you like me to call for medical assistance?" the conductor asked.

Charlie waved him off. "No, thank you. Appreciate it, but I've got to make that train." Pasting a phony smile on his face, he limped bravely toward one of the cars.

No way I'm getting stuck here for the night.

He was settled in the cool interior for only a moment before the train began to roll toward home. He put his sore leg up on the empty seat next to him and pulled up his pant leg for a better look at his injury. Only a bit of brush burn, but quite a bit of soreness.

Ah, well, I'll ice it when I get home.

He leaned back and closed his eyes for a moment, smiling when he pictured himself skinning his knees after tumbling from his bike and being set upon by his mother, a mercurochrome bottle in one hand and a homemade cookie in the other. He opened his eyes again and parted the musty covers of *The Stargazer at Dawn*. Might as well read the thing. It was going to be a long ride.

CHAPTER THIRTY-THREE

On Monday morning Lenora dabbed at her eyes and checked her appearance in the beveled mirror that hung over the little antique sink in the staff toilet. It had been a rough night. She hadn't wanted to spend the night crying over Jason and show up at work with swollen eyes, so she'd crawled out of bed and shuffled down the hall to her office, where she'd worked on the new version of her YA story until there wasn't time to get quite enough sleep to prepare her for the day. However, the outlining and editing had really helped her calm down and center herself. Not for the first time, and probably not the last. *Thank God for writing,* she thought, tossing the tissue into the wastepaper basket and stepping into the break room just as Charlie entered through the back door. Lenora's heart skipped a little. He was walking with the aid of a cane, looking smaller, even a bit frail. For the first time, ever.

"Charlie, what happened?"

"Ah, I tripped when I was hurrying for the train home on Saturday," he said, stuffing his lunch bag into the fridge and heading toward the little private office with his briefcase. "The day was a total failure. I didn't get any information from my friends. Don't look worried. This is nothing."

"Well, it's not nothing," Lenora scolded, hurrying to his side. "Have you seen the doctor?"

"Went to the Urgent Care place yesterday. Seems like it's just a sprain. Nothing broken. Didn't tear an ACLU or anything."

Lenora giggled. "Silly. That's lawyers."

Charlie gave her a smile on his way past. "Whatever. Point is, I'll be fine. But since you've got two good legs, maybe you could open the door and let in the masses while I get myself settled here." He sniffed. "You started the coffee, so I'll get both of us a cup and bring them out front."

"Sure," she said, and was about to turn away when he stopped her to examine her face closely.

"You okay, Lenora?"

She nodded, feeling her cheeks color slightly. "Healing takes time. I'm on my way, though."

He nodded and limped into the office. Gratefully, Lenora turned her steps to the sales floor. Sometimes girlfriends were the best medicine, but sometimes a guy friend's casual dismissal of mushy stuff in favor of soldiering on was helpful in its own way.

Throughout the day, although Lenora often leapt to her feet to take the burden off of him, Charlie insisted upon going about business as usual, even walking to the bank to make the deposit, then taking another short stroll on his lunch break.

"Are you sure—"

"Best to keep moving," he insisted.

It was a busy day, with only one brief lull in the action mid-afternoon. Both partners perched on stools drawn up to the sales counter and leaned wearily on their elbows.

"I have to stop at the market on the way home," Lenora

said, fingering the list she'd scribbled on a post-it. "My niece is driving my mother up to visit for a few days."

"That sounds great. You need any extra time? I can work a shift for you."

"You should rest. I have two days off in a row. That should be fine. They can amuse themselves, or even stop in and hang out here."

"Bullshit," Charlie declared. "I'll work Thursday for you. When's the last time you saw your mother in person?"

"Well, April, I guess."

He nodded, briskly. "And she's like eighty or something, right? Take the three days."

Lenora smiled. "We'll see."

* * *

Charlie tapped at the keys, pausing now and again to read from the list of books beside his laptop while Lenora did a little stocking and schmoozing with a couple of regulars. He had told her that he was posting a kind of "sale" on the Facebook page devoted to his antique books business, designed to clear his shelves of older copies that were in imperfect, but nevertheless readable, condition. He'd taken photos of the more attractive candidates, but some were simply described, such as a Dickens from the early twentieth-century with some water damage, a Tolkien with a missing cover, and a copy of Conway's *The Stargazer at Dawn* defaced by handwritten notes. Charlie actually owned every book save that last one, and, as luck would have it, Lenora herself had suggested the "give a poor old book a good home" advertising gambit last year, so his true purpose, he hoped, would remain a secret. Charlie re-read the ad, included the photos and sat back for a moment to gather his thoughts a bit before he hit "post." A shiver snuck down his spine. The trap was set, and he was the bait.

* * *

"Finally!" Al pulled the Jeep into the last open parking slot and he and Karen hurried out, slamming doors and jogging toward the dock behind the Wilson Lake Visitor's Center. It was a gorgeous summer day, sunny, breezy, warm, but not too humid, the kind of day when everyone would want to be on the water.

"Come, on, hurry," Karen said, moving a few steps ahead of him. "We want to get seats by the railing so we can take pictures."

"Coming." Al smiled, indulgently. He had more than enough photos of Wilson Lake to last a lifetime, but her energy and joy for small pleasures was refreshing, and something he knew damn well he'd always lacked. Maybe that's why she was so good for him. Of course, her cooking didn't hurt, either.

The sightseeing boat bobbed gently at the dock, nudged by the foaming wakes of personal watercraft and a guy in an expensive-looking speed boat. "Are those allowed here?" Al asked, pointing, but Karen just shrugged. "Let's get moving. Looks like the line's not quite as long as I'd imagined."

"That's because it's Wednesday. You couldn't drag me here on a summer weekend." His phone chimed, and Al stopped in his tracks.

So did Karen, about ten feet ahead. "Aaaaal," she whined. "There are still only so many seats at the rail."

"Okay, okay." He trotted toward her, glancing between his phone and his surroundings. "I've got an email."

"Are you kidding me? You're like a teenager. There's a real boat out there, filling up with real people who all want to sit at the railing on this beautiful day—"

"It's from Greg," Al said softly.

Karen's jaw dropped, then she grinned excitedly, lake cruise and seat selection apparently forgotten. "What does he say?"

"Come on," Al said, good-naturedly, taking her arm and hustling her toward the dock. "The message will still be there in five minutes."

They showed their tickets and climbed aboard, the ladies and older men assisted by a strapping young sailor. Al was grateful that he hadn't made the cut and was left to hop on by himself. Karen snagged a pair of seats at the railing and tugged his arm, gesturing to his phone.

"Let's see. What did he say?"

Al squeezed the phone tightly because he felt his hands shaking. Tap, scroll, tap. And there it was. Twelve years of waiting, but there it was. "It's a picture of *very* small Christmas cactus cuttings under a plastic bag tent," he said, turning the phone toward her and letting her guide his hand to tilt it to a glare-free angle so she could see.

"Grandpa, what do you think?" Karen read. "Fingers crossed." Her voice cracked and she swiped a finger under her eye as she smiled up at him.

Al grinned, and took the phone back, gazing at it with rapture, willing the little green bastards to grow into a success for the young gardener. *Fingers crossed, buddy*, he replied. *Let me know how it goes.*

* * *

The tray teetered in Lenora's hands as she pushed the sliding patio door open with her elbow, stepped onto her back porch, then attempted to close it with her shoulder.

Clucking her tongue, Lenora's mother rose from her chair

and shooed Lenora out of the way and closed it for her. "Watch you don't spill our lemonade," she scolded, gently.

Lenora grinned, setting the heavy tray down on one of the wicker side tables. Her mom was even smaller than Lenora herself, dressed, as usual, in a chic casual outfit and costly but tasteful jewelry. Her hair was cut in a style similar to her daughter's but was a mix of silver and iron grey. "Where's Lola?"

Mom resumed her seat, waving an arm in the general direction of the lake. "She went down to look at the dock, and started talking with two young people in kayaks. They're probably still chatting."

"She's a doll to bring you up. It's so good to see you."

"It's good to be here. It was so hot in the city." She chose a glass of lemonade and took a sip. "And it's good to see you looking well. How are you feeling, honey?"

Lenora settled herself in a chair beside her mother and lifted a glass without taking a drink. "It's too soon to really be feeling better about the break-up, but I guess you could say I can see the way forward from where I am today."

Mom nodded, seeming to consider this. "I guess that's good enough, for now."

"You know what's been amazing? I've gotten this idea for a new direction for my Young Adult story, and I've been so excited to work on it that it's really taken my mind off the hurting. I actually forget it for hours at a time while I'm writing."

"Really? I know you had been saying you weren't so thrilled with the story. What changes are you making?"

Lenora turned to face her mother, leaning forward eagerly. "I'm going to give the main character a close friend who tries to commit suicide."

"Lenora! Well, it sounds like it might be therapeutic. But this is an appropriate topic for kids?"

"Believe it or not, yes, it's acceptable. You'd be surprised at the subjects YA authors tackle. Of course, the friend *doesn't* kill herself, and it's thanks in part to the main character's intervention."

Mom shrugged. "I'm sure I'd be shocked to know what's in kids' books nowadays. But what real kids have to deal with is probably worse."

"Exactly. Young people have lots of choices for entertainment now. They're not going to read books unless they're relevant."

"I'd love to read it when it's done. Although I suspect your writer friends will be better at helping you with it. You know, you and your brother can do no wrong in my eyes."

Lenora was pleased. "I'd love to have you read it."

Mom gestured toward the wide back lawn, and Lenora looked up to see her slim, tanned niece trudging up the slope toward them, long dark hair flowing free, her fist full of wildflowers. "Here's Lola coming back. You know, she pointed out a sign for a wine tasting thing at that fancy Victorian restaurant as we were driving up. Maybe we could have dinner there and try it out."

"Of course, Mom. We can do that, we can check out the antiques mall and the craft fair at the high school and take a boat ride. Whatever you two would like to do."

A breeze rushed past, ruffling their hair and bringing along the smell of someone's freshly mown lawn. Mom looked about as pleased as anyone in the world could possibly be. "Life is good, Lenora," she declared.

Lenora felt her eyes brimming with grateful tears, so she just smiled back and nodded.

* * *

"Please be patient, Mr. Zoloty," Rick purred, although his head pounded with rage as he twirled a pencil and tapped his foot on the rug. "Everything is going according to the plan I laid out—it only seems to you like time is dragging on because you're sitting and waiting for a phone call. But trust me, I've got this."

"I've trusted you for five months—and it's been two since you told me you'd discovered the whereabouts of the damned book. I hope you don't expect me to up my offer again."

"Not at all." Better to let Zoloty think that Rick was jerking him around than to know that the expert he'd hired was being played for a fool by a team of amateurs who didn't even know what he was after.

"Because what I'm really considering is putting someone else on the job."

Rick's knuckles whitened as he stopped spinning the pencil and gripped it hard. He held the phone away from his face so his ragged breath wouldn't betray his fury. *Deep breath, phony smile to help sound convincing, try again.* "That would be a mistake," he said, casually. "A new man will have to start from scratch. You can be sure I won't share any information I've gathered. He'll have to begin at square one—it could take another, say, five months perhaps? When is your election day? It might be too late to influence enough people to make a difference at that point."

"You're a son-of-a-*bitch*." Zoloty spat the words out.

"So I've been told." Rick's smile was real now. He leaned back on the sofa and lifted the crossword puzzle to his knee, fingers steady, confident that he retained the upper hand. The finish line truly *was* very near. Santorelli had to have the book, and Rick had spotted the skinny old fool limping up and down Main Street—an easy target. The money was nearly in his hands. And with that stupid bitch, Nina, out of the picture, none of it would have to be wasted on jewelry or trips for her.

Good riddance. There were other pieces of ass in New York. Although he'd been surprised to find her gone, he was certain that she feared him enough to keep her end of the bargain that she herself had offered. He had no reason to mention her name in connection with this search, and she'd likely never mention his.

"One more chance, Foster," Zoloty's voice interrupted these thoughts. "You know where that damned book is and you'll get it to me in exactly one week or the deal is off. I felt I needed it, but I'll not be played forever. If I don't have it, I'll simply have to have faith that the grassroots campaign for the incumbent president will save the day. Remember, that thing is not worth a dime, nor a penny, to anyone else, and you've spent five months of your life chasing it. If you lose me, you might as well shove it up your ass."

Rick gritted his teeth and his knuckles whitened around the pencil again. *Miserable, spoiled-rotten pretty-boy bastard.* "Understood," was the only word he trusted himself with, before ending the call.

The phone clattered when he tossed it onto the coffee table. "*Prick.*" Rick envisioned the long, aristocratic neck of his client as he snapped the pencil in two.

* * *

Felicia leaned out of the car window and craned her neck but still couldn't see any more of the accident scene than she'd been able to glimpse already. Dozens of lights flashed and whirled around, and although the sirens finally had stopped, she could occasionally catch the harsh chatter of two-way radios. Her cell phone rang and Felicia rolled up the window and yelled "Hello," at the hands-free thingy in the car's ceiling.

"Hi, Mom. Is this a good time?"

"Angelina, honey, it's as good a time as any. I'm stuck on Route 6. There's been a huge accident. We haven't moved in almost a half an hour."

"Oh, that's terrible. I hope no one is hurt badly."

"Me, too. So how are you, sweetheart? How's my handsome son-in-law and my grandbabies?"

"Everyone's fine. The kids and I are looking forward to flying up to visit next week."

"I'm thrilled. I've been cooking and baking for days."

"You know, you don't need to go to so much trouble. Just seeing you will be a treat for us."

"Too late. The freezer is full. You'll be able to see your brother's new apartment, too."

"He's found a place, huh? I'm glad. You two will get along much better this way."

"Yes, we will. Thank God we're still speaking. He's even apologized for sneaking around in my study and insulting my manuscript. I was so angry. This has been a life-long dream of mine."

"Bobby and I are excited for you. I've told all my girlfriends about your big break and they've all said they'll buy the book. I made them promise to leave you a review."

"Thanks. That's so important." Up ahead, she noticed a police officer waving and pointing. "Oh! This is good. They're starting to funnel us off onto a side road. Now let's see if I remember how to get home that way."

"Use the GPS."

"If we use these things all the time, our brains will turn to mush," Felicia said, inching forward along with her fellow motorists.

She could hear Angelina's big sigh. "Whatever you say, Mom. Do you think the publisher will send you out on a book tour?"

"There'll probably be something modest. But I'll be responsible for a lot of the marketing. Lenora says she'll help me with that. We're starting to post things on The Paper Pirate website already. You know, to generate interest."

"You guys have such a loyal following. I'm sure it will help you."

"I hope so. I'm going to give it all I've got." Felicia's car crept closer to the pile-up. "Wow, now that I can see better it looks like the accident is worse than I thought. We'll have to say a prayer. I'm sure someone was hurt."

"How many cars involved?"

"Looks like four, and a big box truck. They're all heavily damaged, and there's still smoke coming from one that looks like it burned. What a mess! I think every cop and fire truck in the county is out here tonight."

CHAPTER THIRTY-FOUR

June 29

"The fireworks are fantastic. Don't miss them," Charlie told the middle-aged couple as they stood on the sidewalk outside The Paper Pirate. "Don't let the idea of traffic bother you. There's a bunch of holiday stuff going on until midnight, so folks come and go. There isn't one big Exodus."

The woman smiled, fingering the July Fourth brochure he'd tucked in the bag along with her book purchase. "Thanks for the advice. We'd love to see them, but we were hesitating."

"Have a good night, guys."

"Thank you, my friend," the husband gave a quick wave as the couple headed off into the warm evening.

Charlie limped back inside, locked the door and turned the "closed" sign to face the world. Leaving only the little white nightlights on, he cashed out the register and tidied up the kitchenette area in the breakroom before packing up his laptop and locking the back door behind him.

Everything in the narrow rear lot looked as is always did,

the summer sounds that still rang out from Main Street were nothing out of the ordinary, the aroma wafting from the open door of Vito's Pizza was no different than any other evening, but ever since he'd "told" the partners' tormentor about the location of the valuable *Stargazer,* Charlie knew that his world had become a more dangerous place.

Half-hoping he'd come home to find that their mysterious intruder had already searched his place and gone away, Charlie stalled his return with a trip to the grocery store and the Wine and Spirits shop. Finally arriving at his house, he pulled the Cadillac into the garage and watched the neighborhood disappear as the door descended. What the hell would happen between now and the time he opened it tomorrow? *Would* he leave the house again? Charlie frowned, turning toward the rear door. *Bullshit. You've got protection, and enough nerve to use it.* He crossed the patio and let himself in through the kitchen door.

After a simple dinner—with coffee—and a quick clean-up, he took his laptop out of his messenger bag and placed it on the coffee table in the living room, where he worked until dusk began to settle. Then he made the rounds, checking doors and windows before returning to his recliner and logging off, extinguishing the last light in the house. His fully-charged smartphone was in his pocket, and the Glock was loaded and lying on the seat beside his right hand, just as they had been for the last few nights. He drew a deep breath and willed himself to be alert—and the night's vigil began.

* * *

Charlie's head drooping to the left startled him awake. At first, all had seemed quiet, but he soon heard his prey prowling around the outside perimeter of the house, trying all the windows. It was his cue to retreat to the basement and call the police, but, to his disappointment, he was hit hard by curiosity and a bout of conflicting emotions that ended up keeping him on the main floor until a click, a sliding sound, and a light thud made Charlie realize that he was no longer safely alone in his home.

Listening to the intruder rifle though the stuff in the home office, Charlie at last made the decision to call in the police. Then, a bump, a crash, and an oath issued from the room in quick succession was followed by a growl and the sound of something that belonged to Charlie shattering. That necessitated a change of plans.

He covered the length of the hall in a few seconds, pushed the office door open and slapped a hand on the wall switch, flooding the room with light. A stocky, dark-clad man with a stocking obscuring his features jumped and whirled to face him. The room wasn't large. They stood about ten feet apart. Charlie didn't give him much time to think.

"That's enough. Sit down and keep your hands where I can see them." He pointed the weapon at the desk chair then at the intruder's heart. The man stood frozen for a moment. "I said sit."

This time, his command was obeyed. Charlie hooked the cane over the door handle and slipped his phone out of his pocket. "Let's see if I can call an Uber for you. One with flashing lights on top."

He hadn't meant to taunt—the situation was delicate enough, but the sight of his broken objects had thoroughly pissed him off. Before he could get the phone up to eye level to punch in the three magic numbers, he saw a sneer creep across the guy's face—visible even through the dark stocking. Charlie barely had time to wonder if perhaps the bastard wouldn't flinch at harming a lame old man when his opponent stood and flung the heavy rolling chair at him as easily as if it had been one of those cheap, stacking vinyl chairs that could be tossed around in a light gust of wind.

Instinctively, Charlie flung his hands up to protect himself. The phone clattered to the floor, and the bulky, barrel-chested figure hurtled toward him.

What *coglioni*, Charlie thought, raising the gun and firing twice. He'd aimed for both knees, but only hit the right one—his other bullet hit the man's left thigh, but, no matter, he was down. The intruder let out a blood-curdling howl of pain that mimicked perfectly the one uttered by the rival Don's man forty-some years ago beside that peaceful Catskill stream.

Charlie felt like a bucket of ice water had been dumped on his head. He knew he should retrieve his phone and finally call the police, but he stood transfixed, waiting for the PTSD nightmare to begin. The seconds ticked by; he listened to his attacker's cursing and watched him thrashing around. He bent slowly toward the phone, lifted it and pressed 9-1-1, glancing first to his left, then his right, then tossing a quick squint over his shoulder, wondering where the hell the panic was, almost as if he wondered from which direction it would arrive.

"9-1-1. What is your emergency?"

Charlie quickly gave his name and address. "I need the police and an ambulance," he said in a strained voice. "Someone broke into my home and he rushed me. I had to shoot him, Miss. Please send help. I don't want him to die."

"Yes, sir, I'm getting you assistance right away. I will stay on the line with you until they arrive. Are you in a safe place right now?"

Charlie stood over the writhing, moaning intruder, gun pointed directly at his head. "Yes, Miss. I believe so." Charlie's pulse was elevated, but his breathing was smooth and his hands steady. *Okay, so where's the PTSD? Hmm. Son of a bitch. Could it be that Felicia's trick is working after all?*

The 911 operator had only the chance to get out a couple of comforting lines before Charlie informed her that he heard sirens. "Sir, if the intruder is disabled, please secure your weapon and go to the front door. Open it wide and stay there with your hands up. Okay, Mr. Santorelli?"

Charlie did as he was told, and in what seemed like less than a minute, his house was swarming with activity, and he was sitting on a stool at the breakfast bar giving evidence to a young Brookdale police officer.

"I hope they hurry and get him to the hospital. He was bleeding a lot, and I can only imagine the pain of a shattered kneecap. Can you make them hurry?"

"They're very good at taking care of any kind of trauma, Mr. Santorelli,"

the officer said gently. "It's great that you're concerned, but remember he didn't have to be here tonight."

Charlie ran a shaky hand through his hair. "Okay, you're right. I just don't want to be in any trouble."

"Of course, there'll be a thorough investigation, but from what you've told me, plus the fact that you're a respectable, well-known shopkeeper, and your gun permit is in order, I think you'll be fine."

A ruckus caused both of them to turn their attention to the living room. The intruder, strapped securely to a gurney, handcuffed wrists lying on his chest, was wheeled toward the front door, moaning, bitching, and yelling threats of violence. Someone had pulled the stocking off of his face and Charlie was barely able to prevent himself from speaking the name, *Gronsky! What the—*

The young officer rolled his eyes when the patient threatened a lawsuit as he was trundled roughly over the threshold and out into the night. "He ought to be glad the state will be paying for his knee replacement surgery," he quipped and despite the turmoil of the evening, Charlie chuckled.

After another half hour of questioning the officers left him to get some rest, instructing him to come down to the station tomorrow to finish up a few more details. They seemed concerned about his well-being. Did he want to call someone to stay with him? Charlie assured them he felt safe now, even though his Glock was in a plastic bag in their possession and his office was still cordoned off with yellow tape. As he showed them out, one of the cops casually advised him to consult with a lawyer, but both agreed it was doubtful he'd face any charges.

"This is the real meaning of standing your ground," the younger one said.

Charlie thanked them and stood in the front doorway until they'd gotten into their car and backed down his driveway. He turned and shuffled inside, and closed the door carefully. That done, he felt an enormous grin spread across his face. Twirling the cane, he strutted to the hall closet without a trace of lameness and tossed it inside. No need for *that* ruse any longer. What a nice touch that had been—it was well worth getting the skinned knee to make him think of it. He'd have to remember to bring the thing with him to the police station tomorrow and resume his frightened little old man act for a while, just to be on the safe side.

Good job, soldier, he congratulated himself, pouring a bit of whiskey into a glass over ice. Now, on to the next bit of business —finding that damned book.

CHAPTER THIRTY-FIVE

Charlie pulled into the driveway behind Vinnie's battered Volvo station wagon, cut the engine and emerged into the sunshine. He headed up the pathway to the front door, but a flash of color and movement in the periphery made him turn quickly and see the lady of the manor busy in her garden. Turning his steps, he called to her and she waved him in at the gate.

"Hi, Charlie. Good to see you. No more cane?"

"Nah. I'm doing much better now."

"As befitting the man who has delivered us from our own little corner of hell. I'm glad of it." She handed him the basket into which she was tossing dried up flower heads and proceeded along the row, deadheading as she went. Charlie inched along beside her. "So it was Gronsky, of all people."

"Gronsky, or whatever his real name is, yeah. No one was more shocked than I was. He was just an annoying blip on the screen, and seemed like he couldn't care less when I told him we were keeping the store."

"I suppose the whole story will be told eventually. It's too soon. But I'm dying to know the details."

Charlie just smiled.

"No trouble for you, I expect?" she asked, glancing up with a crease in her brow.

"Not so far. And it doesn't look like that will change. I was within my rights, and his life was never really in danger. I tried to get in a few questions while I was down at the station, but the cops can't say much until the whole mess is wrapped up. Sounds like he acted alone, and he's cooperating—I think he admitted to Al's job, too, but nothing else."

"How strange. I know that I chased a woman, and why would anyone *else* have been searching our homes and the store?"

Charlie shrugged, holding the basket out for a handful of dead marigold and zinnia blossoms. "It'll all come out. Or else it won't. I have a strong feeling we have nothing more to worry about, Vinnie."

Vinnie straightened, and rewarded him with a smile. "I'm inclined to believe you, sir. We're all so proud of you, and so grateful."

Charlie glanced at his shoes. "I'm just glad I could help. You guys mean a lot to me."

Vinnie rounded a corner and reached out with her clippers and Charlie followed her with the basket at the ready. Every bit of that statement had been true, and then some. Which made this next bit a lot harder.

"You know, a buddy of mine gave me some old books when we met for lunch in the city, and I've been reading one of them. Pretty good, although I didn't think it was to my taste at first. Once I got into it, well, I was impressed."

"Oh?"

"Yeah. Guy never got much credit for this one, but he did a

great job. Gave me an odd feeling, though. I'd never read it but it was so damned familiar." Vinnie turned to him with a pretty half smile that he knew he was about to wipe away. "I think you'd like it." He held her eyes for a second. "Benjamin Conway. *The Stargazer at Dawn.*"

Vinnie's hand flew to her throat and she gripped the fence rail for support.

"Sometimes, it's useful for an author to do a little bit of experimenting, play-acting," he said, gently, with what he hoped was his most reassuring expression. "Trying on someone else's style, you know, to see if it can help you work through a mental block with your own story." He chatted amiably, but Vinnie shrank from him. Her face was a mask of disbelief and horror—an expression he'd never seen on her. It hurt to see it now. "I've done it myself, but you know, in the end, I knew I had to be true to my own style. And I'm not even as talented as you are. I'd say you're every bit as good as Edith Wharton or Margaret Atwood or. . . Eve White."

To his dismay, Vinnie let out a little cry, dropped the clippers, clapped both hands over her mouth and began to back away, stumbling on the uneven ground. Charlie set the basket down and took her arm, gently leading her to a bench beneath a bower of climbing roses. Enveloped by their perfume, they sat motionless, listening to the buzzing of the bees and the insistent chattering of jays in the hemlock at the far end of the garden. She sat with clenched hands in her lap, shoulders bent, head bowed, refusing to look at him, although he watched her carefully.

"Vinnie, my friend," he said, softly, "I'm *very* good at keeping secrets. You have no idea. It's just that I have such admiration for your work, I want to read more of the real thing."

"How. . .how did you know?" she stammered, hoarsely.

"It started with *Stargazer*. I recognized the similarity to the chapters you've been submitting lately. It's a great book, but not exactly the same style as your usual. Which is why those submissions have had me puzzled. The rest was dumb luck. I'd pulled out my old copy of *Dauntless* when I thought we might be using it for the reading marathon and there it was, lying on my desk. . .I guess I got bored and flipped it open—I re-read the whole thing, cover to cover. It's unmistakably you, Vinnie. If anybody in the group had done the same thing, they might've known, too. I was just the one who did."

Vinnie smiled ruefully, shaking her head a little. The breeze pushed her blonde hair in front of her face and she brushed it back, languidly. "What now?"

Charlie shrugged. "You tell me."

She sighed, deeply. "I've started a sort of sequel, if you will, to Conway's book. It picks up after Peter's death and follows Julia as she makes a new life. I've got four chapters so far, and I'm quite pleased with them. Of course, there'll be some small references made to events in *Stargazer*, and if I were to get a contract with a publisher, I'd give Conway credit for those and thank him profusely for inspiring the new work."

Charlie chuckled. "*If* you get a contract? You do a good job, do you think there's any way in hell that a publisher would refuse Eve White's comeback novel?"

Vinnie glanced shyly down at her trembling hands, then raised her eyes to his. "I'll only give it a shot when this manuscript is completely finished."

He nodded, one definitive up and down of his head. "Deal. Just one thing. . .I have a demand in return for my silence."

Vinnie cocked her head to the side and looked at him quizzically. Thank God she seemed to take the joke as it was intended.

"I want to see your copy of *The Stargazer at Dawn.* I believe it's the book our man was after."

"Really? But it's defaced. Every conceivable blank space is filled with scribbling in some foreign hand."

"Believe it or not, that scribbling is what makes your copy worth a lot more than the one my buddy gave me." If only Charlie could find Gronsky's client, there would be a handsome sum for the five partners to divide among themselves.

"I'm intrigued. What does it say?"

"Not sure, exactly. Some romantic saga about a fugitive from a nineteenth century Balkan dictator's injustice. And a rich man somewhere in New York who hopes to use the information to influence his country's elections for the better."

"Charlie, you devil. How in the world did you find all of this out?"

"Never mind that," he said with mock sternness. "Ten minutes with that book will buy my silence for a lifetime. Which, at my age, won't be terribly long, but there you have it."

Vinnie beamed a lovely smile upon him, rose from the bench and reached out for his hand. "Come with me."

They entered the house through the kitchen door and climbed two flights of stairs to Vinnie's garret workroom. She led him over to one of the book cases and scanned the lower shelves, holding her long hair back with one graceful hand. Charlie watched as her fingers glided over one spine after another. It looked like she was having trouble locating it. Of course, she would be assured of his silence anyway, but he was dying to see the volume that had caused the group so much misery.

"Now, where is it? I haven't looked at it in a couple of weeks, but I thought I'd put it right—that's strange," Vinnie murmured, poking her hand into an empty slot between books, and retrieving two rumpled dollar bills. She held them up and met his eyes with a thoroughly confounded expression.

"What the hell?"

She fingered the two bills. "It was the price of the book, but, what in Heaven's name is it doing here, and where's my copy of *Stargazer?*" They regarded one another in complete bafflement then shrugged at the same moment.

* * *

Nina stepped from the cab and limped only slightly as she crossed the sidewalk. She was wearing a pretty flowered sundress with a skirt long enough to conceal the bandages on her leg, which, after receiving proper medical attention, was healing nicely. After riding the bus into the city last week, she had stopped by the apartment, gathered up her things and taken a cab to the home of an eccentric aunt, the only relative with whom she'd kept in touch over the years. She didn't know what fate would befall Rick and wasn't even sure she'd ever hear about it. His luck would run out eventually, but she was confident that he would keep her name and her involvement to himself, even if arrested by the Brookdale police. Whatever the sentence might be for breaking and entering, it couldn't possibly compare to the time he'd spend behind bars for a string of burglaries, forgeries, fraud, and manslaughter. Rick was a survivor. He'd do his time and get back to the legitimate part of his business as soon as he was set free. He probably wouldn't look for her and she wouldn't be found, even if he did.

She smiled sweetly at the young man who held the door to the restaurant open for her after having ushered his date inside. The space was sunlit and hung with greenery. Nina shifted her purse higher on her shoulder and glanced around at the diners, absently fingering the pendant at her throat. It was a cubic zirconia, but no matter. It could always be replaced.

Spotting a tall, slim, middle-aged man at a table for two under a potted palm tree, Nina lifted her hand in a quick little wave and walked over to meet him. He stood as she approached, and reached out a hand for her to grasp.

Hmm, Marc Jacobs blazer, a whiff of Dolce & Gabbana's Light Blue. The man has class.

And a wife, she'd heard. *Too bad.* But that hardly mattered to her now. A waiter appeared much too quickly to hold Nina's chair for her and take their drink order. Her companion apologized as soon as the server had hurried away.

"Our eager young friend has spoiled our formal introductions."

Nina waved her hand. "It's quite alright." Although they were not yet acquainted, their one phone conversation had covered all the necessary points.

They made a bit of small talk, received their drinks, chose entrees, and returned their menus to the waiter. Nina's companion was in no hurry to wrap up the business part of the lunch, and she was pleased with his impeccable manners.

Just what I deserve.

"Let's get this one detail out of the way so that we can enjoy our meal." Nina dipped her hand into her purse and placed a small package, wrapped in brown paper, on the table between them.

She paused when the salads arrived, then with two manicured fingers, she gave the package a gentle push towards him.

"Mr. Zoloty. I hear you're a Conway fan. So am I."

ACKNOWLEDGMENTS

One day, Jan Poppendieck, a member of my writers' group, the Delaware Valley Writers' Circle, suggested that we all collaborate on a novel about a similar, fictional group buying a bookstore together. We toyed with the idea, and several of our members created basic sketches of possible characters. In no particular order, Consuela Golden suggested the patrician Lavinia Holcomb, Bernard LoPinto created Charlie Santorelli, the wise, bookish guy with a family he was ashamed of, Lily Briggs dreamed up sweet Felicia Cocolo, Jan outlined the troubled Lenora Stern, I thought of regular-guy Al Rockleigh and Jack Cullen came up with the clever name of the lakeside bookstore, The Paper Pirate, while also postulating that two crooks, a man and a woman named Nina, might be after something valuable, or of historical significance. Somewhere along the way, someone suggested that each of the characters should have a secret. Because everyone was busy with his individual work, we didn't get far with the collaborative project and eventually abandoned it. However, I found the idea immensely inspiring, and my imagination quickly fleshed out the characters and produced a working outline that became the completed *The Paper Pirate*. I want to thank each of my friends for allowing me to use his suggestions and I sincerely hope that I have done justice to all of them.

Many thanks to the Hawley Public Library for the hospitality shown to us in pre-Covid days, when the Delaware Valley Writers' Circle met in person. Although the topography and some details have been changed, Brookdale was intended to mimic the town of Hawley, PA.

I also want to express my gratitude to Lisa Kastner, my publisher, Benjamin White, my editor, and the staff at Running Wild Press for their generosity, talent, and assistance.

AUTHOR BIO

Dawn McIntyre is a New Jersey native and long-time resident of rural Pennsylvania. After years of remodeling houses and working in corporate America, she began devoting more time to her true passion building with words. The result, so far, has been a portfolio of short stories and four novels.

Among them are *Julia's World*, a story about a young girl struggling to emerge from the shadow of an abusive mother to discover the rest of the world and her place in it, *Distant Relations*, about a teen who escapes her stifling extended family to start fresh in the home of her estranged father–a man who realizes too late how much he wants the daughter he left behind, and *The Study*, in which a thirty-something journalist discovers the illicit secrets of a historic figure he's researching and must face a decision to reveal and profit from them, or to conceal and protect the reputations of long-dead people he's come to admire and respect.

Dead Inside, the story of a middle-aged woman who impulsively reaches out to offer comfort to a guilt-ridden stranger and finds that her good deed has only dredged up misery from her own past follows *Nala's Dress*, a quirky tale of a young couple threatened by a hex visited upon them by a jealous ex-lover. *The Festival*, a twice-told yarn about a literary grave robber planning to plagiarize a story entrusted to her by an adoring fan was written in response to a prompt suggested by a friend, as was the all-dialogue historical heart-to-heart between a young gay man and his mischievous aunt, *The Visit*

Her first book, *Chance Hill*, brought to life an ornery, twentysomething woman, viewed during the summer that changed her life, and her first published novel, *Zookeeper*, addressed the prevalence, stupidity and tenacity of prejudice.

She founded, along with two fellow authors, a writers' workshop in 2013 that met at a local library until the Covid pandemic necessitated a switch to virtual gatherings. She continues to write fiction peopled by richly nuanced characters in deceptively simple, familiar settings.

Running Wild Press publishes stories that cross genres with great stories and writing. RIZE publishes great genre stories written by people of color and by authors who identify with other marginalized groups. Our team consists of:

Lisa Diane Kastner, Founder and Executive Editor
Mona Bethke, Acquisitions Editor, Editor, RIZE
Benjamin B. White, Acquisitions Editor, Editor, Running Wild Press
Peter A. Wright, Acquisitions Editor, Editor, Running Wild Press
Rebecca Dimyan, Editor
Andrew DiPrinzio, Editor
Cecilia Kennedy, Editor
Barbara Lockwood, Editor
Cody Sisco, Editor
Chih Wang, Editor
Pulp Art Studios, Cover Design
Standout Books, Interior Design
Polgarus Studios, Interior Design
Nicole Tiskus, Production Manager
Alex Riklin, Production Manager
Alexis August, Production Manager

Learn more about us and our stories at www.runningwildpress.com

Loved these stories and want more? Follow us at www.runningwildpress.com, www.facebook/runningwildpress, on Twitter @lisadkastner @RunWildBooks @RwpRIZE

RUNNING
Wild
PRESS